Whispers of the Heart

Amy N Kaplan

Whispers of the Heart

Published by Misfit Pages

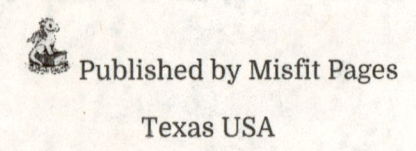

Texas USA

On the World Wide Web at www.misfitpages.com

First Published 2025

Copyright © 2025 Amy N Kaplan

Cover Design
Stephanie Swann

All rights reserved.

No part of this publication may be reproduced, distributed, or transmitted in any form or by any means, including photocopying, recording or other electronic or mechanical methods, without the prior written permission of the publisher, except in the case of brief quotations embodied in reviews and certain other non-commercial uses permitted by copyright law.

ISBN: 978-1-962613-07-1

Author's Note

This novel is a work of fiction. Names, characters, places, businesses, organizations, incidents, and dialogue are either products of the author's imagination or are used in a fictitious manner. While the story draws from certain universal human experiences and emotions, it has been significantly fictionalized and transformed.

Any resemblance to actual persons, living or dead, events, or locales is entirely coincidental. The psychological journeys, family dynamics, and personal challenges depicted in this narrative should not be interpreted as representing any specific individual's life story.

The characters in this novel—including Daphne and her family—face situations that may resonate with readers' own experiences or those of people they know, but they remain fictional constructs designed to explore themes of resilience, healing, and personal growth. These characters and their stories have been crafted to stand independently as literary creations.

This disclaimer affirms the fictional nature of this work in its entirety, and no identification with actual persons or life events is intended or should be inferred.

Acknowledgements

To Beth, my friend and editor extraordinaire, thank you for making my words shine. To my long-suffering husband who endured my writerly mood swings with remarkable patience; you're a saint and so much more than I deserve at times. And to my eldest spawn, Jen, who rescued me from formatting disasters more times than I can count.

Content Advisory

This novel contains themes and situations that some readers may find distressing. I believe in handling these topics with care and authenticity, as they reflect real challenges many people face. For readers who appreciate knowing sensitive content in advance, this story contains:

- Father-daughter sexual abuse and child molestation
- Domestic violence and intimate partner abuse
- Rape, sexual harassment and professional boundary violations
- Emotional abuse and psychological manipulation
- Parental alcoholism and family dysfunction
- Substance abuse, addiction, and recovery
- Overdose and rehabilitation
- Suicide and suicide attempts
- Depression, anxiety, and PTSD
- Grief and loss of loved ones
- Progressive illness (Parkinson's disease)

The journey also includes healing, growth, finding love after trauma, and the creation of chosen family bonds that transcend the cycles of abuse. While these difficult themes are explored with honesty, the narrative ultimately focuses on resilience and the possibility of rebuilding a meaningful life after experiencing profound trauma.

Resources

If you or someone you know is experiencing situations similar to those portrayed in this novel, please know that help is available:

Domestic Violence Support National Domestic Violence Hotline 1-800-799-SAFE (7233) Text START to 88788 www.thehotline.org Available 24/7 in over 200 languages

Sexual Assault Support National Sexual Assault Hotline 1-800-656-HOPE (4673) www.rainn.org Free, confidential support available 24/7

Suicide Prevention National Suicide Prevention Lifeline 988 or 1-800-273-TALK (8255) www.988lifeline.org Available 24/7

Substance Abuse and Mental Health SAMHSA's National Helpline 1-800-662-HELP (4357) www.samhsa.gov/find-help Information, support, and treatment referrals (24/7)

Child Abuse Childhelp National Child Abuse Hotline 1-800-4-A-CHILD (1-800-422-4453) www.childhelp.org Professional crisis counselors available 24/7

Fiction can help us process difficult experiences and show that healing is possible, but real support may be needed on that journey. You are not alone.

Dedication

To my husband Herb, never stop whispering to my heart.

Table of Contents

Chapter 1 – Home 1
Chapter 2 - Akron 13
Chapter 3 - Queens 47
Chapter 4 – The Letter 82
Chapter 5 – High School Memories 99
Chapter 6 - UCLA 129
Chapter 7 - Luke 158
Chapter 8 - Therapy 187
Chapter 9 – Deja Vu 213
Chapter 10 - Sydney 224
Chapter 11 - Justin 238
Chapter 12 - Growth 254
Chapter 13 - Richmond 271
Chapter 14 - Kismet 291
Chapter 15 - Wedded Bliss 322
Chapter 16 - Dallas 348
Chapter 17 – A Writer is Born 371
Chapter 18 - Together 403
Chapter 19 - Moving Day 413
Chapter 20 - Royce and Stacie 422
Epilogue - Tahiti 434

Whispers of the Heart

Chapter 1 – Home
2030

It was moving day. The morning sun spilled through the lace curtains, casting intricate shadows across Daphne's bedroom floor. She lay still for a moment, mentally rehearsing the tasks ahead. Roman would be arriving with his belongings by mid-afternoon, and everything needed to be perfect. Her fingers twitched toward the nightstand where she usually kept her current list, but the polished oak surface was bare except for a small reading lamp and yesterday's coffee mug.

The first flutter of anxiety stirred in her chest. Where had she left it?

Stan's imperious meow broke through her thoughts. He sat regally in the doorway, his black fur gleaming in the morning light, green eyes fixed on her with unusual intensity. Behind him, Loretta wound her way past his legs and trotted to Daphne's bedside, chirping her own breakfast demands. The calico's patchwork tail stood straight up like an exclamation point as she pawed at the duvet.

"Yes, yes, I'm coming," Daphne said, swinging her legs out of bed. The hardwood floor felt cool beneath her feet, grounding her in the familiar sensation. The cats formed an escort party as she made her way downstairs, Loretta weaving between her feet while Stan maintained a dignified distance, though she noticed he stayed closer than usual.

The kitchen welcomed her with its subtle lavender walls and morning quiet. Daphne moved through her routine with practiced precision: filling the coffee maker's reservoir to exactly the eight-cup line, measuring coffee grounds with the special scoop she'd reserved solely for this purpose, pressing the timer button exactly twice to ensure optimal brewing strength. While it brewed, she portioned out the cats' breakfast with equal care—one-third cup each, Stan's in the blue ceramic bowl by the window, Loretta's in the green one near the pantry.

Stan waited with characteristic patience, though his tail twitched when Daphne took an extra moment to ensure the food was centered in his bowl. Loretta, by contrast, danced in excited circles until her breakfast appeared. The familiar routine settled Daphne's nerves, but as she reached for her morning checklist—usually kept by the coffee maker—her hand met empty air.

"Now where did I put that list?" she murmured, opening the drawer where she kept her collection of notepads. Each was labeled by purpose: Grocery Lists, House Maintenance, Garden Planning, Monthly Budgets. Her eyes scanned the neat row of spiral-bound pads, but the moving day checklist was nowhere to be found.

The coffee maker beeped its completion just as Daphne finished checking the kitchen drawers. She poured herself a cup, inhaling the rich aroma. Usually this moment brought pure contentment, but today the coffee's warmth couldn't quite reach the cold knot of anxiety forming in her stomach. That list contained everything she needed to do before Roman arrived—every task carefully planned to ensure his homecoming would be perfect.

Loretta chirped encouragingly and batted at a cabinet door. "No, sweet girl, I already checked there," Daphne said, but she opened it anyway. The spice rack gleamed back at her, each jar perfectly aligned and labeled in her neat handwriting. She adjusted a slightly crooked bottle of oregano, but it brought none of the usual satisfaction.

Her bedroom revealed nothing, though she straightened the already-straight bedding, tucking hospital corners that would have passed military inspection. The living room proved equally fruitless, despite reorganizing the books by author and height—first fiction, then non-fiction. She even color-coded the spines before forcing herself to move on.

Stan shadowed her movements with increasing attention, occasionally brushing against her legs with a soft meow. His typical aloofness had given way to concern—a sure sign her anxiety must be showing. Loretta darted ahead of them both, peering around corners as if the list might be hiding there, waiting to be discovered.

Fresh linens draped over one arm, Daphne paused in the doorway of what had been functioning as their guest room. Soon it would be Roman's again. She flicked on the light, illuminating the generic beige bedding and bland decorative prints that marked it as a temporary space. That would have to change.

"This isn't you at all, is it?" she murmured, setting down her bundle of sheets. The navy blue comforter she'd selected—Roman's favorite color since childhood—waited in the hall closet. She'd bought it last week, after his late-night call about finalizing the divorce papers had left her stomach in knots.

Working methodically, she stripped the guest room bedding, folding each piece with precise corners before storing them away. The generic prints came down next, carefully wrapped in tissue paper. With each item removed, the room seemed to exhale, as if relieved to be shedding its impersonal facade.

Daphne opened the closet, pushing aside hanging clothes to reach the carefully labeled storage boxes at the back. "Hockey Trophies - Roman" read her neat handwriting on the first box. Her hands trembled slightly as she lifted it down.

One by one, she unwrapped each trophy, arranging them chronologically on the built-in shelves. "Junior League MVP, 2010," she read softly, placing it at the start of the line. "Regional Championships, 2012." Each award represented a moment of triumph, a piece of the boy becoming a man. She remembered every game, every celebration.

As she smoothed the navy comforter across the freshly made bed, a memory surfaced with startling clarity. Twelve-year-old Roman, standing in this very room shortly after he and Reuben had moved in. He'd been so serious, trying so hard to be grown up about everything, but his eyes had lit up when she suggested they redecorate.

"We should make a list," she'd said, pulling out a notepad. "That way we won't forget anything important."

The way he'd leaned forward, suddenly interested, suggested no one had ever included him in planning before. Together they'd written everything down: paint colors, bedding options, storage solutions for his hockey gear. She hadn't known then that this shared love of lists would become their special connection.

Daphne tucked the last corner of the comforter under the mattress, adjusting it until the sides hung perfectly even. A hockey stick still waited to be mounted on the wall brackets—she'd save that for Roman to do himself. Some things a man needed to handle on his own.

Stan had settled on the windowsill, watching her work with half-closed eyes. But when she sighed, his head lifted immediately. He crossed to where she stood, rubbing against her legs with uncharacteristic affection.

"I know," she told him, bending to scratch behind his

ears. "I'm worried about him too."

Leaving Roman's room, Daphne's need for the list grew more urgent. Her hands fluttered from surface to surface, straightening items that needed no straightening. In the hall, she realigned three photo frames though they hadn't moved since yesterday. She could feel her pulse quickening, her thoughts scattered like leaves in autumn wind.

Last month, when Roman had first called about the divorce, she'd channeled this same anxiety into organizing the garage. Three days she'd spent out there, cataloging every holiday decoration, every box of memorabilia, every tool in Reuben's workbench. She remembered Reuben finding her surrounded by plastic storage containers, all their contents spread out around her like the aftermath of a yard sale.

He hadn't said a word about her obvious stress response. He'd simply started helping her take down the containers, passing them to her one by one. The next day, he'd surprised her with a set of changeable labels for future reorganizing—a silent acknowledgment of her coping mechanism and how it helped her process worry.

"The list has to be somewhere," she muttered,

moving toward the kitchen again. Stan followed close behind, his occasional meows starting to sound concerned. Loretta had taken to darting ahead, looking back as if to say "Try here next!"

In the kitchen, Daphne found herself opening the pantry door. Each shelf gleamed with organizational perfection: canned goods arranged by type and expiration date, baking supplies in clear containers with printed labels, snacks in matching baskets sorted by category. She'd done this three days ago, after lying awake wondering if Roman was eating properly during the divorce proceedings.

Her fingers traced the labeled shelves, remembering how the simple act of creating order had calmed her racing thoughts that day. But no list revealed itself among the organized supplies.

The den offered no answers either, though she straightened every pencil in the cup on her desk and realigned her reference books by height and color. Her manuscript files sat in perfect alphabetical order, each story idea carefully categorized and labeled, but they couldn't tell her where the list had gone.

That left only one place, and her stomach tightened

at the thought. Reuben's study.

She stood in the doorway, eyeing the organized chaos within. Papers covered his desk in seemingly random piles, yet he could always find exactly what he needed. Scientific journals lay open across every surface, sticky notes protruding from their pages like colorful flags marking territories of thought. A half-empty coffee mug left a ring on what appeared to be important research notes.

Loretta immediately darted inside—she loved exploring the many hiding spots the cluttered room provided. The calico disappeared behind a stack of engineering magazines, her tail the last thing to vanish.

Daphne forced herself to enter without straightening a single paper. Years of marriage had taught her that Reuben's chaos had its own order, one that worked perfectly for him. Just as he'd learned to accommodate her need for structure—keeping his creative whirlwind contained to this one room—she'd learned to let his spaces be.

Her fingers twitched at her sides as she navigated the study. A precariously balanced stack of research papers tilted slightly to the left. Three different coffee cups, all partially full, created a semicircle around Reuben's laptop. Sticky notes decorated every surface like confetti, covered in his distinctive scrawl.

"It has to be in here somewhere," she told the cats. Stan responded with an encouraging meow from his position in the doorway, while Loretta poked her head out from behind a stack of Scientific American magazines, whiskers twitching with interest.

Daphne's eyes scanned the room methodically, fighting the urge to straighten, organize, control. The pendant light above cast shadows that emphasized the wonderful chaos of her husband's mind: engineering sketches taped to walls, mathematical formulas scribbled on whiteboards, paper airplanes made from meeting agendas perched on shelves.

She checked the most obvious spots first: the leather inbox that she'd given him (never used for its intended purpose), the drawer where he kept important papers (filled instead with origami creatures he made during long conference calls), the filing cabinet (which contained everything except files).

"Oh!" The small sound escaped her as she noticed something tucked halfway beneath his keyboard—not where she would put it, but exactly the kind of spot that made sense to him. She reached for the paper, recognizing her own handwriting even from a distance.

Relief and joy flooded through her as she retrieved the list, smoothing the creased paper with trembling fingers. Every task was there, laid out in her neat script: prepare Roman's room, stock his favorite breakfast cereals, make space in the garage for his car, empty the dishwasher....

A smile tugged at her lips as she noticed the additions in Reuben's familiar scrawl:

- *sit down and relax*
- *eat breakfast*
- *I love you*
- *remember to stay hydrated*

Trust him to know exactly what she needed to see. He understood her so well—her lists, her need for order, her tendency to forget self-care when focused on taking care of others. Warmth spread through her chest, easing some of the morning's tension.

The dishwasher. Her eyes caught on the first official item. Yes, start there, something simple and concrete.

She headed to the kitchen, Stan and Loretta trailing behind like a small parade, their missions accomplished.

Golden morning light filled the kitchen now, warming the lavender walls and making the copper pots above the stove gleam. Daphne opened the dishwasher, inhaling the clean scent of the recently finished cycle. With practiced movements, she began removing dishes, each one finding its designated space in the cabinets.

Her hand closed around a large glass tumbler, and she paused. Through the faded image of Daffy Duck, she could almost see herself as a child. A bittersweet smile touched her lips as memories began to surface, clear as photographs.

"I remember when Barbie gave this to me," she said softly. "We must have been 8 years old..."

Chapter 2 – Akron
1975

The sun crept over the skyline, casting a warm golden glow on the bustling streets of Brooklyn. It was moving day for Daphne and her family, a momentous occasion filled with excitement and anticipation. The scents of cardboard boxes and packing tape mingled in the air as they worked together to pack their belongings. With each item wrapped and tucked away, a new chapter awaited them in Akron, Ohio.

Daphne's heart fluttered with nervous energy as she surveyed the now-empty apartment, the echoes of laughter and friendship still lingering in the shadows. As the moving truck pulled up outside, she thought of her closest friends. Their bond was strong, forged by shared experiences and secrets whispered under city lights.

Daphne ran across the street to play with her friends

one more time. She was going to miss these girls. Knocking on the door she called out, "Can Barbie come out to play?" The door burst open, and Barbara Jean ran out and hugged Daphne.

"I wish you didn't have to leave. Maybe we can hide you in my room? I've got five brothers and sisters, mom won't notice one more," she said breathlessly.

"Yeah, but I've only got one brother, so my mom will notice if I'm not there," said Daphne. "Where's Margie, isn't she up yet," asked Daphne.

"Daaaafffeeeee! Don't leave us," screeched Margie, as she ran up the driveway with two boys in tow. Before Daphne could say a word she was swept up into another hug. "Promise me you'll call?" Barbie pleaded, her eyes glistening with tears. She clutched Daphne's hand tightly, searching for reassurance.

"Of course, I promise," Daphne replied, her own voice cracking as she struggled to hold back her emotions. "You're not getting rid of me that easily."

Amidst the tearful goodbyes, Barbie handed Daphne a small package, carefully wrapped in tissue paper. As Daphne unfolded the delicate layers, she discovered a glass tumbler adorned with a drawing of Daffy Duck.

"Remember me every time you use it," Barbie said softly, a bittersweet smile playing on her lips.

"Thank you, Barbie. I will," Daphne whispered, cradling the tumbler in her hands, its cool surface grounding her amidst the whirlwind of emotion.

The glass was more than just a parting gift—it was one of the few tangible connections remaining from their friendship that had changed so abruptly that summer day. Daphne could still see the blood oozing from the gaping wound in Barbie's forehead after she'd tripped on the steps leading to Daphne's house. The memory blurred after that—adults rushing, sirens wailing, and then the aftermath: visits restricted, playdates supervised, as if the accident had somehow been Daphne's fault. The glass remained unbroken when so much else had shattered.

As the final goodbyes were exchanged, Daphne's mind raced with memories of sleepovers and laughter-filled outings. Her friends felt like an extension of herself and leaving them behind was akin to severing a part of her soul. But life was unpredictable, and she knew that, despite the distance, their bond would endure.

♥♥♥

The air buzzed with the terse commands of Preston Blackman as he orchestrated the move with the precision of a drill sergeant. His voice, a relentless drumbeat, pushed everyone to their limits. "Daphne, is your room clear? We need to get moving. Now!"

Rosie descended the staircase, her steps heavy with a weariness that seemed to seep into the very walls of the home they were leaving behind. She clutched a box marked 'kitchen' to her chest, the contents clinking softly with each step. Her eyes lingered on the living room where laughter once filled the air, now only echoing in her mind.

Daphne's small hands carefully wrapped her Daffy Duck glass in a soft sweater before nestling it into her suitcase. Her heart clenched at the thought of leaving behind the only home she had ever known. Her fingers traced the outlines of cartoon feathers as if to etch this piece of her childhood into her memory forever.

She looked around her now-bare room, where shadows played on empty walls and dust danced in sunbeams that no longer had dressers or toys to warm. Closing her eyes, she imagined Barbie's giggles, their shared secrets, and the comfort of knowing that right outside her window was a friend who understood her world.

With one last glance, Daphne zipped up her suitcase and hefted it off the bed. The weight of it felt like an anchor, pulling her back towards all she was leaving behind. But Preston's voice cut through once more, sharp and insistent.

"Daphne! Let's go! We don't have all day."

She took a deep breath and rolled her suitcase out of the room, casting one final look at what was once hers—a space filled with both light and shadows—and stepped into a future unwritten and unknown.

♥♥♥

The Brooklyn street buzzed with the hum of an impending farewell. Cars honked in the distance, children shouted as they played stickball, and neighbors chattered from their stoops. The Blackman family's station wagon sat like a cavernous beast, swallowing box after box of their belongings.

Nine-year-old Daphne stood on the sidewalk, her small fingers tracing the iron railing that lined the steps to her childhood home. She watched her father heave a final suitcase into the back of the car. The fabric of her dress clung to her legs in the summer heat, but she hardly noticed, her gaze lingering on the stoop across the street.

The moving truck rumbled to life, signaling the end of one chapter and the beginning of another. Daphne took a deep breath, steeling herself for the journey ahead as she climbed into the passenger seat. Clutching the glass tumbler tightly in her hands, she reminded herself that no matter where she went or what challenges lay before her, the love and support of her friends would always be with her.

♥♥♥

Miles's whines cut through the hum of the engine, an unwelcome chorus to the symphony of rubber rolling on asphalt. "Are we there yet? This is so boring!"

Daphne would trade this endless stretch of highway for a game of jacks on sun-warmed concrete in a heartbeat.

"I'm tired," Miles moaned, slumping further in his seat. "And hungry."

Rosie glanced back at her son through the rearview mirror, her patience wearing as thin as the treads on their tires. "Just a little longer, sweetheart."

Preston kept his eyes on the road, grip firm on the wheel. "There's a rest stop coming up. Hold your horses."

Daphne returned her gaze to the passing scenery—fields of green that stretched like an artist's canvas to horizons unseen. The car's steady vibration coaxed her into a silent reverie, where memories played like old movies behind her eyes.

Barbie's laughter echoed in her mind—the way it used to ricochet off brick walls and parked cars as they made chalk masterpieces on the sidewalk. Daphne could almost feel the gentle scrape of chalk against her fingertips, Barbie by her side turning gray slabs into rainbows.

"Hey, watch it!" Miles's shout yanked Daphne from her thoughts as his restless legs kicked the back of her seat.

"Mind your brother," Rosie called out softly.

Daphne exhaled slowly, turning to Miles with a smile that didn't quite reach her eyes. "We'll be there soon. Then you can run around all you want."

Miles huffed and crossed his arms, sinking into his

own world of comic books and action figures.

The car rolled on, carrying them toward new beginnings and away from sidewalks marked by hopscotch squares and echoes of childhood chants. Daphne rested her head against the window, watching as each mile unfurled before them like ribbons of possibility. She held tight to memories—her talisman against the tide of change—letting their presence soothe the ache for home that swelled in her chest.

♥♥♥

The Blackman's Akron house, a two-story affair with peeling paint and a front door that stuck in the jamb, sat hunched on the edge of a street filled with similar relics of better times. Inside, the air was thick with tension, a silent pressure that settled over the worn furniture and threadbare rugs like an unwelcome guest.

"Alright, everyone," Daphne's father announced as they stood in the living room, surveying the chaotic jumble of belongings. "Let's get this place set up. We've got a lot of work ahead of us."

Daphne nodded, steeling herself for the challenges that lay ahead. She knew all too well that her father's enthusiasm was a fragile facade, one that could crumble at any moment, leaving destruction in its wake.

"Okay, Dad," she replied, grabbing a box labeled 'kitchen' and heading towards the small, outdated space that would soon be filled with the smells of her mother's sporadic attempts at cooking.

Her mother, already clutching a half-empty bottle of wine, slumped onto the couch with a defeated sigh. "I just need a little break," she mumbled, taking a long swig before closing her eyes.

Daphne gritted her teeth, suppressing the anger and disappointment that threatened to bubble over. This was supposed to be a new beginning, but the same old patterns seemed determined to follow them no matter where they went.

Daphne had learned years ago that her mother's drinking had begun after losing Nathalie, the daughter born a year before Miles who had lived for only a day. The umbilical cord wrapped around her neck had stolen her before she'd truly arrived. Though never spoken aloud, Daphne felt the weight of her mother's unspoken question: why had she survived when Nathalie hadn't? It was a ghost that haunted their relationship, one that no amount of perfect grades or household chores could exorcise.

♥♥♥

Daphne had learned to move through the house with a quiet grace, each step measured and deliberate to avoid the creaky floorboards. She found herself holding her breath more often than not, releasing it only when she was sure her father's attention was fixed elsewhere.

Miles, five years younger and not as adept at navigating their father's moods, often drew his ire. The boy's innate curiosity and restless energy were a dangerous mix in a home where calm was the highest currency.

Their mother, Rosie, once a vibrant presence who filled the rooms with laughter and music, had become a ghost of herself. She floated from room to room, her gaze distant, fingers often wrapped around a glass that never seemed to empty.

On one particularly stifling afternoon, the sound of shattering glass sliced through the house's uneasy calm. Daphne's heart lurched into her throat as she rushed toward the noise, finding Miles standing frozen in the kitchen, eyes wide and brimming with tears.

Their father loomed over him, his face contorted in anger. "Clumsy fool! Can't do anything right!" His voice boomed off the linoleum and formica.

Daphne moved quickly between them, her voice steady but soft. "It's just a glass, Daddy. I'll clean it up." She kept her eyes fixed on the jagged pieces scattered across the floor as if they held some spell to calm the storm.

Miles slipped behind her, small hands clutching at the hem of her shirt. Daphne could feel his trembling against her back as she swept up the shards.

Later that evening, as twilight bled into nightfall and their father's snores echoed from his armchair, Daphne sat at the kitchen table with Miles. They pieced together a jigsaw puzzle in silence — each click of interlocking cardboard a whispered promise that they could create order from chaos.

The next morning brought no respite. Their mother slipped out early, leaving behind only the scent of stale perfume and regret. Daphne stepped into her shoes by default, fixing breakfast and packing lunches with robotic precision.

School offered no sanctuary for Daphne or Miles; it

was merely a different stage for acting out their parts — the studious daughter and the carefree son. They returned home each day as if to a minefield where every step could be their last.

In this house of brittle smiles and hollowed eyes, Daphne clung to her routines like life rafts. The list-making began here: tasks laid out in neat rows on scraps of paper that promised control amidst chaos. She didn't realize then that this coping mechanism would shape her entire life.

At night, Daphne would lie awake listening to Akron breathe around her — cars whispering on distant highways, trees rustling like gossiping old men. In those quiet hours before sleep claimed her weary mind, she would imagine a life different from this — one filled with laughter that didn't have to be checked for fear it might wake something terrible.

She would drift off eventually, cocooned in dreams where families spoke without shouting and mothers' kisses weren't tinged with bitterness. And in those dreams — fragile as spider silk — Daphne dared to hope for more than just survival.

♥♥♥

"Damn it, Daphne! Can't you do anything right?" her father's voice echoed in her mind, the memory as vivid as if he were standing beside her. She recalled the way his features twisted with rage one evening, after she'd accidentally spilled her drink on their new living room carpet. In that instant, the tension in their household had been palpable, her mother and siblings frozen in place like statues, unable to move or breathe for fear of setting him off further.

Daphne remembered how she'd quickly cleaned up the mess, desperate to quell her father's fury. But no matter how hard she tried, there was always something else, another mistake or perceived failing that ignited his anger anew. It was a never-ending cycle of fear and apprehension, a dark cloud that hung over the family like a storm threatening to unleash its wrath.

In the dim light of their new home in Akron, Daphne's mother sat hunched over the kitchen table, a bottle of whiskey clutched in her hand. The once-vibrant woman had grown pale and withdrawn, her eyes hollow and haunted by the turmoil that consumed their family. As her husband's anger and violence escalated, so too did her dependence on alcohol, the toxic liquid offering a temporary escape from the unbearable weight of reality.

"Mom, please... put the bottle down," Daphne pleaded softly, reaching out to touch her mother's arm. But the woman only tightened her grip, turning away with a cold, dismissive shrug. It was as if an impenetrable wall had been erected between them, one that not even the most heartfelt words or actions could breach.

Daphne sighed, feeling a dull ache in her chest as she glanced at her younger brother huddled behind a chair on the living room floor. He seemed so small and vulnerable, his innocence threatened by the destructive force that held sway over their lives. Determined to protect him, Daphne drew on reserves of strength she never knew she possessed, shielding him from the worst of their parents' dysfunction.

♥♥♥

It was during those difficult times that Daphne discovered solace in her studies, her intense focus and determination propelling her to excel academically. She found refuge within the pages of textbooks, immersing herself in the scientific wonders of biology and the poetic beauty of literature. And through it all, she maintained a close-knit circle of friends, their unwavering support a balm for her wounded heart.

"Hey, Daphne, want to come hang out after school?" her friend Sarah asked one day, a warm smile lighting up her face. "We can study for the history test together."

"Sure, I'd love to," Daphne replied, her own smile reflecting the gratitude she felt for the simple gesture of friendship. In those moments, surrounded by laughter and camaraderie, she could almost forget the chaos that awaited her at home.

♥♥♥

As the days turned into weeks, Daphne did her best to establish a sense of order amidst the chaos. She meticulously organized her bedroom, finding solace in the familiar objects she'd brought from their previous home: the worn teddy bear that had been her constant companion since childhood, the collection of books that had seen her through countless sleepless nights, and the small assortment of knickknacks that reminded her of happier times.

The sound of shattering porcelain pierced the tense air as Daphne flinched, her heart racing. The fragments of the vase scattered across the floor like fallen stars, a stark reminder of her father's fury. Preston Blackman stood rigid, his eyes ablaze, glaring at the spot where the vase had once been – a symbol of order misplaced.

"I told you to put it on the mantle!" he roared, his voice a whip that cracked through the silence of the house.

Daphne's breath caught in her throat, her hands clenched at her sides. She willed herself to be still, to be as unnoticeable as the dust motes dancing in a shaft of sunlight.

"I... I thought it would look better by the window," she stammered, her voice barely above a whisper.

"Thought? You thought?" Preston's sneer was like acid. "You don't get paid to think. You do as you're told!"

She nodded, her eyes locked on the jagged pieces of what was once beautiful. Daphne vowed in that moment to escape the unpredictable tempests of her father's moods. The cold floor under her feet seemed to seep into her bones, grounding her resolve.

♥♥♥

Her father's voice, raised in anger, pierced her thoughts. It was a sound that had filled their home far too often, creating an atmosphere of tension and fear.

"Where is your homework?" her father yelled, his face red with rage. "You think you can just do whatever you want around here?"

Daphne flinched at the memory, feeling the familiar knot of anxiety forming in her stomach. Her father's outbursts were unpredictable and violent, leaving the family walking on eggshells in a futile effort to avoid setting him off.

"Please, Dad," young Daphne pleaded, her lip quivering as she fought back tears. "I promise I did it. I just forgot it at school."

"Forgot it at school?" he scoffed, towering over her small frame. "You think I'm stupid, don't you? Well, I'll teach you a lesson you won't forget!"

The sound of his hand connecting with her cheek rang out through the house, an all-too-familiar occurrence.

"Your mother is going to Brooklyn to take care of your grandparents for a few weeks," her father, Preston Wesley Blackman, stated.

"Daphne, you'll have to sleep with your father. You know he doesn't like to sleep alone," her mother,

Rosaline Ginnie Waxweiler, chimed in. Although absurd, the statement seemed normal coming from Daphne's mother.

"Why can't Miles do it? Why does it always have to be me?" asked Daphne.

"Stop being so difficult," said Daphne's mother. "You know your father prefers little girls."

They had this conversation every time her mother went away. And every time Daphne counted the days till her mother came home. By the time Daphne was 11, she had gathered enough courage to talk to her mother about it when she got home.

With hesitation in her voice, Daphne asked "Mom, can we talk?"

"Daphne, I'm trying to get my suitcases unpacked here. Can't it wait? It probably isn't even important." Snapped Rosie.

Daphne's voice caught as she said, "Mom, while you were gone..." She looked at the floor and continued. "Dad insisted on giving me a bath and..."

"So? He's your father! This is a waste of my time, Daphne." Rosie began to walk out of the room with an armful of dirty laundry.

"Mom, wait! There's more."

Sighing heavily, Rosie sat on the edge of the bed. "Out with it child."

"... then, at night, in bed... he... he..."

"Oh for heaven's sake Daphne. Just say it."

"He touched me and said something about making love" mumbled Daphne.

Rosie began to laugh; mean, evil laughter. Looking her daughter up and down, head to toe, "Why would he want *you* when he has me?" And with that, she walked out of the room.

As Daphne navigated the treacherous waters of adolescence, she clung fiercely to the belief that a brighter future lay just beyond the horizon. And though the path was fraught with uncertainty and heartache, she vowed never to lose sight of the dreams and aspirations that burned like a beacon in the darkest night. For it was only through hope and resilience that she would ultimately find the stability and love she so desperately craved.

♥♥♥

In school, Daphne's hands moved deftly over test papers and assignments, each correct answer a brick in the fortress she was building around herself. Her focus was laser-sharp; equations and formulas were constants in a world where nothing else was sure. She saw them as life rafts in an ocean of chaos.

Her teachers noticed. "Brilliant work, Daphne," they would say with approving nods. Their praise was currency she hoarded greedily, knowing it bought her credibility and opportunity.

Nights spent hunched over textbooks weren't just about learning; they were rehearsals for a future performance where she was no longer a character in this grim play at home. Each A+ on her report card didn't just signify academic excellence; it was a silent scream for freedom.

In bed at night, while the house lay quiet and dark save for the occasional creaks and groans of settling wood, Daphne would stare at the ceiling and picture herself elsewhere – anywhere but within those suffocating walls. Her dreams were vivid tapestries woven with threads of determination and hope.

As she lay there night after night, she promised herself that this life would not define her. She would not be broken by misplaced vases or by the shards of her family's fragile peace. No matter what it took, she would carve out a space for herself in the world – a space filled with order and reason.

Daphne understood that grades were her golden ticket – each perfect score another step away from Preston's shadow that loomed over everything she did. The thought alone infused her with strength; it turned fear into fuel.

Her path forward was clear: Excel. Excel beyond expectation, beyond anyone's wildest dreams – except perhaps her own. She had always known that knowledge was power, but now more than ever, it became her mantra. She repeated it to herself like a prayer.

♥♥♥

The moon hung like a silent guardian over the quiet Akron neighborhood, its pale light filtering through the gauzy curtains of Daphne's small, meticulously organized bedroom. Nestled under her grandmother Katherine's quilt, Daphne clutched a worn novel to her chest, its spine cracked from frequent visits to the worlds held within its pages.

Her eyes danced across the lines, devouring words that spoke of courage and warmth, of families knitted tightly with love and laughter—a stark contrast to the strained threads of her own. The house lay still around her, save for the occasional creaks and groans that came with the settling of an old structure.

Daphne's room was a sanctuary, each item carefully placed, each book on the shelf a friend she could turn to when her father's temper flared or when her mother's absence became too palpable. She found solace in tales where fathers bestowed gentle wisdom instead of harsh words, where mothers enveloped their children in tender embraces instead of escaping into numbing oblivion.

A breeze whispered through a slight gap in the window, stirring the papers on Daphne's desk—homework completed days ahead of schedule. It fluttered past her math textbooks, over neatly arranged pencils and notepads filled with orderly handwriting. She breathed in the scent of paper and ink—a comfort as reliable as the calculations and equations that promised predictable outcomes.

Daphne turned another page, lost in a scene where a fictional family gathered around a bountiful dinner table, voices mingling in harmonious conversation. Her heart swelled at the thought of such normalcy. The characters became vessels for her hopes; their joys and triumphs were hers as well.

Eventually, the book slipped from her grasp as her eyelids grew heavy with sleep. The novel lay open-faced on her chest, rising and falling with each quiet breath. Dreams wove themselves into the fabric of her subconscious—a tapestry of longing for a life filled with kindness and stability.

In these dreams, Daphne walked hand in hand with siblings who didn't flinch at sudden movements or sharp tones. She sat at long tables where food was shared generously and stories were passed around like cherished gifts. She smiled at fathers who repaired what was broken with gentle hands and mothers whose laughter was like music filling every corner of a sunlit room.

As slumber deepened its hold on her, Daphne's expression softened. In this place between sleep and wakefulness, she held onto the fleeting sweetness of her imagined family—a fortress against the waking world's unpredictability that awaited outside her bedroom door.

♥♥♥

The school bus groaned to a stop, its doors folding open with a tired hiss. Daphne Blackman stepped down onto the curb, her backpack snug against her shoulders. Her eyes swept over the Akron neighborhood, where every lawn seemed manicured with precision, every flower bed bloomed with care. It was as if each petal and blade of grass stood in silent rebellion against the disorder of her own home life.

As the bus rumbled away, she let out a breath she hadn't realized she'd been holding. She adjusted the straps of her backpack and walked slowly, deliberately, taking in the harmonious arrangements of marigolds and begonias that lined the walkways of neighboring houses. There was something about their vibrant colors and neat rows that whispered promises of stability and peace.

Daphne harbored dreams of creating that same order and beauty in her own life, dreams that felt like distant stars—present, yet untouchable. For now, she settled for the small patch of earth under her bedroom window. It was her canvas, a tiny haven where she could impose order on chaos, coaxing life from the soil with gentle hands.

The little garden was a motley collection—a few marigolds here, some hardy pansies there—but it was hers. She'd salvaged seeds from packets at the grocery store, tucked them into the ground with hope as her only fertilizer. Each day after school, she'd kneel beside the patch, nurturing each shoot with whispered encouragements and careful weeding.

"Hey Daphne," called a neighbor's voice, jolting her from her thoughts.

She turned to see Mrs. Jenkins waving from across the street. The woman's garden was a neighborhood jewel—roses and lilies living in harmonious splendor.

"Hi Mrs. Jenkins," Daphne called back with a smile that didn't quite reach her eyes.

"Your flowers are coming along nicely," Mrs. Jenkins observed with an approving nod.

"Thank you." Daphne's heart swelled with pride. "I'm trying my best."

She lingered at the edge of her own yard, reluctant to step inside and face the unpredictability that awaited.

But there were chores to be done before she could lose herself in the tranquility of tending to her flowers—the only thing in her life that seemed to respond predictably to care and attention.

Daphne pushed open the front door, steeling herself for whatever atmosphere might greet her today. Her father's mood dictated the climate within these walls; it was an ever-changing weather pattern she had yet to master.

But later tonight, under the cloak of dusk, she would be back outside with dirt under her fingernails and determination in her soul. In those quiet moments spent nurturing her flower patch, she could dream about a future where order wasn't just a fleeting visitor but a permanent resident in the home she would one day create for herself—a home filled not just with beauty but also with love and stability, where vases remained whole and laughter wasn't a rare bloom but a perennial joy.

♥♥♥

The air at the bus stop hummed with the energy of school kids shedding the weight of the day's lessons. Daphne stood slightly apart, her book bag clutched tight against her, a silent observer in a sea of laughter and gossip. She mimicked the curve of a smile on her lips, letting out a small chuckle as if she were part of the conversations around her.

"Hey Daphne, you coming?" a voice called, but she only nodded, not trusting her voice to maintain the façade of normalcy. As the bus rumbled into view, its brakes hissing in protest, Daphne's heart pounded in her chest.

Without warning, her feet made the decision for her. They carried her away from the safety of routine and towards an unknown path. She began to walk, letting each step fall in rhythm with her racing thoughts. The bus faded into the distance, along with the sounds of her classmates.

The air was crisp, filled with the musky scent of fallen leaves. Daphne's eyes drank in the vibrant oranges and reds that painted the trees lining the streets. It was as if nature itself had taken up brushes and stroked color across its canvas just for her.

She passed by shops with their windows dressed in seasonal decor, quaint displays that whispered of family dinners and warm laughter – scenes alien to her own life. A pang of longing struck her chest but she pushed it down with a deep breath.

With every step she took on this longer path home, Daphne savored the illusion of peace. Her mind wove tales where she was just another girl with an unremarkable life; where doors opened to hugs and not harsh words; where dinner tables were places of conversation and not battlegrounds.

But reality has a cruel way of reminding one of its presence. Her house loomed into view, its facade a mask hiding what lay behind closed doors. Daphne's pace slowed; each step grew heavier as she approached.

She stood at the threshold for a heartbeat or two, gathering fragments of courage that threatened to scatter like leaves in the wind. She reached for the door handle, steeling herself for what lay on the other side, for now, it was time to face what she could not escape – yet.

♥♥♥

The late afternoon light cast long shadows across the lawn as Daphne rounded the corner to her house. She noted the curtains flapping out of the open windows, an unusual sight that quickened her pulse with unease. Pushing open the front door, a cacophony of voices greeted her, her parents' words sharp and biting as they echoed through the half-empty hallway.

Daphne's father, Preston, towered over a sea of cardboard boxes, his voice booming with a ferocity that made the very air in the room feel heavy. "It's decided, Rosie! Baltimore is our fresh start."

Her mother's retort was a muffled sob, barely audible over the sound of tape ripping and being slapped onto boxes. "And what about the kids, Preston? Another new school?"

Preston didn't look up from his task. "They'll adapt. They're resilient."

Resilient. The word hung in Daphne's mind like a lead weight as she ascended the stairs to her room, each step feeling heavier than the last. The sanctuary she had carefully curated with posters and photographs felt foreign now, stripped of its warmth.

Kneeling by her bed, Daphne pulled out an old suitcase and began folding her clothes with meticulous care. She smoothed out each wrinkle in her shirts, aligned the seams of her jeans just so—her hands moving with a precision that belied the turmoil swirling inside her.

Every item was a decision, every memory evaluated for its weight and worthiness to travel to this unknown new life. But when her fingers brushed against the cool glass of the Daffy Duck memento, she paused. The relic from a time before Akron—a time that seemed like someone else's life—felt like an anchor.

Clutching it to her chest, she closed her eyes and allowed herself a moment of grief for what was and what could never be again. Her breath came out in slow waves as she whispered to herself—a mantra to keep the tears at bay.

In that small room where dreams mingled with despair, Daphne tucked away her treasured glass amid layers of clothing like a fragile bird nestled in a nest. It was a silent vow that no matter where this next road took them, she would hold on to this piece of herself.

Her room bare and belongings packed, Daphne stood at the threshold one last time. The question haunted her—will I ever find home? But deep down, amidst all the uncertainty and change, she knew home wasn't just a place; it was something she would have to build for herself.

With one last look back, Daphne carried her suitcase

downstairs, past the arguments still raging in the living room. She set it by the door and walked outside into the fading light. For now, she would watch the sun dip below the horizon and imagine a world where everything stayed put—where roots grew deep and strong.

And maybe one day, she thought as dusk settled over Akron like a soft blanket, maybe one day that world could be hers.

♥♥♥

"Another move?" she asked her parents, trying to suppress the tremor in her voice. "Why? We just got here."

"Your father found a new job," her mother said, avoiding eye contact and taking a sip from her ever-present glass of wine. "It's a good opportunity for him."

Daphne could see the weariness etched into her father's face as he sat on the couch, his fingers drumming nervously on the armrest. He didn't look particularly enthused about the news either, but there would be no argument. It was decided.

So Daphne began to pack up her belongings once again, this time with a heavy heart and a creeping sense of despair. As she wrapped the delicate glass tumbler featuring Daffy Duck that Barbie had given her, she couldn't help but feel a dull ache in her chest. The promise of staying in touch seemed more fragile than ever, their friendship stretched thin by the relentless miles that would soon separate them.

"Goodbye, Akron," she whispered to herself, looking out the window of her nearly empty bedroom one last time. "Goodbye, Sarah. Goodbye, Cathy." The words tasted bitter on her tongue, like the unwanted remnants of a dream that refused to fade away.

As the moving truck pulled away from the house, Daphne tried to hold back her tears. She knew better than to hope for lasting stability or comfort, but deep down, a small part of her still clung to the belief that someday, things might be different. Someday, she would find her place in the world—a place where love and happiness could take root and finally flourish.

But the illusion of stability was short-lived, as it so often was in Daphne's life. The news of another move came like a swift punch to the gut, leaving her reeling with a mix of disbelief and resignation. This time, they were headed to Baltimore, Maryland.

"Are you going to miss Akron, Daphne?" her younger brother asked, breaking the silence in the car as they drove away from the only home she had known for the past few years.

Daphne hesitated before answering. "I guess so," she admitted softly. "There were some good memories here, after all."

"Like what?" her brother pressed, genuinely curious.

"Like... making new friends, exploring the parks, and the quiet moments when everything felt almost normal," Daphne replied with a wistful smile.

Her father glanced over at her from the driver's seat. "Well, let me tell you something, kids," he said, his voice heavy with an unspoken weight. "We're not moving to Baltimore, Maryland like I told you before. We're actually going back to New York."

"Really?" Miles exclaimed, his eyes lighting up with excitement. "Back where we came from?"

"New York, but not our old neighborhood," their father clarified, a hint of nostalgia in his tone. "It'll be a fresh start for us, in Queens."

Daphne's heart twisted with mixed emotions. She

was relieved to return to familiar territory, but the thought of starting over yet again left her weary. As she watched the landscape change outside her window, she couldn't help but wonder if this move would bring about the stability she longed for or if it was just another stop on a never-ending journey.

Chapter 3 – Queens
1981

It was moving day. It didn't feel like a moving day, though. There were no movers coming to drop off furniture. There were no boxes to unpack. There were, however, suitcases everywhere.

The brick facades of the row houses on Daphne's new block in Queens absorbed the afternoon sun, their warm hues inviting a sense of permanence she craved. Fourteen-year-old Daphne stood on the sidewalk, her gaze lingering on the one that would be hers. Could this place, her grandmother's house, with its symmetrical windows and stoop, become the home she longed for?

Her father gripped her shoulder, his touch felt cold and controlling. Her mother fumbled with the keys, her hands shaky from years of alcohol abuse.

"Welcome to your new life, kiddo," Preston declared with a tight smile, his eyes scanning the neighborhood for any perceived threats to their reputation.

As Daphne looked around the house, she was acutely aware of the weight of starting over. New school, new friends, and new expectations – all tangled up in her parents' toxic relationship. She felt an overwhelming desire to find something she could control amidst the chaos. "I think I'll unpack my suitcase," she murmured, retreating upstairs.

Her new bedroom was smaller than the last, but it held promise. She placed her suitcase on the bed and unzipped it slowly, the familiar sound offering a whisper of continuity in her life of change. She lifted out clothes and books, each item finding its temporary place in the room.

Then came the glass tumbler, her talisman from a childhood that felt both distant and achingly close. She unwrapped it from its cocoon of socks and held it up to the light streaming through the window. The faded lines of Daffy Duck's face danced in her palm. A sigh escaped her lips as she set it carefully on the windowsill.

Other small treasures followed: a seashell from a

rare beach outing, a postcard from her grandmother, a smooth stone she found on a particularly hard day. Each object had a story, a fragment of stability that she clung to through every upheaval.

She stepped back to survey her work, her eyes tracing the neat line of memories basking in the sunlit glow. Her hand brushed against something else in her suitcase—a notebook filled with meticulous notes and doodles from school. It joined the array on the windowsill.

Her fingers hesitated over another item—a framed photo of her and Barbie, taken just before she left Brooklyn. Their smiles were frozen in time, but Daphne could still hear Barbie's laughter echoing in her mind. With gentle reverence, she placed it beside her glass tumbler.

The room around her felt less empty now, each cherished item anchoring her to moments of joy and resilience. Daphne flopped onto the bed, allowing herself a moment's rest amid boxes still begging to be unpacked.

Her eyes closed briefly, and she could almost imagine this was it—the final move, the end of transient beginnings. But even as hope flickered within her chest, experience tugged at its edges with reminders not to hold too tightly to this new sense of place.

For now, though, Queens was home. And for Daphne, that was enough to unpack another box.

♥♥♥

Over time, Daphne found solace in a group of friends from the neighborhood that seemed to understand her struggles. Each one of them had their quirks and secrets, but together they formed an unbreakable bond.

"Hey, Daphne!" called out Claire, a girl with raven-black hair and a penchant for vintage clothing. "You're coming to the park with us later, right?"

"Of course!" Daphne replied, grateful for the invitation.

"Good," chimed in Kevin, always quick with a sarcastic quip that somehow managed to put everyone at ease. "We don't want you to miss out on our legendary kickball games."

"Legendary? That's a bit of a stretch, don't you think?" teased Jessica, flipping her long blonde hair over her shoulder. Although she appeared confident, Daphne knew she struggled with anxiety and often sought refuge in their little group.

"Alright, alright," conceded Kevin, laughing. "Maybe 'infamous' is a better word,"

The friends spent countless hours together, finding solace in each other's company and navigating the treacherous waters of adolescence. They shared secrets, fears, and dreams, forming a tapestry of experiences that would stay with Daphne for years to come.

"Hey, Daph," whispered Claire one day as they sat under their favorite tree in the park, "do you ever think about what life will be like when we're older?"

Daphne contemplated the question, the leaves rustling above them like whispers of the future. "Sometimes," she admitted. "I wonder if I'll find something that makes me truly happy – something I can control, you know?"

Her friends nodded in understanding, their hearts beating in unison with hers as they faced the uncertainty of growing up. In those moments, Daphne found strength in their bond, a feeling of belonging that would carry her through even the darkest days ahead.

It was during one of those treasured afternoons, when the sun cast a golden glow on everything it touched, that Daphne first met John Michael Hannigan. He approached their group, the confidence in his stride betraying an aura of self-assuredness. His sandy blond hair framed his face, drawing attention to his striking blue eyes. As he got closer, Daphne couldn't help but notice his uncanny resemblance to a young Leif Garrett.

"Hey, you're the new girl, right?" John asked, flashing Daphne a warm smile. The immediate connection they felt was palpable, and Daphne felt as if she had known him for years.

"Uh, yeah," she stammered, taken aback by his magnetic presence. "I'm Daphne."

"Nice to meet you, Daphne. I'm John," he said, extending his hand. She shook it, feeling a spark of electricity pulse through her veins. It was the beginning of something special.

♥♥♥

The chatter and clatter of high school life swirled around Daphne as she navigated the hallways on her first day of ninth grade. She clutched her books close to her chest, a shield against the jostling crowds of students. Her eyes flitted across the colorful lockers, each adorned with stickers and magnets that spoke volumes about their owners.

As she turned a corner, a soft melody sliced through the noise, drawing Daphne's attention. There, sitting cross-legged against a wall, was Phoebe, her fingers dancing over guitar strings. A small circle of students gathered around her, enchanted by the music that flowed as naturally as the sunlight through the high windows.

"Hey," Phoebe called out, catching sight of Daphne's curious gaze. "You're new here, right? Come join us."

Daphne hesitated for just a moment before stepping closer, her heart fluttering at the unexpected invitation.

"I'm Phoebe," said the musician with a warm smile that matched the twinkle in her hazel eyes. "And you are?"

"Daphne," she replied, easing into the circle.

From behind them came a lyrical voice. "That's a lovely name." Lucy emerged from the throng, notebook in hand. "Names carry stories within them. I try to capture those stories in my poetry."

Nina swept in next, her arms wide in a dramatic flourish that caused several passersby to smile. "And I bring those stories to life on stage," she proclaimed with confidence that seemed unshakable.

Daphne watched them, this eclectic trio who spun art from thin air. She felt an unfamiliar sense of belonging stir within her.

"You seem like you have a story too," Phoebe observed gently.

Daphne nodded slowly. "I guess everyone does."

Lucy beamed at her. "Exactly! We're all walking novels, waiting for someone to read us."

The bell rang then, signaling the end of their impromptu gathering. But in that short span before they dispersed to their respective classes, Daphne knew she had stumbled upon something special—her tribe.

As they walked together toward their classrooms, Phoebe strummed a final chord on her guitar, Lucy scribbled another line of verse into her notebook, and Nina practiced expressions in her compact mirror. And Daphne? She marveled at how quickly she'd found kindred spirits in this new chapter of her life.

♥♥♥

Under the glare of Friday night lights, the football field at Queens High School buzzed with excitement. Bleachers packed with cheering students, parents holding thermoses of coffee, and banners flapping in the cool breeze created a mosaic of school spirit. Daphne huddled with her friends in the stands, a colorful knit scarf wrapped snugly around her neck, hands clutching a steaming cup of hot cocoa.

"Go, Wildcats!" Phoebe yelled next to her, strumming an air guitar every time their team made a good play. Lucy scribbled lines of poetry in her notebook, inspired by the game's ebb and flow. Nina mimed dramatic interpretations of the cheerleaders' routines, eliciting giggles from their little group.

Daphne's gaze wandered across the bleachers. Between swaths of royal blue and gold pom-poms, she spotted him. The boy with shaggy blonde hair that brushed his shoulders and a grin that lit up the autumn night. It was John, from the neighborhood. Their eyes met and held; his smile deepened as if he recognized her from a dream.

Her heart did an unfamiliar dance in her chest,

skipping beats and then racing to catch up. She smiled back before she could stop herself, warmth flooding her cheeks despite the chill in the air.

"Who's that?" Nina whispered, following Daphne's gaze.

"Just some guy," Daphne mumbled, trying to sound indifferent.

Nina's eyes sparkled with mischief. "He's been staring at you for the last ten minutes."

Daphne feigned interest in the game below but sneaked another glance at him. He hadn't looked away; their connection felt like a live wire stretching across the stands.

As halftime approached and the band filed onto the field, John Michael rose from his seat and navigated through the crowd. Each step he took toward her sent Daphne's pulse racing faster.

Phoebe elbowed Daphne gently. "Incoming," she teased under her breath.

Daphne swallowed hard, her hands suddenly clumsy with her cocoa cup. She straightened up as he stopped before their row, his face open and expectant.

"Hey," he said simply, his voice smooth as vinyl.

"Hi." Daphne couldn't help but smile again, surprised at how natural it felt to talk to him.

The band launched into a spirited rendition of the school fight song, brass notes soaring over their heads.

"Want to walk around? It's too noisy to talk here," John Michael suggested over the music.

Daphne glanced at her friends who nudged her encouragingly. She nodded and followed him down the bleacher steps into the throng of halftime wanderers.

They strolled side by side along the track that bordered the field, weaving through clusters of students discussing plays and gossiping about teachers. They chatted about trivial things—favorite bands, most hated cafeteria food—yet it felt significant somehow, each word a step closer to understanding this kindred spirit who had appeared so unexpectedly in her life.

As they circled back toward the bleachers, John Michael turned to face her fully. "You know," he began with an earnestness that caught Daphne off guard, "I saw you on your first day of school and thought you looked cool."

She blushed again but met his gaze boldly this time. "Thanks," she said softly.

The whistle blew for the second half of the game to start but neither moved to rejoin their friends in the stands. Instead they stood there under those bright lights, two teenagers momentarily lost in a world of their own making—a world where time stood still and only possibilities stretched out before them.

As the weeks rolled into months, John seamlessly integrated himself into Daphne's circle of friends. They spent countless hours together, exploring the nooks and crannies of each other's basements or attics, uncovering hidden treasures and memories tucked away in dusty corners. On weekends, they could be found roller-skating along the sidewalks, laughter and youthful exuberance trailing behind them like an echo of simpler times.

"Come on, slowpoke!" John called out, playfully teasing Daphne as she struggled to keep up with his effortless glide.

"Be patient! Some of us weren't born on wheels!" Daphne replied, half-laughing, half-gasping for breath. But despite her initial struggles, she soon found her rhythm – not just on the sidewalk, but in the ebb and flow of life in Queens.

The crisp autumn air carried the scent of fallen leaves and distant bonfires as Daphne walked through the streets of Queens, her steps buoyant with anticipation. The Halloween spirit infused the neighborhood, with carved pumpkins perched on stoops and cotton cobwebs draped over hedges. Daphne clutched a plastic bag filled with old newspapers and a flour canister, the essential ingredients for an afternoon of crafting with John Michael.

She approached the row house where John lived, its facade unremarkable but for the vibrant mural that adorned the garage door—a testament to the artist who resided within. Daphne hesitated at the gate, heart fluttering like a trapped bird against her ribs. She smoothed her hair, tucking a loose strand behind her ear before she mustered the courage to push open the gate.

John greeted her with a grin that could outshine any jack-o'-lantern's glow. "Hey, Daphne! You made it. Come on in."

Inside, John's home was a treasure trove of creativity. Canvases cluttered corners and art supplies held court on every available surface. In the kitchen, a cleared table awaited their messy endeavor.

"Hope you don't mind getting your hands dirty," John said as he spread a plastic sheet over the table.

Daphne laughed, tying her hair back with an elastic band she had wrapped around her wrist. "I think I can handle a little mess."

They worked side by side, tearing newspaper into strips and whisking flour and water into a sticky paste. The papier-mâché mixture squelched between their fingers as they dipped and layered, forming the rudimentary shapes of their masks.

John's hand brushed Daphne's as they reached for the same strip of paper, sending an electric jolt up her arm. She glanced at him to find his eyes already on hers, a silent conversation passing between them in that fleeting contact.

"You've got... uh..." John gestured toward his own cheek.

Daphne touched her face, coming away with a dollop of paste. She attempted to wipe it off but only smeared it further.

"Here, let me," John offered. He stepped closer, his breath warm on her skin as he wiped away the paste with gentle precision.

Daphne's heart hammered in her chest, her cheeks flushing not from embarrassment but from the proximity to John.

They continued their work amidst laughter and shared stories, talking about favorite Halloween costumes from years past and scary movies that still haunted their dreams. Every now and then, one would catch the other stealing a glance when they thought themselves unobserved.

As their masks took shape—his a dragon with curving horns, hers an elegant cat with pointed ears—Daphne felt something shift inside her. Here in this kitchen filled with laughter and goopy paste, she wasn't just Preston Blackman's daughter or Rosie's protector; she was simply Daphne, crafting memories with someone who made her feel seen.

The afternoon waned into evening as they finished their masks. John held hers up to her face, tilting his head as he appraised his work.

"Perfect," he declared with a satisfied nod.

Daphne mirrored his movements, fitting the dragon mask to his face. "You look terrifying."

Their eyes met through the eyeholes of their creations—a moment suspended in time—before they erupted into giggles at the absurdity of it all.

Daphne couldn't remember the last time she'd felt this light-hearted. With John Michael and papier-mâché masks as her companions, Queens suddenly felt less like another stopover and more like a place where roots could take hold—even if just for now.

In those fleeting moments, Daphne and John shared something magical. A connection that transcended words, forged through laughter, inside jokes, and stolen glances that spoke volumes about the depth of their feelings for one another.

"Remember when we tried to roller-skate backward?" Daphne reminisced, laughing at the memory. "You were such a show-off!"

"Hey, I was just trying to impress you!" John protested, feigning innocence. But the truth was, he had been smitten from the moment he laid eyes on her. And as the days turned into weeks, and the weeks into months, he realized that what he felt for Daphne went beyond mere infatuation. It was a love that would last a lifetime.

One of their most memorable experiences together was the day they visited the Museum of Modern Art. They were both mesmerized by the vibrant colors and bold brushstrokes of artists like Van Gogh and Picasso. Daphne, who had always been captivated by the idea of control in her own life, found herself drawn to the timeless beauty of art that seemed to defy all boundaries. John, on the other hand, marveled at the raw emotion and unbridled passion that each painting conveyed.

"Isn't it amazing how a single canvas can hold so much feeling?" Daphne mused, her eyes lingering on a particularly evocative piece.

"Definitely," John agreed, his gaze never leaving her face. "It's like capturing a moment in time, preserving it for eternity."

They continued with their shared adventures, attending movies where they would compete to see who could quote more lines from classic films, and festivals where they attempted to win stuffed animals for each other at carnival games. And there were the dinners with John's family, where Daphne felt warmly welcomed as if she were already part of them.

But as the seasons changed, and the leaves began to turn from green to gold, Daphne and John slowly came to the bittersweet realization that their time in Queens was drawing to an end. Despite their best efforts to hold onto the magic of those halcyon days, life inevitably pulled them in different directions.

♥♥♥

Golden light spilled through the basement windows of Nina's brownstone, where a motley crew of teenage dreamers gathered around an old television set. The air hummed with the scent of buttery popcorn and the anticipation of a cinematic adventure. Nina, draped across an armchair like a Hollywood siren of yore, pressed play on the VCR.

Daphne nestled into the plush folds of the couch, a bowl of popcorn cradled in her lap. On screen, 'The Rocky Horror Picture Show' sprang to life, a kaleidoscope of color and sound that captivated the room. Nina mimicked the characters with exaggerated gestures, her laughter a melody that danced around the stone walls.

Lucy, with her ink-stained fingers, scribbled lines of

verse in her journal, inspired by the film's flamboyance. Phoebe strummed an unplugged electric guitar, her chords syncing with 'Time Warp.' The energy was infectious; even Daphne's toes tapped along.

"Isn't this just divine?" Nina twirled a lock of hair around her finger. Her eyes sparkled like stars destined for Broadway's sky.

Daphne glanced at her friends, each lost in their own creative reverie. A smile tugged at her lips—she had never known acceptance like this. No judgments for her spreadsheet dreams or laundry love; just unity in their quirks and aspirations.

The film unfurled its madness and mayhem, and Daphne felt herself unwind. For once, the worries of moving boxes and parental storms seemed galaxies away. Here in this basement sanctuary, possibilities bloomed like roses in an unkempt garden.

Nina tossed a handful of popcorn at the screen during a musical number. "One day, I'll be up there—not on screen but on stage, you know? And you guys will be front row."

Phoebe looked up from her guitar. "With backstage passes?"

"Of course! And Daphne will keep track of all our show finances with her killer math skills," Nina replied with a wink.

Daphne chuckled at the thought; her mind often wandered to balance sheets and equations as naturally as breathing. Yet tonight, imagination painted a different picture—a life where numbers served dreams rather than simply order.

As Tim Curry's Frank-N-Furter took his final bow on screen, Daphne leaned back into the couch's embrace. She let herself drift into fantasies of futures bright with potential—a home filled with laughter instead of tension, careers sparked by passion rather than necessity.

She looked at each face lit by television glow—Nina with dreams as big as the city skyline, Lucy weaving beauty from words, Phoebe making music from silence—and she saw it clearly: happiness wasn't just an act in someone else's script; it was there for the writing.

And as 'The Rocky Horror Picture Show' rolled credits against a backdrop of applause from four teenage girls in Queens, Daphne dared to believe that happy endings weren't only for fairy tales or movies—they could be hers too.

♥♥♥

In the dimly lit gymnasium, crepe paper streamers swayed above the heads of the high school students, casting shadows that danced along the walls. The Homecoming dance was in full swing, the air thick with teenage excitement and anticipation. Girls in glittering dresses and boys in ill-fitting suits mingled awkwardly, trying to act more mature than their years.

Daphne, in a simple blue dress that brought out the color of her eyes, lingered on the outskirts of the dance floor. She watched her classmates sway and shuffle to the music, a sense of longing tugging at her. Then, from across the room, John Michael caught her gaze. His smile was an unspoken invitation.

He weaved through the crowd with a grace that seemed at odds with his shaggy hair and lanky frame. Reaching Daphne, he extended his hand with a confidence that made her heart flutter. "May I have this dance?"

Her fingers slipped into his, and he led her onto the dance floor just as the DJ transitioned to a slow song. The lights dimmed further, leaving only the soft glow of fairy lights strung across the ceiling. John Michael pulled

Daphne close, his hands resting lightly on her waist as hers found their place around his neck.

She could feel the steady beat of his heart against her cheek as she laid her head on his shoulder. His cologne was a mix of musk and something woodsy, a scent that would forever be etched in her memory as synonymous with comfort and youthful romance.

The music enveloped them—a melody that seemed to exist solely for them in that moment. The chatter and laughter of their peers faded into a distant hum. Daphne's mind quieted, all thoughts of family troubles and future uncertainties slipping away.

As they moved together in time with the song, Daphne closed her eyes and let out a contented sigh. She wished she could capture this feeling—this perfect slice of time—and lock it away forever.

John Michael's voice was soft in her ear, barely above a whisper. "You look beautiful tonight."

Her cheeks warmed with a blush that thankfully went unseen in the low light. "Thank you," she murmured back.

They continued to dance even as the song neared its

end—the final notes stretching out as if reluctant to conclude this magical interlude.

In this fleeting embrace with John Michael, Daphne found an oasis of serenity amidst life's chaos—a moment she'd cherish long after the last note played and the lights came back on.

♥♥♥

Under a canvas of gray, the world seemed to slow down at the outdoor rink in Queens. John Michael's hand found Daphne's, a lifeline as they stepped onto the slick surface. The ice beneath their blades whispered secrets of balance and motion, each one eager to reveal itself through trial and error.

John Michael's laughter melded with the crisp winter air, a warm sound in the cold expanse. He wobbled on his skates, his grip on Daphne tightening. She mirrored his grin, her heart buoyant despite her shaky legs.

"Careful there," she teased, her breath forming clouds between them.

"I'm more of a canvas guy than an ice guy," he confessed, cheeks flushed from more than just the chill.

The rink's perimeter welcomed them with open arms, forgiving their stumbles and awkward strides. Around them, seasoned skaters weaved intricate patterns, their confidence as bright as the strings of lights framing the rink. But in their own unsteady orbit, Daphne and John Michael created a world that required no expertise—just presence.

Their fingers laced together like the perfect dovetail joint. She marveled at how something so simple could anchor her so fully in this moment—a far cry from the tumultuous waves of home life.

A daring move saw John Michael release one hand to sweep back his shaggy hair. His other arm snaked around Daphne's waist, pulling her closer. The gesture sent a cascade of butterflies fluttering through her stomach.

"You're brave," she whispered.

"For you? Always."

They circled the rink again, gaining confidence with each lap. A smile danced on Daphne's lips as she leaned into him, her eyes capturing every nuance of his expression—the curve of his smile, the spark of mischief in his eyes.

Near the Zamboni entrance, where shadows draped themselves like curtains on a stage, John Michael tugged her into an alcove. Their laughter faded into soft breaths as they drew each other near. His lips met hers in a kiss that tasted like promise and new beginnings—sweet as hot cocoa on a winter day.

As they reemerged into the rink's bustle, hands clasped once more, Daphne allowed herself to feel something akin to freedom. It was not just from gravity's pull as they glided across the ice but from the weight of expectation that often pressed down upon her young shoulders.

The rest of the world might be chaotic—a blur of moving boxes and parental storms—but here with John Michael on this slab of frozen water, she could imagine a life where love and laughter were as plentiful as snowflakes in a Queens winter sky.

♥♥♥

Perched atop the shingled roof, John Michael and Daphne dangled their legs over the edge, the cool breeze tousling their hair. The cacophony of Queens traffic dwindled to a soft hum, surrendering to the night's serene whisper. The city's constellation of lights winked and flickered below them, a terrestrial mirror to the stars above.

Daphne glanced over at John Michael, his features half-lit by the glow of a distant billboard. His eyes shimmered with the reflection of the night sky, an artist's palette of dreams and colors.

"You know," he began, breaking the silence, "sometimes I imagine escaping to Paris. Just me, my brushes, and endless inspiration."

Daphne's lips curled into a smile. "Paris? With all those romantic cobblestone streets?"

He nodded. "Exactly. And every day I'd set up my easel by the Seine and paint whatever caught my eye."

Daphne leaned back on her hands, her gaze drifting skyward. "I see myself in a skyscraper office, floor-to-ceiling windows overlooking the city. Numbers and equations laid out before me like a puzzle only I can solve."

"Sounds just like you," John Michael said with an affectionate chuckle. "Queen of Order amidst the chaos."

A blush warmed Daphne's cheeks as she tucked a strand of hair behind her ear. "And you'd send me paintings to hang on my walls?"

"Of course," he promised with a grin. "To remind you there's beauty in spontaneity too."

Their shared laughter mingled with the rustling leaves around them. The city sprawled beneath them—a canvas of possibility—felt both vast and intimate from their rooftop retreat.

"You think we'll make it?" Daphne asked after a moment, her voice tinged with hope and uncertainty.

John Michael reached over, squeezing her hand gently. "We'll make it," he affirmed with conviction. "We're dreamers, Daphne. And dreamers find a way."

As they sat there side by side, silhouetted against the jeweled skyline, their dreams didn't feel like distant stars but rather destinations waiting for their arrival.

♥♥♥

Morning light filtered through the grease-smeared windows of the Queens Boulevard diner, casting an amber glow over the red vinyl booths. Daphne perched on a stool, a half-finished milkshake sweating in front of her. John Michael slid onto the seat beside her, their knees touching beneath the chrome-edged table. The clink of spoons against thick glass and the hiss of the griddle played a melancholy soundtrack to their final moments together.

He pushed the milkshake toward her, urging her to take another sip with a bittersweet smile. Daphne wrapped her fingers around the cold glass, tracing the ridges as she had done countless times before. She glanced at him, his eyes mirroring the turmoil swirling inside her.

"Remember when we couldn't even finish one of these between us?" John Michael's voice cracked slightly as he gestured to the tall glass.

Daphne chuckled, a fragile sound. "And now look at us, acting like we can handle our own."

The corners of his mouth lifted, but his smile didn't reach his eyes. "I guess we have to start getting used to doing things on our own."

She took a long draw from the straw, not because she was thirsty, but because it delayed the inevitable. "I don't want to get used to it," she whispered.

John Michael reached across the table, his fingers

brushing hers. "Neither do I."

Their shared silence filled with unspoken words and dreams that had sprouted wings too fragile for the distance about to separate them. He stood abruptly, dropping a few crumpled bills onto the table. "Let's walk you home."

Outside, Queens buzzed with its usual fervor. Cars honked while pedestrians weaved past them in a hurry to be somewhere else. Daphne and John Michael moved slowly through it all, two figures adrift in the city's ceaseless current.

The air between them crackled with every step closer to her house—every step closer to goodbye. John Michael's hand found hers, their fingers entwining like vines clinging desperately to each other.

They stopped in front of Daphne's building, an unremarkable structure that had been her world for what now felt like both an eternity and a fleeting moment.

"This isn't it for us," John Michael said firmly, his voice a mix of conviction and hope. "We'll see each other again."

Daphne nodded, fighting back tears that threatened to break free. "You'll paint your masterpieces and I'll come see every exhibition."

"And you'll conquer numbers and markets," he countered with pride in his voice.

They stood there on the threshold of her departure, holding each other as if they could somehow merge souls to weather what lay ahead.

Daphne buried her face in his chest, memorizing everything—the feel of his jacket under her cheek, the rhythm of his heart against her ear, the scent of paint and cologne that was uniquely him.

"Promise me something?" she murmured into his shirt.

"Anything," he replied without hesitation.

"Promise me you won't forget this—us." Her voice was barely audible against the fabric.

John Michael pulled back just enough to look into her eyes. "Impossible."

Their lips met in a kiss that carried all their unspoken promises and sealed them with a tenderness that belied their youth. They pulled apart slowly as if breaking away would undo them completely.

Daphne took a deep breath and stepped back from him. With one last glance that held all their memories and wishes for what might have been, she turned toward the building entrance.

John Michael watched until she disappeared inside before turning away with heavy steps—a young artist about to paint a world without his muse.

♥♥♥

Moving day finally arrived. Daphne didn't want to go. She never really *did* want to move, but this time was different. Something in her gut was telling her to stay... but, how?

"Grandma, can't I just stay here with you instead," she pleaded. "Mom and Dad won't even miss me." Daphne's parents were silent.

Miles said, "Nope! We won't miss her at all. Can I have her stuff, Mom?"

Caroline sighed and looked to her daughter, Rosie, for some help before she replied, "Daphne, your grandfather and I would love for you to stay with us..."

Preston cut her off, saying, "Daphne Allison stop being foolish! Finish your breakfast, we're leaving in 20 minutes."

Miles shoved the rest of his breakfast into his mouth and ran to the car mumbling, "I'm ready! Let's go now!"

Rosie looked at her daughter disapprovingly and said, "Why do you always have to cause trouble, Daphne? Why can't you just be more like your brother, Miles, and do as you're told?"

Miles had always been Rosie's favorite, a position cemented after his kidney surgery when he was six. Daphne remembered the hospital visits, the hushed voices of doctors, and most vividly, the transformation in her mother. Afterward, Miles could do no wrong in Rosie's eyes. His every whim catered to, his transgressions overlooked with a tenderness never extended to Daphne. Understanding came years later— the fear of losing another child had twisted something in Rosie, leaving Daphne forever on the outside of that protective circle of love.

Daphne looked at her grandmother and whispered, "It's going to be a long car ride."

The station wagon idled at the curb, its rear crammed with boxes and suitcases. Daphne, her fingers wrapped tightly around the Daffy Duck glass, lingered on the sidewalk. She cast a lingering gaze upon the brick house that had cradled her moments of joy and self-discovery. Each window seemed to flicker with the ghost of a memory, each first a stepping stone to who she was becoming.

"Come on, Daphne! We have to hit the road," Preston called out, his voice slicing through her nostalgia.

She took a deep breath, her eyes tracing the contours of the home one last time. With each step toward the car, the fabric of her life in Queens seemed to fray, threads of friendship and love pulling taut with distance. Yet she clutched the glass—a talisman from one temporary home, a symbol of permanence in her transitory world.

As she slid into the back seat beside Miles, she nestled the glass safely between folded sweaters. The car pulled away from the curb, and Daphne peered through the rear window at the receding house.

The only bright spots during family gatherings had been Uncle Doug and Aunt Winona. Her mother's brother would always bring his guitar, filling the room with songs he'd written himself. Despite her parents' obvious disdain for Aunt Winona's talk of empathic abilities and spiritual connections, Daphne had been drawn to her warmth. In their presence, family gatherings became bearable, even joyful at times. But Queens was far from them, another loss in a childhood defined by them.

"You okay?" Miles asked, his voice softer than usual.

Daphne managed a smile. "Yeah, just saying goodbye."

Her thoughts drifted to John Michael—their shared laughter echoing off Nina's basement walls, their hands entwined as they glided across ice. The warmth of his embrace at the Homecoming dance still lingered on her skin.

Miles followed her gaze as houses and shops blurred past them. "You'll make new friends," he said.

She nodded but knew it wasn't about making new friends. It was about leaving pieces of herself behind with each goodbye. The glass was heavy in her hands—not just with soda pop and ice cream sundaes shared with Barbie but with whispered secrets under city lights and tentative kisses by a Zamboni entrance.

As Queens gave way to open highways, Daphne's heart twinged with loss but fluttered with hope. John Michael's parting words—"Remember us when you look at those city lights"—were a promise etched in her mind.

She leaned back against the seat, her fingers tracing the faded edges of Daffy Duck's face on the glass. Her past was contained within its fragile curves—her foundation—and now she faced forward toward Charleston, toward possibility.

The future was an unwritten chapter, but Daphne had a knack for mathematics and equations; she'd find a way to balance it all out. For now, as towns and trees whizzed by outside her window, she allowed herself to dream—of stability, of love unbroken by distance or time—a dream where she was no longer running but arriving at last.

Chapter 4 – The Letter
2030

The afternoon light streamed through the window, casting a golden hue over the mahogany surface of Reuben's antique rolltop desk. Daphne's fingers worked methodically, her movements precise as she cleared away the detritus of days gone by. Receipts, a mountain of them, formed neat stacks to one side. Newspaper clippings, each chronicling a snippet of Reuben's professional accolades or community involvement, were gathered in a growing pile to be sorted and filed later.

She relished the order taking shape before her, an outward reflection of the internal calm she so coveted. The desk was an old friend, its nooks and crannies familiar from years of shared secrets and stored memories. Lining up pens in the old cup that had seen better days brought a quiet satisfaction. She arranged framed photos—snippets of smiles and warm embraces—each capturing a frozen moment of joy.

Daphne paused, her hand hovering over an engineering magazine with a cover boasting the latest in aeronautical design. Beneath it lay an envelope, yellowed with age, its edges curling slightly like autumn leaves preparing to fall. Her heart skipped, curiosity piqued by this unexpected discovery.

She slid the envelope free with gentle fingers, respecting its apparent age. A faded stamp clung to the corner; its postmark was smudged but hinted at decades past. Who had tucked it here beneath these pages filled with dreams of flight and fancy? What words lay dormant within, waiting to bridge the gap between then and now?

With reverence usually reserved for sacred things, Daphne set aside the magazine and held the envelope up to the light. The contents remained hidden, yet their significance was as palpable as the quiet that now enveloped the room.

Stan sauntered in, tail held high like a flag of conquest as he surveyed his domain. He jumped onto the desk with a soft thud, his gaze drawn to the envelope as if sensing its importance.

"Not now," Daphne whispered more to herself than to her feline companion. "We'll uncover this mystery together." She stroked Stan's sleek fur as he purred contentedly.

Loretta appeared in the doorway then, her whiskers twitching with interest as she watched her human engage with an object she couldn't understand but knew must be important.

The envelope lay between them—a silent invitation to delve into history's embrace—but for now it remained sealed. The stories it contained would have to wait just a bit longer before they unfolded in Daphne's hands.

♥♥♥

The yellowed paper crackled under Daphne's fingers as she extracted the inner envelope, its edges softened by time. Her name, Mrs. Daphne Stainthorpe, looped across the front in her mother's hand—her mother's constant refusal to acknowledge her first husband still lingered. The script was meticulous yet bore a heaviness, each letter weighed down by the burden of its message.

She hesitated, tracing the ink, transported to the day she'd first broken the seal. Daphne unfolded the letter with care. As her eyes scanned Rosie's bitter words once more, she recalled the tangle of emotions that had seized her then—relief, guilt, a hollow victory over a man who had defined fear for her.

Dear Daphne,

I hope this letter disrupts the blissful ignorance you've managed to cocoon yourself in. Life isn't all sunshine and rainbows, and I've grown tired of pretending otherwise. So, here it is – the truth you've conveniently danced around for far too long.

Preston is dead. Gone. And while the world may shed a tear for the departed, I can't muster any false grief. It happened suddenly, a fittingly abrupt end for a man who reveled in causing pain to everyone around him. I thought you should know, though I doubt you'll lose any sleep over it.

I've spent too many years drowning in regret, and your absence during the darkest times was just one more disappointment in a long line of them. Your conscience may be clear, but I can't help but wonder if things might have been different had you been there to witness the hell we endured together.

Miles is left to pick up the pieces, just like me. We're left to sift through the wreckage of a family that never really was, thanks to your convenient disappearances. It's amusing how you manage to distance yourself yet still find a way to cling to the edges of our lives.

I don't expect you to feel responsible for everything but make no mistake – your choices have consequences. You can't keep running from the past, though I'm sure that's your preferred method of dealing with life's messes.

Take care of yourself, Daphne, as I try to do the same for Miles and myself. Life moves forward, whether you choose to acknowledge the wake of destruction you left behind or not.

Sincerely,

Your Mother

Her thumb brushed over the paper where Rosie's pen had pressed hardest: "Preston is dead." No warmth there, no mourning; just a statement of fact from a woman who'd shared her life with a tyrant.

The cats, sensing their human's stillness, paused in their play to glance up at her. Daphne folded the letter with precision that mirrored her mother's handwriting and placed it back inside its aging cocoon.

"Preston may be gone," she whispered to herself as

much as to Stan and Loretta, "but some ghosts refuse to rest."

With the envelope now resting atop Reuben's tidy desk, Daphne gazed out at the peaceful scene beyond her window. Her hands moved to smooth out imaginary wrinkles on her blouse—a gesture of composure. She'd learned long ago that no spreadsheet could chart the complexities of family history or predict how its echoes would ripple through time.

Yet here she stood amidst it all—the past's relentless surge met with her unyielding quest for order and tranquility.

♥♥♥

The paper crinkled under Daphne's fingers, the ink a stark contrast against the aging background. Rosie's words cut through the years, as sharp as the day they were penned. Daphne winced, each sentence devoid of the warmth or solace one might expect in such a message. It was just like Rosie, always distant, always ready with a barbed comment rather than a comforting embrace.

Daphne leaned back in her chair, her mother's script a visual echo of her voice—cold, precise, indifferent.

Memories swirled like leaves caught in an autumn gust, bringing her back to times when vulnerability was met with venom rather than virtue.

She recalled a particularly icy evening when the wind howled outside their Akron home. Daphne had reached for Rosie's hand, seeking a harbor in the storm of their family's discord. Instead of a refuge, she found a tempest. Rosie's eyes had flared with the familiar fire fueled by liquor and loathing.

"Look at you," Rosie had slurred, her words dripping with disdain. "Always needing something. Can't you see I have my own problems?"

Daphne could still feel the sting of rejection, the way her young heart had crumbled like brittle leaves underfoot. She had learned to tread carefully around her mother, navigating the treacherous landscape of her moods like a mapmaker charting perilous territories.

Now, years later, with each word from that old letter etching deeper into her consciousness, Daphne reaffirmed the fortress she had built around herself. She folded the letter with mechanical precision and placed it back in its envelope. Her gaze drifted to the window where Stan and Loretta lounged in the sunbeam, their serene presence a stark contrast to the storm that raged within her.

She stood up and moved to the window, letting the light wash over her face. The warmth did little to thaw the chill that had settled in her bones—a legacy of Rosie's coldness that seemed determined to linger.

The phone rang then, its shrill tone slicing through the silence of Reuben's study. Daphne shook off the shadows of her past and answered with practiced composure.

"Hello?"

Her voice was steady, betraying none of the turmoil that Rosie's words had stirred within her. The present demanded attention; she couldn't afford to drown in yesteryears' sorrows—not when there was so much yet to do before evening fell and life marched on into another chapter without regard for past wounds or present pains.

A sheepish apology crackled through the line, "Mrs. Feldman, I'm afraid we're running behind schedule. Got tangled up with a bit of a situation here."

Daphne's heart sank. The careful choreography of

her day was slipping from her grasp, every minute planned to stave off the chaos that once ruled her life. She pressed the phone closer to her ear, struggling to keep the edge from her voice. "How late are we talking?"

"We're looking at a couple hours, ma'am. Again, really sorry for the inconvenience."

The words hung heavy in the air as she replaced the receiver in its cradle. A couple of hours. Time she hadn't accounted for. Time that now stretched out before her, filled with memories she'd rather not entertain.

She leaned against the window pane, staring out at the familiar landscape of her garden as a single tear betrayed her stoic facade. Images flashed unbidden through her mind: Rosie's face twisted in scorn, staggering through their cramped apartment with a bottle clutched like a lifeline, spewing vitriol about overdue bills and wasted opportunities.

"Why can't you be more helpful? You think your grades make you better than us?" Rosie's words echoed through time, sharp as ever.

Daphne brushed away the tear with a swift movement, chastising herself for this momentary lapse. She refused to let Rosie's ghost disrupt her sanctuary, not today.

She straightened and exhaled slowly, reclaiming control. Her gaze drifted to Stan and Loretta, watching her with curious eyes from their respective perches.

"Well," she addressed them with a wry smile tugging at her lips despite herself, "looks like we've got some extra time on our hands."

She decided then to turn this delay into an opportunity—time to start that book she'd been eyeing on the shelf for weeks or perhaps even take a stroll through the garden she had nurtured into an oasis of tranquility.

♥♥♥

Daphne's hand hovered over the aged paper, the loops and whirls of Rosie's handwriting like chains linking her to a past she could never fully escape. The letter lay open, its words a stark reminder of a time when hope had been as tangible as the trembling in her fingers.

She remembered how, as a child, she would sit at the kitchen table, legs swinging beneath her, eyes fixed on the door each time it creaked open. Anticipation would bloom in her chest—a misguided wish that Rosie would walk through with clear eyes and open arms, transformed from the distant specter of a mother into the warm presence Daphne craved.

Instead, Rosie would stumble in, the stench of liquor preceding her like an unwelcome herald. Each time, hope would crumble into dust, leaving Daphne to sweep it under the rug along with the shards of another broken promise.

The house echoed with silence now, filled only by Stan and Loretta's soft purrs. It was clean, ordered, a stark contrast to the chaos of her childhood home. Yet even amid the calm she'd cultivated so carefully, Daphne could feel the tug of old longings—a child's yearning for maternal love that had never materialized.

Her gaze drifted from the letter to the window where Loretta lounged in a sunbeam. The cat stretched languidly, utterly content in her solitude. Daphne envied that ease. She had worked hard to emulate it—to build walls high and thick around her heart.

The sound of fabric rustling brought her back. She folded Rosie's letter with meticulous care, placing it back in its envelope as if tucking away a fragile relic. The words were mere echoes now—echoes that no longer held power over her.

The light caught in her hair, turning strands to silver and gold. She let out a slow breath and watched as it fogged up a small patch of glass before fading away.

In that fleeting mist was a symbol of all she'd overcome—the clouded vision of a life once suffocated by others' failings now cleared by her own resolve. She'd learned to nurture herself when no one else would.

Turning from the window, Daphne resolved once more to focus on what lay ahead. Her list awaited action—items to check off, tasks to complete—each one an affirmation of control in an uncontrollable world.

She headed toward the kitchen to making herself a cup of tea—the good kind, with leaves steeped in a pot. She'd learned long ago that rituals could smooth over life's unexpected edges. As she walked away from Rosie's letter and all it represented, Daphne didn't look back—not even once.

The next item on the list beckoned her to start the laundry. The hum of the washing machine soon filled the room, a symphony of normalcy. Daphne meticulously sorted colors from whites, taking pleasure in the crisp snap of fabric as she shook out each garment before placing it in the machine.

As the water swirled and soaked into fabrics, Daphne turned to her next task: grocery shopping. She needed to stock up on essentials before her stepson arrived. With a glance at the clock, she calculated how much time she had left before she needed to leave.

The refrigerator door opened with a gentle suction sound, and she surveyed its contents with an appraising eye. Lettuce for salads, chicken breasts for grilling, and her favorite vanilla yogurt for breakfast—she mentally checked off items and added what was missing to her grocery list.

In quick succession, Daphne moved through the house, ticking off tasks with a precision that would make a Swiss watchmaker nod in approval. She fluffed cushions on the couch, wiped down surfaces until they shone, and aligned books on shelves by height and color.

A faint purr broke her focus as Loretta sauntered into the room, rubbing against Daphne's leg. A smile tugged at the corners of Daphne's lips as she scooped up the feline, burying her face in its soft fur for a moment of comfort.

"Alright, Loretta," Daphne murmured as she set down her companion. "Let's keep moving."

Her fingers brushed against smooth wooden hangers in the closet as she selected an outfit for later—something comfortable yet presentable. As each article of clothing settled into place on her bed, she envisioned how they would look together.

With every completed task, Daphne's confidence grew; she was reclaiming control from chaos with every checkmark on her list. She didn't just do these chores; she mastered them—a small victory against life's unpredictability.

The sunlight shifted across the floorboards as time marched forward, bringing with it change and challenge. But for now, Daphne reveled in the sanctuary of order within these walls—a testament to her resilience and resolve.

♥♥♥

Daphne stood before the assorted recyclables, cardboard mingling with plastic and glass. She found solace in separating them, piece by piece, each into its rightful bin. The rhythmic motion of her hands provided a simple distraction from the more complicated fragments of her past that often clamored for attention.

The clink of glass echoed through the room as she

methodically placed jars and bottles into a blue container marked with the recycling symbol. The task was tedious to some, but to Daphne, it was a small act of reclaiming power over her environment, an echo of the order she longed to instill in every aspect of her life.

With each item sorted, the chaos of her emotions settled into a calm tide. Her focus narrowed to the colors and shapes in her hands—the green of a wine bottle, the brown of a beer bottle, the clear lines of a milk jug. She relished the monotony, how it silenced the noise in her head.

The afternoon sun began its descent, casting a warm glow through the kitchen window. Shadows danced across the clean surfaces as Daphne worked in silence. She moved from room to room with quiet efficiency, ensuring that every space within her home reflected her need for precision.

Daphne stood back to admire her work. The recycling was done; the bins lined up neatly against the wall of her garage. She walked through her house, noting how every cushion sat plump on its seat, how every picture frame aligned perfectly straight.

Her home was more than just a space; it was a

testament to her resilience—a sanctuary she had built amidst life's unpredictable storms. Daphne smiled softly at this thought, acknowledging that despite everything, she had fashioned something beautiful from the disarray that once defined her existence.

She returned to the living room where Stan and Loretta had taken their respective posts—one curled on a sunlit patch of carpet and the other perched regally on the back of an armchair. They seemed to understand that their world was ordered and safe because Daphne made it so.

Sitting down on her couch, she allowed herself a moment to just breathe—to simply be in this space that resonated with calm and care. Yes, there were wounds that time alone could not heal; there were memories that would always sting with fresh pain when poked. But here in this moment, she could celebrate how far she'd come from the chaos of her youth.

Daphne glanced around at the walls that held both laughter and tears—memories of children growing up and love taking root amidst life's ever-turning pages. This house was more than structure and foundation; it was an emblem of who she had become: steadfast, enduring.

Healing may be an odyssey without end, but Daphne knew each day brought its own small victories. As dusk painted her orderly world in shades of pink and orange, she cherished these triumphs—the mundane yet profound acts of sorting recycling or fluffing pillows—that strung together like pearls on a necklace formed a life not just survived but lived with intention.

Inhaling deeply, Daphne closed her eyes and allowed herself this momentary respite—a fleeting whisper promising that while some scars may never fade entirely, each day offered new grace to weave into the tapestry of her healing heart.

Chapter 5 – High School Memories
2030 / 1981

Daphne stood in the familiar warmth of her living room, bathed in the golden light that streamed through the window. Her gaze fell upon the list she held in her hand, a meticulously organized spreadsheet detailing every task that awaited her. The crisp lines and neatly typed words brought her comfort, each completed chore a small victory over the chaos that often threatened to overwhelm her.

"Alright," she murmured to herself, a determined glint in her eyes. "Let's keep going."

With a sense of purpose, Daphne began to move through the room, carefully dusting the mantelpiece and rearranging family photographs just so. Her hands were steady and practiced, her movements precise. She reveled in the quiet satisfaction of watching order take shape from disorder, like a sculptor shaping beauty from raw marble.

Her focus shifted to the stacks of books on the nearby shelf, their spines a colorful mosaic of knowledge and adventure. As she sorted through them, her thoughts drifted back to her college days when she was a cheerleader, filled with boundless energy and enthusiasm. It seemed like a lifetime ago, and yet some things never changed. The same drive for perfection and control that had propelled her through those years now fueled her tireless efforts to maintain order in her home.

"Ah, 'To Kill A Mockingbird,' my favorite," she whispered, running her fingers along the well-worn spine before carefully returning it to its designated spot on the shelf.

Daphne ran her cloth along the spines of well-thumbed novels, each one aligned with precision on the bookshelf. The dust particles danced in the slanting sunlight before settling on the polished wood surface. Her fingers paused on a leather-bound edition, a ghost of a smile tugging at her lips. She could almost hear the echo of her children's laughter, recalling nights spent huddled together, lost in stories of adventure and magic.

Lowering herself to the floor, she reached for the bottom shelf, where years had gathered forgotten trinkets and treasures. As she pulled out a miniature cedar chest, its polished wood gleaming in the soft light, memories flooded back. Stephen had given her this keepsake box during their junior year in Charleston—a perfect replica of a full-sized hope chest, complete with intricate carvings along its edges and a tiny brass lock that still worked. "To keep your dreams safe," he'd said, his eyes tender as he placed it in her hands.

The cedar scent still lingered faintly as she lifted the lid, unleashing a mosaic of emotions that lay neatly stacked within. Inside, a silk scarf, patterned with paisleys and swirls of colors now muted by time, unfurled in her hands. Beneath it lay an assortment of photographs—snapshots of youthful faces frozen in time—and letters tied with ribbon grown brittle..

She sifted through the photographs: there was Royce on his first bicycle, Morgan in their ballet recital costume, Caroline's toothless grin beaming up at her. Each image tugged at a different chord within her heart, resonating with silent melodies of nostalgia.

A photo slipped from between its brethren—a candid shot capturing Daphne and Reuben at a company picnic.

Reuben's arm slung casually around her shoulder as they both sported wide grins, oblivious to the camera's gaze.

Her hand hovered over the letters. The loops and flourishes of handwriting on faded paper beckoned, tempting her to delve into words penned by hands long stilled. The first piece she withdrew was a bundle of love letters, tied with a ribbon that had once been crimson but now bore the muted tones of an old bruise. The ink had faded, yet the swooping script still whispered promises and sweet nothings.

Daphne unfolded one of the letters, her eyes dancing over the words. She remembered how they'd made her pulse quicken, how they'd been a balm on days when the world seemed too harsh. A soft smile touched her lips as she recalled the eager anticipation of each new missive.

Beneath the letters lay a brittle bouquet of dried roses, their petals fragile as tissue paper. She lifted them to her nose, though their scent had long since dissipated into whispers of what once was. Each thornless stem was a token of affection from dances and dates long past.

A mix CD rested at the bottom of the box, its surface scratched but its contents unforgotten. She could still see herself in younger years, huddled by a boombox as melodies filled the room—a soundtrack to memories both bitter and sweet.

♥♥♥

Daphne's thoughts drifted back to the family's move from Queens, NY to Charleston, WV. It had been a difficult transition, trading the familiar cacophony of the city for the quiet hush of the Appalachian hills. She recalled the jarring shift in landscape, the way the towering buildings melted into rolling green hills that seemed to swallow her whole.

In truth, forming friendships in Charleston had been daunting. Daphne remembered the anxiety that gripped her chest as she navigated unfamiliar hallways, searching for a friendly face amidst the sea of strangers. Lunchtime was the worst; sitting alone, picking at her food, willing someone to notice her. Slowly, though, she began to find her footing – joining clubs, attending events, and putting herself out there despite her fears.

The impact of her mother's alcoholism and her father's multiple jobs weighed heavily on Daphne. The constant chaos at home made it difficult for her to concentrate on her studies, and she often found herself seeking solace in the quiet corners of the school library. It was there that she discovered her love for literature – a passion that would carry her through even the darkest times.

Rosie stumbled noisily into Daphne's room. Slurring her words she said, "Daphne, wake up. It's too hot in here and your father's not home."

Flipping on the light, Daphne blearily opened her eyes. "OMG Mom, you're naked"

But Rosie had already begun to climb into bed with her.

♥♥♥

Sophomore year of high school found Daphne navigating the social landscape with newfound confidence. Her friendship with Suzie had been a game-changer, providing her with a sense of belonging she'd never experienced before. Suzie was the life of the party, her infectious laughter and boundless energy drawing people to her like a magnet. Her wild red hair, an unruly cascade of fiery curls, seemed to match the spirited nature that defined her personality. She had an uncanny ability to make everyone feel special, and Daphne was no exception.

One fateful day, Suzie dragged Daphne to a pep rally, insisting that she needed to experience the school spirit she'd been missing out on. As they cheered and chanted alongside their classmates, Daphne felt a sense of camaraderie she'd never known before. It was then that Suzie turned to her with a mischievous grin, her braces catching the gymnasium lights, and said, "You know what would really make you popular around here? A date with my brother."

Daphne raised an eyebrow in surprise. "Benji?" she asked, recalling their brief encounter at the station wagon years ago. "He's nice enough, but we barely know each other."

Suzie just laughed and gave her friend a playful shove. "Trust me," she said confidently. "All the boys need to see someone like Benji take you out. Then they'll know you're dateable."

Daphne's cheeks flushed at Suzie's blunt assessment, but she couldn't deny the logic. Being new to Charleston had made dating difficult, and Suzie's plan to raise her social stock made practical sense.

And so it was that Benji found himself asking Daphne out on a date—a double date with Suzie and her boyfriend, Vinny—to the Spring Fling dance later that month. Daphne hesitated for a moment before agreeing, sensing that this could be an opportunity to finally establish herself in Charleston's social hierarchy.

The night of the dance arrived, and Daphne found herself dressed in a flowing blue dress that made her feel like Cinderella. She fixed her hair in front of the mirror one last time before heading downstairs to meet Benji at his car. As she approached his sleek black Mustang convertible, she couldn't help but feel a flutter of nervousness in her stomach—this was her first real car date, after all.

Benji greeted her with a warm smile as she slid into the passenger seat beside him. He looked handsome in his suit and tie, his sandy-brown hair slicked back neatly, his hazel eyes reflecting a maturity beyond his years. As they drove to the dance together, they chatted easily about their favorite bands and movies—their conversation flowing naturally despite the awkwardness of their arranged date situation.

The Spring Fling was everything Daphne had hoped for—a sea of twinkling lights and pulsating music that made her want to dance until dawn. She laughed and joked with Benji as they swayed together on the crowded dance floor. Although Daphne had a great time, she sensed that Benji's heart wasn't fully in it; his attention occasionally drifting to a pretty blonde across the room whom Daphne later learned was his ex-girlfriend.

After the dance, Benji drove them to a secluded spot overlooking the city—her first time "parking" with a boy. Yet true to his nature, Benji was a complete gentleman. They talked about their dreams and aspirations under the stars, and when he drove her home, he gave her a chaste kiss on the cheek that somehow felt more meaningful than any passionate embrace could have been.

Their "relationship" lasted three months, during which Daphne's social status at school noticeably improved. The boys who had once overlooked her now saw her in a different light—as someone worthy of attention. But as summer approached, Benji reconnected with his old girlfriend, and he and Daphne amicably parted ways, having served each other's purposes and formed a genuine, if not romantic, friendship in the process.

Years later, Daphne would look back on those months with Benji with a bittersweet fondness. She had no way of knowing then that the quiet, kind-hearted boy who had been her first car date would eventually be serving a life sentence for beating a man to death. The Benji she knew had been gentle and respectful—a stark contrast to the man he would become.

♥♥♥

In the quiet of her orderly living room, Daphne paused, the ticket stub pinched between her fingers. The faded ink bore the name of an old cinema in Charleston, the date etched alongside it a bridge to another time. Her pulse quickened as the scene unfolded in her mind's eye, crisp and vivid as if plucked from yesterday's embrace.

There she stood, fourteen and tentative on the outskirts of a bustling school courtyard. A throng of students ebbed and flowed around her, laughter and chatter riding the autumn breeze. Her gaze wandered, snagging on a face unfamiliar yet instantly intriguing.

"I'm Steve," he introduced himself, extending a hand roughened from work unseen. His smile crooked like a secret shared between conspirators, beckoned her closer. Warmth spread through her cheeks as she reciprocated, "I'm Daphne."

The casual lean of his frame against the sun-warmed bricks of Charleston High whispered tales of ease and confidence. Yet his eyes held a kindness that belied his relaxed demeanor—a contrast to the detached coolness of boys she had known.

Their conversation unfolded effortlessly like linen sheets in the wind—topics fluttering from favorite bands to classes they found tedious. His laughter punctuated her words, genuine and unguarded. She savored the cadence of their dialogue, a rhythm that felt both new and exhilaratingly familiar.

The ring of the school bell tolled like an unwelcome interloper, yet Steve dug into his pocket, pulling out a pair of movie tickets. "You should come with me," he said, a hopeful lilt coloring his voice.

Daphne hesitated only for a heartbeat before accepting. The promise of shared popcorn and whispered commentary under the dim glow of the cinema's marquee lit an eager spark within her.

♥♥♥

In the thickening Charleston heat, summer flirted with the edges of fall, and so did Daphne with Steve. The town, with its tree-lined streets and neighborly chatter, became a canvas for their burgeoning affection. Every glance shared across the school courtyard or the local grocery store felt like a secret they both were privy to, an unspoken promise of something more.

She found herself looking for him whenever she stepped outside, her heart leaping whenever she spotted his familiar stride or caught the sound of his laughter. Their encounters were brief yet charged with an energy that left her skin tingling long after he'd gone.

On one such afternoon, they found themselves side by side at the local cinema. The lights dimmed, and as images flickered on the screen, Daphne felt the brush of Steve's hand against hers in the darkened room. Her pulse quickened; her focus shifted entirely from the film to the warmth spreading from her hand to the rest of her body.

The movie ended all too soon, and they spilled out into the golden twilight, eyes sparkling with shared excitement over their clandestine touch.

"Did you enjoy the movie?" Steve asked, a knowing smile tugging at his lips.

"The best part was...unexpected," Daphne replied, her voice barely above a whisper as she met his gaze.

Another day brought them together outside an ice

cream parlor where they leaned against the counter, shoulders touching. Daphne savored a scoop of vanilla as Steve regaled her with stories about his latest woodworking project. Their laughter mingled in the air, drawing curious glances from passersby.

These moments with Steve became her sanctuary from the storm brewing at home. Each shared smile and lingering look offered respite from her mother's bitter tirades and her father's increasing detachment.

Lying in bed at night, Daphne would replay their interactions in her mind, weaving fantasies where she and Steve were free from parental scrutiny and disapproval. She imagined picnics in the park under wide oak canopies and stargazing on warm nights when curfews didn't exist.

But reality always crept back in with the dawn. The weight of her family's dysfunction pressed down on her chest as she rose to face another day of walking on eggshells and managing chaos... like the time she was sitting in her favorite rocking chair in front of the fireplace. It was snowing outside, but she barely noticed the chill as she read "The Telltale Heart."

Hands came up behind her and slid from her

shoulders down to her chest. Daphne jumped and screamed. She didn't think her father was here today.

"What's wrong with you? Don't you like this? You should." slurred Rosie.

Grabbing her book and running to her room, Daphne said "No mom, I don't."

♥♥♥

The kitchen clock ticked in the background, counting away the seconds as Daphne traveled back to those humid Charleston nights when cicadas serenaded the dark. She could almost feel Steve's fingers tracing circles on the back of her hand as they sat on the porch swing, talking about everything and nothing until the stars dimmed.

Their love had been their own secret garden—hidden from disapproving eyes—where they could dream of a life unburdened by past shadows. They shared whispers of escape and fantasies of a future where they could shape their destiny without interference.

But walls have ears, and secrets in small towns have a way of unfurling in the wind. Her mother's voice still echoed in Daphne's mind, sharp as shattered glass.

"You're too young to know what love is," Rosie had snapped after discovering their relationship. "You'll thank me one day."

Steve's parents had echoed the sentiment, convinced that their son's potential would be squandered on a teenage romance. Meetings were forbidden; calls went unanswered. They were pulled apart as swiftly as they'd been drawn together.

Daphne gazed at their faces in the photo booth strip again. Her younger self didn't know yet that this was goodbye—that within weeks, Steve's family would move him across state lines to ensure their separation.

Their last encounter played before Daphne's eyes like an old movie—the hurried exchange at the bus station where they'd first met, his hand gripping hers tightly one last time. "We'll find each other again," Steve had promised with all the conviction of youth. "Someday."

But life had other plans. Letters sent went without reply; distance grew into silence. Daphne held onto hope until it frayed at the edges like the worn copy of "To Kill a Mockingbird" that sat by her bed.

Now here she stood in her quiet kitchen decades

later, with only memories and what-ifs for company. The photo strip returned to its resting place amid relics of a past life—one where each item was a marker on her journey toward who she'd become.

♥♥♥

The clang of locker doors and the cacophony of adolescent chatter filled the Charleston high school hallways. Daphne shuffled through the throng, her books clutched to her chest, an island in a sea of laughter and friendship she couldn't seem to navigate. Each smile shared between classmates, each secret whispered, felt like a world away from her. The ghosts of her Queens friends haunted her steps; their absence was a weight around her ankles.

She turned a corner and collided with a shoulder, books tumbling to the ground. A flurry of apologies erupted from both parties as Daphne crouched to gather her scattered belongings. The boy who'd bumped into her paused to help, his face etched with genuine concern.

"Sorry about that," he offered, handing her a math textbook.

"It's okay," Daphne replied, forcing a smile. "Thanks."

As he walked away, Daphne's gaze lingered on his retreating back, longing for the easy camaraderie she'd once had with John Michael and her artsy friends. With a sigh, she hoisted her backpack and continued on to class.

The empty house greeted Daphne that afternoon with silence heavy enough to smother. She flicked on lights as she made her way through the rooms, checking for signs of life. Her mother's presence was there in the empty wine bottles that peeked out from beneath the sofa, the smell of stale alcohol lingering like an unwelcome guest.

Miles sat cross-legged on the living room carpet, his action figures arrayed in some grand narrative only he understood. At the sight of Daphne, his face brightened.

"You're home!" He scrambled to his feet and wrapped his arms around her waist.

Daphne ruffled his hair affectionately. "Hey there, champ. Did you have a good day?"

Miles nodded enthusiastically but then his expression dimmed as he glanced toward the kitchen. "Mom's sleeping again."

A pang of responsibility tightened Daphne's chest. She was all too familiar with this routine: checking on their mother, ensuring Miles had something to eat, keeping up with chores that Rosie neglected in her stupor.

"I'll make us some dinner," she said more cheerfully than she felt. "How about grilled cheese sandwiches?"

"Can we have tomato soup too?" Miles asked with hopeful eyes.

"Of course." She ushered him toward the kitchen table and set about preparing their simple meal.

Later that evening, Preston Blackman returned home as shadows stretched across the front lawn. He entered without fanfare or greeting, sidestepping Rosie's slumbering form on the couch without so much as a glance. Daphne heard him ascend the stairs to bury himself in paperwork or whatever other excuse he had for avoiding reality.

Dinner passed quietly with Miles chattering about school projects and comic book heroes. Daphne listened and nodded at all the right moments while her mind churned with worry over Rosie's decline and Preston's indifference.

As night settled in and Miles lay tucked under his blankets—innocent dreams far removed from their troubled household—Daphne lingered by his door. Her gaze traced the stars glow-in-the-dark stars stuck to his ceiling, a feeble attempt at bringing light into their world.

Returning downstairs, Daphne found herself standing over Rosie's sleeping form. Her mother's face seemed softer in sleep, lines of stress smoothed away by unconsciousness or drink—or both.

"Why can't you see what you're doing to us?" Daphne whispered into the silence.

But no answer came—just the gentle rise and fall of Rosie's chest as she slept off another day lost to liquor and lamentations. With heavy steps, Daphne retreated to her own room where she surrounded herself with textbooks—the reliable constants in an otherwise chaotic existence—and began studying long into the night.

♥♥♥

Daphne smiled, recalling the vivid memories of her first meeting with Jeffrey. "It was at the Kanawha County Fair," she told Loretta, her voice thick with nostalgia. "I was working at our family's lemonade booth, serving drinks to thirsty fairgoers. My father had taken one of his rare days off from his multiple jobs for what he called 'family time,' though that mostly meant him wandering the fairgrounds with my mother and Miles while I stayed behind to run the booth."

"Despite being stuck working while they enjoyed themselves, I remember feeling strangely free that day," Daphne continued. "As if the universe was offering me a brief reprieve from the turmoil at home."

She could still see him clearly in her mind's eye: Jeffrey Walter Haley, with his tousled brown hair and mischievous grin, approaching her booth with an air of confidence that was both alluring and infuriating.

♥♥♥

"Can I get a lemonade, please?" he had asked, his green eyes twinkling with amusement as he handed over his money.

"Sure," Daphne replied, doing her best not to let her irritation show. She couldn't help but wonder what he found so funny.

"Thanks," he said, taking a sip of his drink. "So, do you come here often?" He smirked, as if aware of the cliché nature of his question.

"Every year," Daphne replied, rolling her eyes. "It's kind of hard to avoid when your family runs the booth."

"Ah, I see," he said, nodding thoughtfully. "Well, in that case, I guess I'll have to make a point of stopping by more often."

Despite her initial annoyance, Daphne found herself drawn to Jeffrey. Their conversations were easy and natural, as if they'd known each other for years. Over the course of the fair, they began to form a deep connection – one that would prove to be the foundation of their relationship.

♥♥♥

"Father hated him, of course," Daphne told Stan with a rueful smile. "But there was something about him...something that made me feel alive, like I could face anything as long as he was by my side."

As she spoke, the memory of Jeffrey's touch – warm and reassuring – filled her with a sense of longing. The vivid recollections of their time together, both bitter and sweet, reminded her of just how much they had endured – and how far they had come.

Daphne's heart fluttered as she spotted him across

the crowded fairgrounds. Tall and lean, with a shock of curly, chestnut hair, he was unlike any boy she had ever seen before. His eyes were a piercing blue, and his smile was infectious. She couldn't help but feel drawn to him.

As fate would have it, they bumped into each other at the Ferris wheel. They struck up a conversation about their favorite rides and soon found themselves laughing together as they soared high above the fairgrounds. It was clear from the outset that there was something special between them.

Over the next few weeks, they spent every spare moment on the phone, sharing their deepest thoughts and fears. They bonded over their dysfunctional families - Daphne's abusive father and alcoholic mother, Jeff's distant stepfather and overbearing mother who disapproved of his wild streak. Their connection grew stronger with each passing day.

One night, as they talked late into the evening, Daphne felt her heart racing in her chest. She knew she was falling in love with Jeff. He made her feel understood in a way that no one else ever had before. And she could tell that he felt the same way about her.

Their relationship blossomed over the course of their

senior year. They were inseparable - going to movies, hanging out at each other's houses, and exploring the nearby woods together. They shared a passion for adventure and a desire to escape from their troubled homes. And most importantly, they had each other's backs through thick and thin.

But as much as they loved each other, their families disapproved of their relationship. Daphne's father saw Jeff as a bad influence on his daughter, while Jeff's mother thought Daphne wasn't good enough for her son. Despite these obstacles, Daphne and Jeff refused to give up on each other. They knew that they had found something special in one another - something worth fighting for.

♥♥♥

In the cramped kitchen of the Charleston home, textbooks sprawled across the table formed a fortress around Daphne. She hunched over her calculus problems, the soft scratch of her pencil against paper the only sound breaking the tense silence. Rosie slouched in a corner chair, a glass of amber liquid cradled in her hand, her eyes dull and unfocused.

Daphne's concentration never wavered as her father

stormed in. His presence filled the room like a brewing storm. "UCLA?" he thundered, waving the application form she'd left on the counter. "What nonsense is this?"

Rosie's gaze flickered briefly towards them before she took another sip, retreating back into her stupor.

Daphne straightened up, steeling herself against the impending onslaught. "It's not nonsense," she replied, her voice steady despite her racing heart. "It's my future."

"Your future?" Preston scoffed. "You think you're too good for West Virginia now?"

Daphne held his gaze. "I want something different."

"Different..." Preston's lip curled in disdain as he dropped into a seat opposite her. The table seemed to shrink under his scrutiny.

Rosie chimed in with a slur, "Why you gotta be so difficult?"

Ignoring the sting of Rosie's words, Daphne gathered her courage like armor. "I've worked hard for this."

Preston slammed his fist on the table, causing the textbooks to shudder. "You'll go where we say," he growled.

Daphne met his anger with quiet resolve. "I'm going to UCLA," she said simply.

Applying there was against her parents' wishes – they wanted her close to home, safe, secure and controllable – but Daphne yearned for independence and a life of her own.

The defiance hung heavy in the air. Rosie muttered something unintelligible, while Preston's face reddened with rage.

But Daphne had learned something crucial over the years—when to push and when to stand firm yet silent. She returned to her studies, her pencil resuming its dance across the page as if nothing had occurred.

Preston rose abruptly, crumpling the application in his hand before tossing it at Daphne. He stormed out of the kitchen without another word.

The application landed amidst her notes, a crinkled beacon of hope amidst chaos. Daphne smoothed out the paper gently, tracing her fingers over each word she'd meticulously filled out weeks ago.

Rosie's gaze lingered on her daughter before she too pushed away from the table and staggered from the room.

Left alone with her dreams spelled out on paper and numbers that made sense in ways people didn't, Daphne allowed herself a small smile. It was a silent vow—a promise to herself that no matter what battles lay ahead, she would carve out a place where chaos had no dominion.

Daphne had always been determined, even as a child. As her parents' marriage crumbled around her, she focused on her studies and extracurricular activities with a single-minded determination that surprised even herself. She could control laundry, after all. She knew the science behind getting stains out and folding clothes properly; it was something she could hold onto when everything else felt chaotic.

♥♥♥

Nostalgia could be a powerful force, but Daphne understood that dwelling on the past wouldn't bring her happiness. Instead, she needed to take the lessons she'd learned from her experiences with Stephen and Jeffrey and use them to guide her decisions in the present.

Daphne stood in the center of her living room, the afternoon light casting a warm glow over the immaculate space. She allowed herself a moment of pride at the sight of her home—every cushion plumped, every surface gleaming. Her eyes traced the lines of the room, pausing on objects that held memories like a child's hands cupping water, careful not to let them spill.

The memory box she'd tucked away earlier seemed to call to her from its resting place on the shelf, its contents a mosaic of her past. Daphne understood that each letter, each photograph, was a fragment of the person she had become. These pieces were not always joyful—some jagged, some worn—but each was essential.

She meandered to the curio cabinet and opened it gently. Her fingers danced over her grandmother Caroline's bone china—a treasure from another era. She remembered the strength and grace her grandmother carried, qualities Daphne hoped she'd inherited. With a soft cloth, she wiped an imaginary smudge from a teacup's delicate curve.

Daphne's gaze fell upon the quilt that draped over the back of the sofa—her other grandmother Katherine's handiwork. It was a patchwork of history in fabric and thread, some pieces faded more than others. She ran her hand over it as if to smooth out time itself.

The sound of Stan and Loretta's purring brought a small smile to her face as they curled up together on their favorite armchair. Daphne appreciated their simple contentment; they sought comfort in each other's company, unconcerned with yesterday or tomorrow.

♥♥♥

The musical chimes from the dryer woke Daphne from her reverie. She walked to the laundry room and began folding the clothes, the methodical task soothing her frayed emotions, she felt a strange sense of peace. In the end, she knew she had done what was best for both herself and Stephen, and that knowledge brought her a small measure of comfort. The memories they shared would always be a part of her, but she had learned to carry them with grace and poise, as a testament to the woman she had become.

The scent of fresh linen filled Daphne's nostrils as she pressed her hands firmly into the fabric, folding it with precision. She inhaled deeply, allowing the comforting aroma to remind her of the strength within herself. Each fold was a representation of her ability to put things in order, and in doing so, find balance in her own life.

As she moved through the remaining tasks on her list, Daphne found herself reflecting on those moments with Stephen that had shaped her – the laughter they shared, the conversations that stretched long into the night, and even the painful tears they shed as they faced their challenges together. Each memory was like an intricate thread woven into the tapestry of her life, providing depth and color to the person she was today.

"Grandma?" a small voice called from behind her, pulling Daphne from her reverie. Her granddaughter Emily stood in the doorway of the laundry room, pigtails slightly askew.

"Hi, sweetheart," Daphne replied, flashing a warm smile. "What are you doing back here?"

"Mommy said to see if you need help," Emily said, skipping into the room and twirling once before leaning against the counter. "You were making your thinking face."

"Was I?" Daphne admitted with a soft laugh, placing the neatly folded laundry into a basket. "I was just daydreaming about when I was younger, but I'm getting back to my list now. Tell your mommy I'm fine and that I'll see you both for dinner later tonight."

"Okay!" Emily chirped, bouncing over for a quick hug and sloppy kiss on Daphne's cheek before racing back down the hallway. "Mommy! Grandma says she's okay!"

"Thanks, Em," Daphne called after her, feeling a swell of love for her energetic granddaughter. She knew that without the experiences she had, her life would be vastly different, and she wouldn't have the family she cherished so deeply.

Chapter 6 – UCLA
1985

Daphne's footsteps echoed on the brick pathways as she wandered aimlessly across the sprawling UCLA campus. The sun beat down on her shoulders, but she barely noticed. Her mind was occupied with thoughts of Jeff, her high school sweetheart back in Charleston. They had promised to make their long-distance relationship work, but Daphne couldn't shake the feeling that something was missing.

She tried to immerse herself in her new surroundings, taking in the vibrant energy of the college town. Students bustled around her, chatting animatedly and laughing loudly. But Daphne felt like an outsider, disconnected from the world around her. She missed Jeff's easy smile and comforting presence more than she cared to admit.

As she passed by a group of fraternity brothers playing a game of ultimate frisbee, Daphne couldn't help but feel envious of their carefree camaraderie. She longed for that kind of connection, something more than just phone calls and occasional visits. But with each passing day, it seemed like Jeff was slipping further away from her grasp.

Determined not to let her homesickness consume her, Daphne forced herself to focus on her studies instead. She had come to UCLA with big dreams and even bigger ambitions, determined to make something of herself despite the challenges she had faced in her past. And as she walked across campus towards the library, clutching a stack of textbooks close to her chest, she reminded herself that this was where she belonged now - not back in Charleston with Jeff.

But deep down inside, Daphne knew that no matter how hard she tried to move on, a part of her would always belong to him. And as she sat down at a quiet table in the library and opened up her math textbook, she couldn't help but wonder if their love story was truly over - or if there was still hope for them yet.

♥♥♥

The September air held a crisp edge as Daphne

hurried across the UCLA campus. She hugged her books closer to her chest, quickening her pace when she noticed the familiar figure lounging against the building ahead. Mark hadn't been in any of her classes—that much she'd confirmed after the third time he "coincidentally" appeared outside her lecture hall. His presence had evolved from puzzling to unsettling over the past two weeks.

"Hey, beautiful," he called, pushing off the wall and falling into step beside her. "Done for the day?"

"I have another class," she lied, veering toward a more populated path. "And I'm meeting someone."

Mark's smile never wavered, but something cold flickered behind his eyes. "No problem. I'll walk you there."

"That's not necessary." Daphne managed to keep her voice steady despite the quickening of her pulse. "Really."

He shrugged, maintaining pace beside her. "Just being a gentleman. Campus isn't always safe for pretty girls alone."

The irony wasn't lost on her. Daphne spotted her roommate Lisa near the library steps and altered course, relief washing over her when Mark finally peeled away with a casual "See you around" that sounded more like a promise than a farewell.

"That guy again?" Lisa asked as Daphne reached her, face flushed. "He's persistent."

"Too persistent," Daphne murmured, glancing over her shoulder to ensure he was really gone. "I've told him I'm not interested."

"Maybe you should report him to campus security," Lisa suggested, but Daphne shook her head.

"He hasn't actually done anything wrong. He's just... there. All the time." The words sounded hollow even to her own ears—an excuse born from a lifetime of minimizing her own discomfort to avoid conflict.

Three days later, Daphne would wish she had listened to Lisa's advice.

The Kappa Sig party was in full swing, bass vibrating through the floorboards as Daphne navigated through clusters of students. She had come with a group of girls from her dorm but had lost track of them in the crowd. As she searched for a familiar face, a hand caught her wrist.

"Dance with me," Mark said, his breath hot against her ear, alcohol evident in his slurred words.

"I can't," Daphne replied, trying to pull away. "I'm actually looking for my friends. I'm leaving soon."

His grip tightened. "One dance won't kill you. Don't be such a tease."

Before she could protest further, he was pulling her through the kitchen and down a darkened hallway. Alarm bells screamed in her mind as he pushed her against the wall in an empty corner, his body pressed against hers, pinning her there.

"I have a boyfriend," she gasped, turning her face away from his attempted kiss. "Back home. I'm not looking to date anyone."

"That's not what your eyes have been saying," he growled, one hand roughly grabbing her breast through her blouse while the other forced its way down the front of her jeans. His tongue invaded her mouth, muffling her protests.

Panic surged through Daphne, her mind cycling through all the lessons from childhood—freeze, appease, survive. She couldn't breathe, couldn't think, couldn't move as his weight crushed her against the wall.

"Daphne? Are you back here?"

Lisa's voice broke through her paralysis. Mark pulled back slightly, enough for Daphne to twist away and stumble toward her roommate's voice.

"Here!" she called, voice cracking. "I'm here!"

Mark melted back into the shadows of the hallway as Lisa appeared, concern etched on her face. "Are you okay? You look—"

"I want to go home," Daphne interrupted, hands trembling as she straightened her blouse. "Please, can we just go?"

That night, Daphne showered until the hot water ran cold, scrubbing at skin that felt permanently marked by unwanted hands. She didn't report the incident—a decision she would later scrutinize in therapy sessions—convincing herself it could have been worse, that maybe she had somehow encouraged him without realizing.

Three days later, Daphne returned to her dorm room after calculus to find the door unlocked. Strange, since Lisa had an afternoon lab on Thursdays. As she pushed the door open, the sight that greeted her stopped her heart mid-beat.

Mark sat on her bed, casual as if invited, one hand stroking the teddy bear Jeff had given her before she left for college.

"How did you get in here?" she demanded, rooted to the spot, hand still on the doorknob.

His smile was benign, chilling in its normalcy. "You should be more careful about who you trust with your spare key."

Daphne swallowed hard. There was no spare key. Dormitory policy required two separate keys to access any room—the building entrance and the individual room. No one but Lisa and the residence advisor had copies of either.

With a calmness that would later amaze her, Daphne said, "I think you should leave now."

"Don't be like that," he replied, patting the space beside him on her bed. "I just wanted to talk. We got interrupted at the party."

"I'm calling campus security," she stated flatly, reaching for the phone on her desk. "Right now."

Something in her tone must have convinced him she was serious. He stood, the mattress creaking beneath his weight. As he brushed past her in the doorway, he leaned close, whispering, "This isn't over, beautiful."

But it was. The campus police escort arrived minutes later, followed by a locksmith to change both her room and building keys. The incident report she filed felt inadequate—just words on paper that couldn't capture the violation of finding him in her most private space.

Three days later, a sophomore from the Tri-Delt house was found at dawn, naked and bound to the campus flagpole. The girl had been drugged, abducted, and raped. Her description of her attacker matched Mark's appearance down to the small scar near his right eyebrow. Campus police found him in a stolen maintenance van with duct tape, rope, and enough Rohypnol to subdue a dozen victims.

The revelation sent shockwaves through Daphne's already fragile sense of security. She spent the next week sleeping on Lisa's floor, unable to touch her own bed where he had sat. Nightmares plagued her sleep—dreams of being trapped, bound, violated. The what-ifs haunted her waking hours.

What if Lisa hadn't found her at the party?

What if she had returned to her room just minutes

later?

What if the next victim had been her?

She channeled her anxiety into studying, into organizing her notes and books with near-obsessive precision. Her room became a sanctuary of order, everything in its place, doors and windows checked multiple times before bed. Control became her shield against chaos, schedules her armor against uncertainty.

The police had taken her statement, assured her she'd never have to see Mark again. But Daphne knew better. Some predators wore uniforms and wedding bands; they came disguised as fathers and husbands and students. They could be anywhere, anyone.

♥♥♥

Amidst the thrumming excitement of the lacrosse match, Daphne stood at the edge of the field, her UCLA cheerleading uniform swaying slightly in the breeze as she completed a final sideline routine. Her freshman year had been a whirlwind of new experiences, but cheering at collegiate games gave her a sense of belonging she'd been searching for. As the teams battled on the field, her gaze was drawn to the figure wearing jersey number 42 on the visiting Temple University squad. The player moved with a grace that seemed almost out of place on the rough field, his sharp cheekbones catching the sunlight as he wove through his opponents with ease. His sandy hair, damp with exertion, clung to his forehead, and every muscle in his body appeared to thrum with purpose.

She felt a pull in her chest, an inexplicable intrigue as she watched him command the game. Daphne had come to enjoy these matches, to lose herself in the college spirit that always seemed to surround these events. Yet here she was, captivated by an athlete from a rival school.

The match ended in a blur of cheers and groans, depending on which side one supported. As Daphne walked away from the field, her pom-poms tucked under her arm, her thoughts lingered on number 42. It was not just his athletic prowess that had caught her attention; there was something in his focus, a silent intensity that resonated with her own inner drive.

It wasn't until later that evening at a local diner where Daphne and her friends gathered to dissect the day's events that she learned his name. A group from the visiting Temple team walked in, their laughter and camaraderie filling the space. There he was among them—Reuben Feldman.

"Reuben's like some kind of machine learning genius or something," one of her friends commented as they observed the athletes from their booth. "I heard he's a junior at Temple and already has tech companies trying to recruit him."

Daphne sipped her coffee slowly, watching Reuben laugh at something a teammate said. His smile reached his eyes and softened his otherwise stern appearance. He caught her looking and for a moment their eyes held. She quickly looked away, but not before a hint of a smile graced her lips.

She skimmed the menu, but her mind lingered on the game, particularly on #42's impressive maneuvers. A shadow fell across her table, and she looked up to find Reuben standing there, a tentative smile on his face. His sandy hair was tousled from the helmet he'd worn earlier, and his sharp cheekbones were more pronounced up close.

"Mind if I join you?" Reuben asked, gesturing to the empty seat opposite her. "I saw you cheering in the stands. Has anyone ever told you that your smile lights up the whole stadium? Because I couldn't take my eyes off the sidelines, even when I was supposed to be watching for the ball."

Daphne's pulse quickened at the corny yet charming line that seemed straight out of a John Hughes movie. "Sure," she said, motioning for him to sit, fighting back a blush. "You played a great game."

"Thanks." Reuben settled into the booth, his athletic frame a stark contrast to the tired students slumping at nearby tables. "I noticed you weren't rooting for my team though."

She chuckled, tucking a strand of hair behind her ear. "Guilty as charged. But I can appreciate talent when I see it."

Extending a hand, Reuben said, "My name's Reuben, but my friends call me Ben."

Daphne took the offered hand in hers and felt the world melt away around her as she replied, "I'm Daphne." The conversation flowed as naturally as if they were old friends catching up.

Their food arrived—burgers and fries—and they ate while discussing their college experiences. Reuben talked about his engineering studies at Temple with an enthusiasm that was infectious.

"What about you? What are you studying?" he asked between bites.

"Mathematics and economics," Daphne replied, sipping her soda. "I'm just a freshman, but I like things that have clear answers."

"That makes sense," Reuben nodded thoughtfully. "But sometimes it's the questions we don't see coming that define us."

His words lingered in the air like a challenge to her orderly world.

Daphne leaned back in the booth, a milkshake straw between her lips, watching Reuben's animated expression as he explained his latest engineering project. The way his eyes lit up, hands gesturing to emphasize a point, she couldn't help but be drawn in.

Across from her, Reuben took a bite of his burger, pausing mid-sentence. "You know, it's rare to find someone who actually understands the intricacies of machine learning outside my lab." He flashed a grin, his voice warm with genuine appreciation.

She sipped her shake, chocolate flavor clinging to her taste buds. "I can't say I know all the ins and outs, but the economic models we work with aren't too different. It's all patterns and predictions."

Reuben chuckled, pushing his plate aside to lean forward. "Exactly! And that's why talking to you feels like such a breath of fresh air." His hand reached across the table, fingers brushing against hers. "Most people's eyes glaze over when I get into the technical stuff."

Daphne blushed but didn't withdraw her hand. Instead, she intertwined her fingers with his, feeling an electric connection that went beyond their shared academic interests. "I guess we're both nerds at heart then," she teased.

He squeezed her hand gently. "The best kind of nerds." His smile was infectious, and Daphne found herself smiling back without reservation.

Their conversation meandered from artificial intelligence to economics, touching on favorite books and music along the way. Reuben shared anecdotes from his childhood in New York, painting vivid pictures of family dinners and holidays steeped in tradition.

Daphne listened intently, captivated not just by the stories but by the cadence of his voice. She shared her own memories in return, describing the various places she had called home and the sense of transience that came with each move.

"I think that's why I'm so focused on creating stability now," she admitted after recounting a particularly poignant memory of leaving Ohio. "I want something that's mine, something that doesn't change every time you blink."

Reuben nodded sympathetically. "I get that. There's something comforting about knowing where you belong." He glanced around the bustling diner. "But I have a feeling you're going to find that place for yourself soon enough."

As they finished their meal and the waitress cleared their table, Daphne realized hours had passed in what felt like minutes. Reuben had a way of making time stand still, each topic unfolding into another seamlessly.

The check came, and they both reached for it at once, hands brushing lightly.

"I've got it," Reuben insisted with a warm smile.

"No arguments here," Daphne said with a laugh.

They exited Joe's Grill into the crisp evening air. The campus was quieter now as students retreated to dorms and apartments.

"Thanks for dinner," Daphne said, wrapping her arms around herself against the chill.

"It was my pleasure," Reuben replied, shrugging off his Temple University jacket and draping it over her shoulders—a gentlemanly act that warmed more than just her body.

Standing under the glow of a streetlamp outside the diner, they hesitated before parting ways. Daphne felt as though she was on the verge of something new and thrilling—a chapter yet unwritten but promising all the same.

"Tonight was... unexpected," she said softly.

Reuben looked into her eyes with an intensity that took her breath away. "The best things usually are." His hand brushed a stray lock of hair from her face, lingering against her cheek.

Time seemed to slow as he leaned in, his eyes asking a silent question. Daphne felt herself nodding almost imperceptibly, her heart racing as she tilted her face toward his. Their lips met in a gentle kiss that sent electricity coursing through her veins. It was brief—just a tender moment of connection—but in that heartbeat of time, Daphne felt something shift inside her, as if a piece that had been missing suddenly clicked into place.

When they pulled apart, Reuben's smile was soft, slightly dazed. "I definitely wasn't expecting that," he murmured, his voice husky.

"The best things usually aren't," she replied, echoing his earlier words with a shy smile.

She reluctantly pulled away from his touch. "I guess this is goodnight then."

"For now," he said confidently as he watched her walk away, his Temple jacket still draped around her shoulders. "Just for now."

With each step back toward her freshman dorm, Daphne replayed their conversations in her mind—the ease of it all, the laughter shared over burgers and milkshakes, the unexpected perfection of that first kiss—and felt a spark ignite within her heart that promised more than just intellectual kinship with Reuben Feldman.

♥♥♥

The evening light cast a warm glow across the walls of Daphne's dorm room, illuminating the stark contrast between her organized desk and the bed where she sat, knees drawn up to her chest, enveloped in thought. She had always prided herself on her ability to sort through complex equations and analyze economic trends with a clinical detachment. But the tangled web of her emotions resisted such neat categorization.

The echo of Ben's laughter mixed with the memory of Jeff's whispered promises over late-night calls. Daphne traced the edges of her calculus textbook, yet her mind roamed far from derivatives and integrals. The sensation of Ben's gaze, both intense and gentle, lingered with her, sparking a flurry of butterflies in her stomach.

A heavy sigh escaped her lips as she pondered the serendipity of meeting someone like Ben so unexpectedly. Their connection was immediate, a resonance she hadn't known was missing until their conversation had flowed like a symphony. He challenged her ideas and shared his own with an openness that was both exhilarating and daunting.

She picked up a pen, twirling it between her fingers as she considered Jeff. Reliable, understanding Jeff, who had been a steady presence through her family's latest upheaval. His voice was a comforting beacon during their nightly conversations—a lifeline to a semblance of normalcy amid the chaos of college life.

But was comfort enough? Daphne questioned as she stared at the collage of photos taped above her desk—a mosaic of high school memories with Jeff's face peeking out from several corners. They were snapshots of familiarity and shared history, but did they encapsulate passion? Growth?

With Ben, it felt different—like diving into an unknown ocean, depths unseen but promising discovery. His words still echoed in her mind: discussions about artificial intelligence that shifted into debates about philosophy and ethics. Their banter was sharp but playful, intellectual sparring that left her energized rather than drained.

Daphne let out another sigh, placing the pen back on the desk. She recognized the need to make decisions not just about relationships but about the path she would carve for herself. A future built on more than just escape from her past or the pursuit of stability—she craved something that ignited her spirit.

The quiet hum of the campus outside filtered through the window as she glanced at the clock—time for economics study group. Daphne shook off the cobwebs of introspection and stood up, straightening her blouse with a determined tug. Her feelings would have to wait; there were more immediate challenges to tackle.

She took one last look around the room that held both order and confusion before stepping out into the hallway. The numbers would make sense; they always did. It was everything else that remained a beautifully intricate puzzle—one she was slowly learning to solve.

♥♥♥

The scent of freshly brewed coffee and the murmur of intense conversation drew Daphne to the dimly lit corner of the campus café. She eased into an empty chair, her presence barely causing a ripple among the group of artsy students huddled around a mosaic-tiled table.

A girl with streaks of lavender in her hair, known as Elise, animatedly discussed the symbolism in Virginia Woolf's prose. Beside her, a guy with wire-rimmed glasses and a beret named Marcel dissected the layers of existentialism in Camus's works. Daphne listened, interjecting with her own insights, her mind alight with the thrill of intellectual exchange.

Hours ticked by as the group debated over Kierkegaard's leap of faith and Nietzsche's perspectives on morality. Daphne felt alive in these discussions, valued for her sharp mind and analytical skills. But as laughter punctuated a particularly witty remark from Marcel, Daphne's smile didn't quite reach her eyes.

The clock tower chimed midnight, signaling the end of another evening. The students gathered their books and scarves, preparing to depart into the cool California night. Daphne remained seated for a moment longer, wrapped in a shawl of solitude.

She appreciated these people – their creativity, their depth – but as they said their goodbyes and disappeared into the darkness, Daphne sensed a void within herself that even the most profound philosophical debate couldn't fill. She yearned for something more tangible, a connection that went beyond intellectual compatibility.

With a soft sigh, Daphne gathered her belongings and stepped out under the stars. The campus lay quiet now, paths winding through shadowed groves and silent buildings. She wandered without direction, lost in thought beneath the celestial tapestry above.

Perhaps what she missed was the simplicity of laughter not followed by analysis, or moments shared without the need for deeper meaning. Maybe she longed for connections rooted not just in mind but also in spirit and shared experience.

Daphne paused beside a fountain, its waters murmuring secrets into the night. She gazed at its undulating surface, reflections dancing like elusive dreams just out of reach. In its depths, she sought an answer to the restlessness that gnawed at her heart.

Her time at UCLA had opened doors to worlds she never knew existed, but none had yet felt like home. Home – that elusive concept that seemed more feeling than place – continued to evade her grasp no matter how hard she studied or how many discussions she immersed herself in.

With a deep breath that mingled with the mist from the fountain, Daphne made her way back to her dorm room. There was comfort in routine and stability in schedules. Tomorrow offered another day filled with classes and conversations – another chance to find what was missing.

But tonight? Tonight was for quiet reflection on all that had been and all that was yet to come. Tonight was for acknowledging that even amidst knowledge and culture, one could still feel adrift on an open sea – searching for a beacon to guide them home.

♥♥♥

Daphne lingered near the entrance of the student center, watching streams of students pour in and out. Posters lined the walls, advertising everything from political debates to poetry slams. Her gaze settled on a discreet sign near the counseling services office, offering free sessions for students in need.

She approached the sign-up sheet with trepidation, her hand hovering over the paper as if it were a crystal ball capable of revealing her deepest fears. Her heart raced, each beat echoing the uncertainty that gnawed at her insides. For years, she had become adept at suppressing her emotions, keeping them as neatly folded as her clothes.

Yet here she was, considering laying bare her tangled thoughts to a stranger. The idea was both terrifying and liberating.

Taking a steadying breath she scrawled her name on the next available line. The pen felt heavy, each letter a commitment to face the chaos she'd worked so hard to control.

As she left the student center, Daphne's steps felt lighter. It was as if by signing up, she had acknowledged a truth long buried beneath meticulous lists and organized shelves: she needed help.

The days that followed saw Daphne wrestling with doubt. She attended lectures and pored over textbooks with diligence, but the act of seeking counseling nagged at her conscience. Would this be another failed attempt at finding peace? Would they understand her longing for stability amid life's relentless upheaval?

When the day of her first session arrived, Daphne stood outside the counselor's door, pulse quickening. She knocked softly and entered upon invitation.

The room smelled faintly of lavender, with warm light filtering through sheer curtains. A woman with gentle eyes gestured toward a cozy armchair.

"Welcome, Daphne," she said with a calm smile. "I'm glad you reached out."

Daphne settled into the chair, clutching her hands in her lap. Words escaped her in hesitant fragments as she tried to articulate feelings she had never dared voice aloud.

"I feel... adrift," she began. "Like I'm always searching for something I can't quite grasp."

The counselor nodded, encouraging Daphne to continue without rushing or pressing.

"And it's not just about fitting in or knowing my major... It's deeper," Daphne confessed. "I need to find where I belong—not just here on campus but... in life."

As Daphne spoke, an unburdening began. Each shared memory—of moving trucks and fleeting friendships—each acknowledgment of her family's dysfunction brought a sense of release.

They delved into discussions about Daphne's compulsive organizing and how it served as an armor against chaos—a way to exert control when none seemed possible elsewhere in her life.

The counselor listened without judgment, offering insights that helped unravel some of Daphne's tightly wound self-reliance.

"You've built strong walls, Daphne," the counselor observed softly. "But it's okay to let others see beyond them."

An hour passed like moments in a dream. When it was time to leave, Daphne felt a surprising reluctance—a desire to stay cocooned in this newfound space where vulnerability wasn't weakness but strength.

She stepped out into the sunlit quad with new clarity flickering within like candlelight in darkness. The journey ahead would be long and undoubtedly challenging, but for once, Daphne allowed herself to feel hope without restraint.

This choice marked not an end but a beginning—one where understanding herself could finally bring the sense of belonging she craved so deeply. And as Daphne walked back toward her dormitory under an expansive sky, it seemed even nature conspired to whisper promises of brighter days ahead.

♥♥♥

In the softly lit room, Daphne perched on the edge of a leather couch, her fingers working at the frayed edges of her nails. The therapist, a woman with gentle eyes and a soothing voice, watched her patiently from across the room. "Take your time," she offered. "This space is for you."

Daphne drew in a deep breath, feeling the weight of countless unspoken thoughts pressing against her chest. The silence stretched between them, punctuated only by the muted sounds of the campus outside.

"I guess..." Daphne started, her voice barely above a

whisper. "I'm just tired of feeling lost."

The therapist nodded encouragingly. "Feeling lost can be disorienting. Do you want to explore what's behind that feeling?"

Daphne glanced around the room — walls adorned with diplomas and certificates, shelves lined with psychology books — seeking an anchor in the sea of uncertainty that seemed to engulf her life.

"It's like I'm on this path," she continued, "and everyone else seems to know where they're going. They have plans, dreams... And I'm just... wandering."

A small frown creased Daphne's brow as she wrestled with the words, trying to give shape to her internal chaos. "I've always needed to have control over things. It's how I coped at home... But here? I don't even know what I'm controlling anymore."

The therapist leaned forward slightly, bridging the gap between them with her presence. "Control can provide a sense of safety," she acknowledged. "Especially if your past was unpredictable."

Daphne's eyes flashed with recognition, and she found herself nodding before she even realized it. Memories of her tumultuous childhood home life flickered across her mind — the need for order amidst disorder, for calm within the storm.

"And now," Daphne said, "it feels like I'm holding onto control so tightly because it's all I have." She paused, noticing the way her hands had balled into fists.

The therapist gave a small smile of understanding. "What if we tried to look at control not as something you have to hold onto so tightly but as something you can manage more gently? Like steering a bike rather than gripping onto the handles for dear life."

Daphne let out a shaky laugh at the imagery. It was an odd comfort, this notion of loosening her grip on life without careening off into chaos.

"You're starting a new chapter here at UCLA," the therapist continued. "It's natural to feel unmoored during transitions."

"But it's more than that," Daphne confessed. "Back home in Charleston... there was someone." She felt a pang as Jeff's face came to mind — his laughter on late night calls that now seemed worlds away.

"And here," she hesitated before confessing further, "there was someone else too... Ben." The memory of their effortless conversation over milkshakes lingered sweetly yet confusingly in her thoughts.

The therapist observed Daphne closely as she grappled with these revelations. "Relationships can often bring our deepest hopes and fears to the surface," she suggested gently.

Daphne sighed deeply, feeling the beginning threads of understanding weave through her confusion. She didn't have all the answers yet — far from it — but articulating her feelings was like lighting a candle in a dark room.

As their session drew to a close, Daphne stood up slowly, smoothing out the creases in her jeans. The therapist offered some parting words: "Remember, Daphne, it's okay not to have all the answers right now."

Daphne managed a small smile as she stepped out into the bright California sunshine. Her heart felt lighter somehow — still unsure but open to whatever might come next on this winding path ahead.

Chapter 7 – Luke
1987

The first time Daphne laid eyes on Luke Kaleb Stainthorpe, she was sitting in a physics class during her junior year at UCLA. The murmurs of her classmates settled into a low hum as Professor Engels announced the term project, a partnership endeavor that would span several weeks.

"Pair up, everyone," Professor Engels instructed, adjusting his spectacles. "And remember, I want groundbreaking ideas, not just regurgitated concepts."

A flurry of activity ensued as students shuffled to find their partners. Daphne hesitated for a moment, feeling the familiar flutter of apprehension in her stomach. Her gaze drifted across the room and locked with Luke Stainthorpe's, who sat a few rows back, his head propped on his hand, a hint of amusement playing on his lips.

"Excuse me," a deep voice interrupted her thoughts. She looked up to see a tall, broad-shouldered young man with a mop of curly dark hair standing beside her. His striking blue eyes were fixed on her with an intensity that made her heart skip a beat. "Is this seat taken?" he asked, gesturing toward the empty chair next to her.

"Uh, no," Daphne stammered, feeling a sudden warmth rise in her cheeks. "Please, sit."

"Thanks," Luke replied, offering her a dazzling smile before taking his seat.

As the class continued, it became evident that Luke was just as passionate about physics as Daphne was. They exchanged knowing glances and whispered insights, their shared enthusiasm creating an undeniable spark between them.

When the lecture ended, they walked together, shoulders brushing, down the sunlit corridors of the university. They discovered they had more in common than just their love for science; both were meticulous planners who found solace in structure and order.

Over the next few weeks, they met regularly in the library, their project slowly taking shape amid stacks of textbooks and scribbled notes. Luke's sharp intellect challenged Daphne's own ideas, pushing her to think beyond the confines of standard physics theories.

"You know," Luke said one evening as they debated the practicalities of time travel, "I've always wanted to see the pyramids of Egypt... but as they were being built."

Daphne chuckled. "Time travel isn't exactly within our reach yet."

"But imagine if it was," he mused, his eyes alight with wonder. "To witness history unfold."

Their conversations often veered into the realms of science fiction novels they both loved. Daphne found herself looking forward to their study sessions, not just for the academic collaboration but for the shared dreams and laughter that accompanied them.

It wasn't long before Luke asked her out on a date. They found themselves wandering through a used bookstore downtown, their fingers brushing as they pointed out their favorite authors and hidden gems nestled in the crowded shelves.

"You've read Asimov?" Daphne asked with raised eyebrows as Luke pulled out a well-worn copy of 'Foundation'.

"Of course," he replied with a grin. "And Clarke, Heinlein... You?"

"I may have a slight obsession with 'Dune'," she confessed.

Their conversation flowed easily from literature to personal aspirations. Luke spoke of his desire to travel across Europe, to experience different cultures and cuisines. Daphne shared her dreams of exploring every corner of the globe.

"Speaking of plans," Luke said, a mischievous grin playing on his lips. "Would you like to grab a coffee with me after class tomorrow? We can discuss our theories on entropy and chaos over lattes."

Daphne felt her pulse quicken at the thought of spending more time with this intriguing young man who seemed to understand her so completely. "I'd love that," she replied, her voice barely above a whisper.

"Great," Luke said, his eyes locked on hers, full of promise and anticipation. "It's a date."

As they sipped coffee in a quiet café the next day, surrounded by the aroma of roasted beans and hushed chatter, Daphne felt an unfamiliar sense of connection.

"This feels right," Luke said quietly, reaching across the table to take her hand.

Daphne smiled in agreement. There was an undeniable bond forming between them—one rooted in mutual respect and shared passions. It was exhilarating to find someone who not only matched her academically but who also ignited a spark within her adventurous spirit.

Their relationship blossomed alongside their project. As they constructed models and formulated hypotheses late into the night, Daphne felt an ease she hadn't experienced before. With Luke by her side, she dared to envision a future where her childhood dreams didn't seem so far-fetched after all—a future where control and order melded seamlessly with discovery and freedom.

"Sometimes I imagine us living in a beautiful home, surrounded by trees and flowers," Daphne confided one evening as they lay entwined beneath the stars, the scent of jasmine perfuming the air around them. "A place filled with laughter and love, where our children can grow up safe and happy."

"I want that too," Luke murmured, his voice thick with emotion. "I can see it now – a big yard for the kids to play in, a cozy living room with a fireplace, where we can curl up together on cold winter nights."

As their dreams took shape in the dim light of the moon, it became increasingly clear that their futures were intertwined. And so, on a warm summer day not long after, Luke got down on one knee, presenting Daphne with a ring that sparkled like the stars they had once wished upon. With tears in her eyes, she accepted his proposal, setting the stage for the next chapter in their lives.

♥♥♥

Amidst the blush of early summer, Daphne stood beside Luke in the quaint chapel nestled on the outskirts of Richmond. Sunlight streamed through the stained glass, casting kaleidoscopic patterns over the couple as they exchanged vows. Daphne's white dress shimmered with a simple elegance, a stark contrast to the vibrant flowers clasped in her hands.

The small gathering of family and friends echoed with heartfelt applause as they were pronounced husband and wife. Luke's uniform bore the crispness of a man proud to serve his country, his smile reflecting a similar pride as he turned to Daphne. They walked down the aisle, hands entwined, stepping into a future they envisioned full of love and shared ambitions.

Days turned into weeks as the newlyweds pored over blueprints sprawled across their temporary dining table. They deliberated over every detail for their dream home – from the color of the bricks to the design of the ironwork that would grace their front porch. Their enthusiasm for this project became a beacon for their hopes, a tangible manifestation of the life they wanted to create together.

"Imagine waking up to coffee in our sunroom," Daphne mused, her finger tracing the outlines of their future sanctuary.

Luke leaned over her shoulder, his breath warm on her neck. "And evenings by the fireplace," he added, envisioning cold winter nights made cozy by firelight and shared blankets.

They settled on a farmhouse design that offered both charm and space for their anticipated family. Luke's commitments with the Navy meant he was often away, but Richmond promised a stable base – a place where Daphne could nest and flourish during his absences.

Excitement swelled as they broke ground on their plot of land. Each visit to the construction site brought new progress; foundations poured one day, walls erected another. They marked milestones with pictures – Daphne standing in what would be their kitchen, Luke perched on beams that would soon support their bedroom ceiling.

Their dreams took shape in wood and mortar, every nail and plank infused with their shared vision. The house stood as a symbol of their union, each room holding promises of memories yet to be made. They imagined holiday dinners in the dining room and summer barbecues in the backyard.

The process wasn't without its stresses. Budgets were scrutinized, and compromises made. Yet each challenge was met with determination – this was their creation, a labor of love that fortified their bond.

As they turned keys in locks for the first time, crossing the threshold into their completed home, Daphne's heart swelled with accomplishment and affection. They wandered through each room, discussing where furniture would go and which walls would host family photos.

"Here," Luke said, placing his hand against an empty wall in the living room, "this is where we'll hang our wedding picture."

Daphne nodded, her eyes bright with visions of years to come – children playing on lush carpets, holiday decorations adorning mantles. She wrapped her arms around him from behind, resting her cheek against his back.

"We built this," she whispered, pride lacing her voice.

Luke turned within her embrace, his hands cradling her face. "We built this," he agreed before sealing their promise with a kiss under the roof they had raised together.

♥♥♥

Sunlight bathed the new brickwork of the Stainthorpe residence as Daphne affixed the polished plaque beside the front door. Her fingers traced the engraved letters, a symbol of a fresh start and enduring commitment. She stepped back, Luke's arm wrapping around her shoulders, their smiles as bright as the promise of their shared future.

The interior of the house gleamed, untouched by time or trouble. Floors unscuffed, walls pristine, each room awaited memories yet to be made. They wandered through their creation, hands clasped, hearts full. Daphne's meticulous nature found satisfaction in the symmetry of furniture and the calculated hues of decor.

Yet as weeks folded into months, a subtle shift began to creep into their domestic bliss. A cup left out on the counter became a catalyst for Luke's displeasure, his brow furrowing over such minor disarray. Daphne took note, adjusted habits, and tucked away concern with a practiced smile.

Soon, Luke's criticisms extended beyond household matters. When Daphne's pregnancy with Morgan left her exhausted and queasy, his eyes would rake over her changing body with undisguised displeasure. 'You're letting yourself go,' he'd remark coldly, as if her body's transformation to nurture their child was a personal failure. Daphne would swallow her hurt, remind herself of the gentle man she'd married, and try harder to please him—a pattern that only deepened with each passing day.

It was during their first year in the new house that Daphne began to notice subtle changes in Luke's behavior. At first, it was nothing more than a few controlling tendencies – an insistence on picking out her clothes or dictating which friends she could spend time with.

"Darling, don't you think that dress is a bit too revealing for dinner?" he'd ask, his voice dripping with concern as he tugged at the hem of her skirt. "I wouldn't want anyone getting the wrong idea."

Daphne found herself acquiescing to his demands, not wanting to upset him. But as time went on, she couldn't help but feel suffocated by his constant need for control.

The outbursts of anger came next – seemingly unprovoked explosions that left Daphne feeling shaken and confused. She tried to rationalize them away, attributing Luke's behavior to the stress of his naval career or adjusting to life in their new home.

"Maybe I should have been more careful with my words," she mused one evening after a particularly heated argument, her fingers absently tracing the delicate china patterns of her grandmother's tea set. "I just never expected him to react so violently."

As the months wore on, Luke's abusive behavior grew increasingly difficult to ignore. Daphne's once-cheerful demeanor gave way to a quiet sadness, her eyes betraying the weight of the burden she now carried.

Her world – once filled with laughter and love – had become a place of fear and uncertainty, each day bringing with it new challenges and obstacles to overcome. And while she longed to escape the oppressive confines of her marriage, she knew that such a decision would come at a steep price.

One evening, Daphne hummed softly while aligning spices in alphabetical order when a crash echoed from the living room. She flinched at the sound. Luke stood over a toppled lamp, its shattered remains scattered like fractured dreams.

"This is your fault," Luke's voice sliced through the quiet, accusatory and cold.

Daphne blinked back confusion, her thoughts scrambling for reason. "I... I don't understand how—"

"You distract me with all this... this constant need for order!" Luke's hand swept across the air as if to disperse an invisible presence.

Daphne retreated a step, her voice emerging small but steady. "I'm sorry you're upset. Let me help clean this up."

He watched her kneel and gather broken pieces with careful hands. The air hung heavy with unsaid words and mounting tension.

Nights turned restless; conversations became minefields. Daphne tiptoed around Luke's moods like she once did her father's wrath. The irony did not escape her that she had recreated the very atmosphere she vowed to leave behind.

Friends inquired about bruises masked under long sleeves or makeup; Daphne parried with tales of clumsiness or mishaps during home improvements. They nodded, but suspicion lurked behind their eyes.

In solitude, Daphne faced her reflection, tracing the line of her jaw where Luke's anger had left its mark. How had she missed the signs? Was there something she could've done differently? She cycled through questions with no satisfying answers.

The spreadsheet that once cataloged their dreams now held entries of incidents and apologies – a ledger of pain she could not balance no matter how many times she recalculated.

Yet Daphne clung to moments of warmth like precious embers among ashes—shared laughter on good days, Luke's fingers dancing over piano keys filling their home with haunting melodies—a man she loved despite it all.

In time though, even those flickers dimmed beneath the looming shadow of his temper until they were mere whispers in a storm.

Luke stood framed in the doorway one afternoon, eyes dark as storm clouds. "Why can't you do anything right?" he thundered over an incorrectly filed receipt.

Daphne's heart pounded against ribcage walls built sturdy over years of survival. "It was an honest mistake," she breathed out in defense.

His retort cut short as a car pulled into view outside—the reality of others' eyes perhaps staying his hand or his words.

In that moment of reprieve, Daphne felt the facade crumble—a realization that no list or plan could protect her from what lay beneath this roof they had so lovingly built. It was not merely about misplaced objects or imperfect order; it was about control and fear—elements no spreadsheet could quantify or contain.

Silent vows formed behind weary eyes as Daphne gathered strength from shards of broken promises and plans. This was not her forever home; it was a lesson hard-learned—a stepping stone toward a future where she would reclaim her life and her peace—one where happiness would not be contingent on another's volatile whims.

♥♥♥

The morning sickness had subsided, but a different kind of unease settled over Daphne as she folded the tiny onesies and placed them in the nursery dresser. The room, painted in soft hues of green and yellow, should have been a sanctuary. Instead, each brush stroke felt like a silent witness to Luke's tightening grip on her life.

As her belly swelled, so did Luke's list of demands and decrees. He hovered over her diet, her activities, even her rest, with the intensity of a hawk eyeing its prey. "You need more protein, Daphne. Remember, you're eating for two now," he would insist at every meal, his eyes narrowing if she reached for a second helping of dessert.

The baby shower came and went—a parade of pastel gifts and well-meaning advice from friends she seldom saw these days. Luke had orchestrated the guest list, trimming it down to those he deemed 'appropriate' company for his wife. Daphne plastered on a smile as she unwrapped presents, but her heart ached for absent faces.

Labor brought relief in the form of focus; contractions eclipsed her concerns about Luke's temper. When Morgan finally arrived, cradled in her arms was a beacon of hope—perhaps this new life could soften Luke's harsh edges.

But the respite was short-lived. Nighttime feedings were met with Luke's impatient sighs from across the hall. "Can't you quiet that child?" his voice would slice through the darkness.

Daphne rocked Morgan gently, shushing and soothing, while tears of frustration mingled with postpartum exhaustion dampened her cheeks. The nursery's rocking chair became both cradle and prison as she sang lullabies into the wee hours, trying to cocoon Morgan from the tension that permeated their home.

With each milestone—Morgan's first smile, first word—Daphne clung to moments of joy amidst the criticism. "Why are you still carrying that extra weight?" Luke would chide as she bounced Morgan on her hip. "You need to set a good example."

She retreated further into herself as friends stopped calling, family visits dwindled to awkward holiday gatherings. The vibrant woman who had once charmed Reuben Feldman at a campus diner was now a shadow in her own house—a specter flitting from room to room, attempting to keep peace.

Luke scrutinized every decision Daphne made for Morgan, second-guessing her methods of soothing colic or introducing solids. "I read an article that said you're doing it all wrong," he'd declare with infuriating certainty.

On walks around the neighborhood with Morgan bundled in the stroller, Daphne would smile at passersby—a master at wearing masks by now. Behind sunglasses hid weary eyes that once dreamed of adventure and laughter shared with family.

She began to weave dreams for Morgan instead; aspirations unburdened by control or critique. She whispered promises during diaper changes and bath time: "We'll explore parks and libraries together. We'll find stories that lift us up and away from here."

And yet those whispered dreams clashed with reality every time Luke's car pulled into the driveway—an ominous herald signaling another evening walking on eggshells. With each day's end came another night spent rehearsing apologies she didn't owe and explanations for imperfections that weren't hers.

Daphne clung to what little agency she had left: spreadsheets tracking household expenses became intricate works of art; laundry turned into ritualistic sorting—colors from whites—an attempt to impose order where she could find none.

Isolation bore down on her like the summer heat through the windows—oppressive and stifling—but within its suffocating embrace lay a quiet determination growing stronger beneath her ribcage. For herself and for Morgan, Daphne knew this was no life; this house was no home.

And so she began to plan—a list here, a secret account there—each step forward an inch toward liberation from Luke's iron-clad world. She held Morgan close, whispering strength into tiny ears while plotting their escape into a future where control would fall away like shackles at their feet.

♥♥♥

Daphne clutched the edge of the kitchen counter, her knuckles white, as Luke's fury filled the room like a toxic fog. The sound of her own heartbeat pounded in her ears, drowning out the distant laughter of children playing outside. She took a measured breath, steadying herself against the force of his anger.

"You just don't know when to stop pushing me, do you?" Luke's voice was low and menacing, a stark contrast to the man who had once charmed her with talk of dreams and shared aspirations.

Her eyes locked onto the fine china they had received as a wedding gift, now teetering on the edge of the shelf. It was a metaphor for her life at this moment—precarious, fragile, threatening to shatter with the slightest nudge.

"I'm just worried about you," Daphne whispered, the words barely slipping past her lips. "The stress... it's not good for any of us."

Luke's laugh was humorless as he stepped closer. "Worried? Or trying to control me? I know what you're doing."

She tried to move away, but he was faster. His hands found her shoulders, gripping them tightly. She winced at the pressure but didn't dare let out a cry that might bring their children running.

"It's not like that," she protested, her voice a mix of fear and desperation. She thought of Royce, his innocent eyes and easy smile that so resembled Luke's on their better days.

"Isn't it?" Luke pushed her back against the wall with a force that stole her breath. A framed picture rattled against the drywall as she collided with it.

Silence enveloped them—a thick, choking silence that seemed to wait for her response. Daphne's heart raced; she could feel every beat echo through her body. But she held his gaze, refusing to show the full extent of her fear.

Luke released her abruptly and stepped back. His chest heaved with ragged breaths as he struggled to regain composure. Daphne remained still against the wall, not trusting herself to move or speak.

He turned away from her then, running a hand through his hair in frustration. "You need to stop questioning me," he said over his shoulder. "I'm handling things."

She watched him leave the room without another word, leaving behind a chilling silence that wrapped around Daphne like a shroud. Her body began to tremble from adrenaline and shock.

Slowly sliding down to the floor, Daphne drew her knees up to her chest. She closed her eyes against tears that threatened to spill—tears for herself, for what had become of their marriage, for their children who deserved so much better.

The moment stretched on as she sat there on the cold tile floor of their kitchen—a room that had once been filled with dreams and laughter now tainted by fear and uncertainty. She knew something had to change but feared what that might mean for all of them.

For now, she gathered herself up from the floor—each movement deliberate and slow—and checked on Royce in his crib, brushing a gentle hand over his soft curls before turning to tend to Morgan's needs with a forced smile plastered on her face.

The house settled around them in an uneasy quiet—a fortress that held within its walls secrets too heavy for its foundation. And at its center stood Daphne—a woman holding together broken pieces while dreaming of escape.

♥♥♥

Richmond sunlight streamed through the kitchen windows, casting a warm glow on the linoleum floor. Daphne moved about the space with a quiet efficiency, her belly rounded with the life soon to be welcomed into a fractured household. She prepared snacks for Morgan and Royce, their laughter a rare but cherished soundtrack to her day. Her movements were deliberate, avoiding the creaking floorboard that might disturb Luke's concentration as he worked from home.

Caroline's arrival loomed like an uncharted territory, a mixture of joy and trepidation in Daphne's heart. Each contraction was a reminder of the delicate balance she strove to maintain. In this home, where whispers carried more weight than shouts, Daphne found solace in the rituals of motherhood. She folded onesies with care, each crease a silent prayer for her unborn child's future.

"Mommy, when is the baby coming?" Morgan asked with childlike curiosity as she clutched a crayon in her tiny hand.

"Soon, sweetheart," Daphne replied with a gentle smile that didn't quite reach her eyes. "We'll have another little one to love before you know it."

The air hung heavy with unsaid words, the truth of their reality lurking in the shadows cast by the afternoon sun. Luke's presence loomed even in his absence, his demands echoing in the quiet moments between Daphne's tasks.

In the sanctuary of her bedroom, Daphne caressed her swollen abdomen, whispering promises to Caroline. Promises of protection and a love unmarred by the darkness that clouded their home. She hummed lullabies composed of hope and resilience, melodies that defied the silence demanded by Luke.

The days crawled by as Daphne juggled doctor appointments, playdates and school runs with precision. She fabricated excuses for missed gatherings and declining invitations with an apologetic tone that fooled no one who truly knew her plight.

Labor arrived like a thief in the night—sudden and without permission. Contractions wracked Daphne's body as she called for help with trembling hands. The paramedics arrived to a scene carefully curated to conceal any evidence of discord.

In the sterile environment of the hospital room, baby Caroline entered the world with a robust cry that pierced through years of stifled sobs. Daphne cradled her newborn daughter close, inhaling the scent of innocence and new beginnings.

Morgan and Royce met their sister with wide-eyed wonderment, each touch a balm to Daphne's weary soul. Luke hovered at the periphery—his smiles practiced, his congratulations hollow.

As they returned home from the hospital, Daphne fortified herself for what lay ahead. She clung to fleeting moments of peace amidst chaos—a giggle from Morgan or Royce's curious questions about stars.

Each day was an exercise in vigilance as Daphne shielded her children from Luke's unpredictable temper.

The house echoed with secrets too heavy for its foundation—walls bearing witness to silent cries for help that never came.

Caroline grew under watchful eyes—a beacon of light against an ever-darkening backdrop. Her first smile was a secret triumph shared between mother and daughter—a silent vow that love would always find a way.

In this home where fear often reigned supreme, Daphne wrapped her children in layers of affection—a fortress against the storm raging just beyond their reach. Her resolve hardened like steel tempered by fire; she would endure for them.

Baby Caroline's presence was a reminder that life continued despite adversity—a symbol of resilience born from strife. And within those walls filled with secrets and abuse, Daphne held fast to hope—an anchor amidst turbulent seas.

♥♥♥

"Mommy, why does Daddy get so angry sometimes?" Morgan asked one morning, her voice barely audible above the sound of the rain pattering against the windowpane.

Daphne hesitated, her heart aching at the thought of her children being subjected to Luke's unpredictable wrath. "I don't know, sweetie," she replied softly, her fingers gently brushing a stray curl from her daughter's face. "But I promise you, we'll find a way to make it better."

As the weeks passed, the instances of abuse became more frequent and severe. There were times when Luke's rage knew no bounds, his hands flying in a flurry of violence that left Daphne bruised and shaken. Other times, he employed manipulative tactics, belittling her until she felt like nothing more than a shadow of her former self.

"Can't you do anything right?" he would sneer at her, his voice dripping with disdain.

Daphne would shrink away from him, her eyes welling up with tears as she struggled to maintain her composure. The memories of their once-happy life seemed to taunt her, a cruel reminder of all that she had lost.

♥♥♥

In the muted glow of the kitchen, a glass tipped and milk spilled like slow-moving clouds across the table, cascading onto the floor in silent, white rivers. Six-year-old Morgan's eyes grew wide with fear, their small hands trembling as they stared at the spreading mess.

Luke's face contorted into a mask of rage, a tempest brewing behind his eyes. His voice erupted, harsh and jarring against the quiet morning. "Morgan! Clumsy child! What have you done now?"

Morgan shrank back, their little frame quivering. "I'm sorry, Daddy," they whispered, their voice barely above a breath.

Daphne rushed in with a cloth, her heart pounding in her chest. She knelt beside Morgan, her touch gentle on their shoulder. "It's okay, darling. It was just an accident."

But Luke loomed over them both, his shadow engulfing the sunlight that had moments ago bathed the room in warmth. "This is your fault," he spat at Daphne, his words sharp as daggers. "You coddle them too much!"

Before Daphne could respond, Luke's hand struck out like lightning, connecting with her cheek with a crack that silenced the morning birds outside. Pain radiated from her face as she caught herself on the edge of the table.

Morgan gasped, their eyes locked on Daphne's reddening cheek.

In that moment, clarity pierced through Daphne's shock like a cold winter breeze through bare branches. The echo of the slap reverberated through the years of apologies and empty promises. Her children's wide-eyed innocence flickered under Luke's darkening cloud.

No more.

She stood up slowly, holding Morgan close to her side.

Morgan clung to her leg, their presence grounding Daphne to the gravity of what came next. The path forward was uncharted and frightening – yet she knew they had to walk it together.

♥♥♥

The conference room at the law firm felt sterile, the hum of the air conditioning a stark contrast to the turmoil swirling inside Daphne. Across the glossy mahogany table, a lawyer with a sympathetic crease between his brows shuffled papers, while beside him, a domestic abuse counselor nodded encouragingly.

"We'll need all financial statements, any evidence of the abuse—photos, doctor visits, witness statements—anything that can substantiate your claims," the lawyer explained.

Daphne clutched her notepad tightly, each item he listed another stone in the fortress she was meticulously building for her escape. Her meticulous nature had served her well; she had already begun to compile what she needed.

"And you mentioned that the house is in your name?" The lawyer peered over his glasses.

"Yes," Daphne confirmed, a small victory in her voice. "The deed is solely in my name."

The counselor leaned forward. "It's good you have a safe place to stay. Have you thought about where Luke will go once you take action?"

Daphne hesitated for a fraction of a second. "He won't have a choice."

They outlined each step with precision—a financial safety net tucked away, copies of all personal records secured, and an emergency bag hidden but ready. They spoke in hushed tones about custody and restraining orders, about how to shield her children from the fallout.

With the help of her friends, family, and a local women's shelter, Daphne meticulously planned Luke's arrest. She collected evidence of his abuse, documenting every bruise, every harsh word, and every cruel manipulation. It was difficult to relive those moments, but she knew it was necessary for her case.

Later that week, Daphne stood in the shadows outside the naval base's legal office, her heart hammering as she watched Luke being led away in handcuffs. His face contorted with rage and disbelief when he saw her standing there—no longer the victim but the architect of his downfall.

"You bitch!," Luke spat as they read him his rights. "You think you can just take everything from me?"

Daphne remained silent, an island of calm in the chaos he had created. Her only response was a slow exhale—a release of years of suppressed fear and anguish.

As Luke's military career unraveled with each charge read against him, Daphne felt an unfamiliar weight lift off her shoulders. She had weathered storms of manipulation and violence but now stood resolute.

She watched as they escorted him to a waiting vehicle bound for Leavenworth. Only when the car disappeared from view did she allow herself to crumble into the driver's seat of her car.

For a long moment, Daphne sat there alone, breathing deeply in and out. She let herself feel it all—the terror, relief, sorrow—and then slowly wiped away tears that had escaped her control.

With trembling hands, she started the engine and drove back to the sanctuary of her home—a place that would soon be purged of shadows and filled with light once again.

Chapter 8 – Therapy
2000

Dr. Fischer listened intently as Daphne recounted the trauma of Luke's abuse. He could see the pain etched on her face, the way her hands clenched and unclenched in her lap. She spoke softly, her voice trembling at times, but she didn't falter in her recollection of events.

"It started with verbal abuse," Daphne began, "small things at first, but they escalated over time. He would criticize me for the smallest mistakes, make me feel like I was never good enough."

Dr. Fischer nodded sympathetically, offering words of encouragement as Daphne continued to share her story. He could sense the fear and shame that still lingered within her, even after all these years.

"Then it turned physical," Daphne said, her voice barely above a whisper. "After our son Royce was born, he started hitting me. At first it was just slaps across the face or shoves against the wall, but it quickly escalated to more violent attacks."

"It wasn't just the physical abuse," Daphne continued, her voice steadying as she faced these painful truths. "Luke used everything as a weapon—even his affairs. He'd leave his wedding ring on the dresser when he went out, telling me he didn't want to 'scare away the fishes.' Sometimes he'd leave love letters from these women where I'd find them, as if daring me to confront him." She paused, her fingers twisting together. "Once, I discovered that a woman he was seeing had a son named Royce. Our son's name—the name Luke had insisted on—wasn't even original. It was as if he wanted me to know I was replaceable, that even our children's identities were under his control."

Dr. Fischer felt a surge of anger at the thought of what Daphne had endured. He wanted to protect her from this man who had caused so much pain and suffering in her life. But he knew that his role was to help Daphne heal from these experiences and find a way to move forward.

"How did you manage to escape?" Dr. Fischer asked gently, his voice filled with concern for Daphne's safety and well-being.

Daphne took a deep breath before answering. "I knew I had to get out for the sake of our children," she said firmly. "I met with a lawyer and a domestic abuse counselor on base to plan my exit strategy."

Dr. Fischer could see the determination in Daphne's eyes as she spoke about taking control of her life and protecting her children from further harm. He felt a renewed sense of hope for her future as she continued to share her story with him.

"It wasn't easy," Daphne admitted, "but I managed to gather documents and save money so that I could leave without any financial issues." She paused for a moment before adding, "I also had Luke arrested for conduct unbecoming an officer."

Dr. Fischer felt a sense of pride swell within him as he listened to Daphne recount these brave actions she had taken on behalf of herself and her children. It was clear that she was strong and resilient, capable of overcoming even the most difficult challenges life had thrown at her thus far.

♥♥♥

The room, usually a haven of clinical neutrality, suddenly felt charged with an undercurrent of discomfort. Daphne sat, her posture rigid, her hands clasped tightly in her lap. Dr. Fischer had been a steady presence through the tumultuous aftermath of Luke's arrest—a professional ear for the raw spillage of her pain. But now, the lines blurred.

A soft tap on the door had preceded the session's start, a gentle reminder of the world outside this intimate space. Daphne exhaled deeply, bracing herself to peel back layers of hurt. She hadn't expected to fend off more than memories.

"Tell me about your mother," Dr. Fischer prompted gently.

Daphne's fingers twisted in her lap. "She never recovered from losing Nathalie—my sister who died at birth. I think she resented that I lived while Nathalie didn't." The admission hung in the air, heavy with decades of unspoken pain. "Then Miles got sick when he was six... kidney surgery. After that, he became the golden child and I was... I was just the reminder of what she'd lost."

Dr. Fischer nodded thoughtfully. "And how did you cope with that dynamic?"

"I tried to be perfect," Daphne said softly. "I thought if

I could just be good enough, organized enough, successful enough... but it never worked. Not with her."

As she delved into a particularly painful recollection, Dr. Fischer leaned forward, his expression one of concentrated empathy. His hand found its way to her knee—a gesture meant to comfort or something more?

Daphne's voice faltered mid-sentence, and her gaze snapped down to the warm weight against her leg. Her heart rate picked up, betraying her cool exterior.

"Dr. Fischer," she began, her tone laced with caution as she eased his hand away and placed it back on his own knee. Her eyes met his, searching for an explanation.

The therapist cleared his throat and pulled back, a flicker of something unreadable crossing his face before he donned the mask of professionalism once again.

"I apologize if that was inappropriate," he offered with a slight nod, but his words felt hollow against the cold twist in Daphne's stomach.

She nodded curtly in response, unsure whether to accept the apology or challenge him further. The safety she had found in this room felt compromised—tainted by the unwelcome touch.

Daphne redirected the conversation back to her healing process, erecting an invisible barrier between herself and Dr. Fischer. Her responses became measured, each word calculated to maintain distance.

As the clock ticked toward the end of their hour, Daphne gathered her belongings with brisk efficiency. She avoided Dr. Fischer's attempts at scheduling their next appointment, muttering something noncommittal about checking her calendar.

Once outside, Daphne allowed herself a deep breath—the air tasting fresher than it had moments before behind closed doors. The uncertainty lingered though; she'd trusted him with her vulnerability and now questioned every interaction they'd ever had.

She pulled out her phone and scrolled through her contacts list until she found Rosie's number. It rang twice before Daphne hung up without leaving a message—some rifts were too wide to cross even in moments of need.

With every step away from the office building, Daphne fortified herself with resolve. No matter what it took, she would reclaim control over every aspect of her life—no one would make her feel powerless again.

Daphne sat nervously on the leather couch, her heart pounding in her chest as she recounted the horrifying details of her abusive marriage to Luke Stainthorpe. The memories were fresh and painful, but she knew it was important to confront them in order to heal.

Dr. Fischer listened intently, his eyes locked on Daphne's face as she spoke. His demeanor was calm and reassuring, but there was an undercurrent of tension that Daphne couldn't quite place.

As Daphne described the final, violent fight with Luke, her voice trembled with fear and anger. She spoke of how Luke had lost control, striking her and their children with terrifying force. She recounted how she had managed to escape with her life and the children, but how the trauma would haunt her for years to come.

Suddenly, Dr. Fischer leaned forward in his chair, his eyes fixed on Daphne's lips. Without warning, he reached out and placed a hand on her knee. Daphne flinched at the sudden contact, her heart racing as she tried to process what was happening.

Before she could react further, Dr. Fischer closed the distance between them and pressed his lips against hers in a forceful kiss. Daphne froze in shock and fear, unable to comprehend what was happening or why this man she trusted would betray her in such a cruel way.

As Dr. Fischer pulled away from her, Daphne felt a wave of disgust wash over her. She pushed him away roughly, tears welling up in her eyes as she struggled to make sense of what had just happened. How could someone who claimed to be helping her turn out to be so cruel and manipulative? How could she ever trust anyone again?

Dr. Fischer looked at Daphne with a mixture of surprise and regret in his eyes, but he said nothing as he stood up and left the room without another word. Daphne sat there for several minutes after he left, trying to process what had just happened and wondering if there was any hope for healing after such a devastating betrayal.

♥♥♥

Daphne's heart pounded in her chest as she walked through the door, her children's laughter echoing through the house. She had to keep it together, for their sake. She hugged them both tightly, trying to push the horrifying memory of Dr. Fischer's betrayal from her mind.

As they sat down for dinner, Daphne forced a smile and asked about their day. Morgan recounted a story about a new friend at school, while Royce excitedly told her about "Nigel Needs a Home" a new book Mrs. Pine had read to him after kindergarten. Daphne listened intently, her mind racing with thoughts of what she would do next.

After dinner, Daphne gave Caroline her bath while Morgan and Royce did puzzles at the kitchen table. As she gently washed Caroline's tiny body, Daphne felt a surge of protectiveness wash over her. She would do anything to keep her children safe from harm, even if it meant facing her own fears and demons head-on.

As Caroline giggled and splashed in the water, Daphne made a silent vow to herself: no matter what happened next, she would never let anyone hurt her children again. She would fight for them with every ounce of strength she had left in her body. And if that meant confronting Dr. Fischer or anyone else who threatened their safety, so be it.

With Caroline snuggled up in bed and asleep, Daphne sat down at the kitchen table to write out her shopping list for the coming week. Her mind was still racing with thoughts of Dr. Fischer and what to do next, but she knew that she couldn't let this incident derail her life any further than it already had. She had come too far to let someone else control her destiny once again.

As the night wore on and the house grew quiet, Daphne felt a sense of calm wash over her despite everything that had happened that day. She knew that there would be more challenges ahead, but she also knew that she was stronger than any obstacle that came her way. And as long as she had her children by her side, nothing could break them apart or diminish the love they shared for one another.

♥♥♥

In the dimly lit community center, nestled between the town library and a quiet park, Daphne took a tentative seat in a circle of folding chairs. Around her sat a mosaic of faces, each carrying the weight of stories untold, pain unshared. She wrapped her hands around the warmth of a paper cup filled with tepid coffee, the steam no longer rising.

The group leader, a woman with empathetic eyes named Joanne, nodded at Daphne, her gesture an invitation to speak. Daphne's voice wavered at first, like the flicker of a candle in a soft breeze. She began recounting her tale in fragmented sentences.

"It's like... you're walking on shards of glass," she described, "and each step could cut deeper, but you can't stop walking."

Nods of understanding rippled through the group. Another woman, her hair threaded with silver, reached out and placed a hand over Daphne's clenched fist.

"We walk that path too," she said, her voice a soothing balm. "But here, we walk it together."

Daphne drew strength from their solidarity. As others shared their own struggles and triumphs over past demons, she realized she wasn't adrift in an ocean of despair; she was part of a fleet weathering the same storm.

Later that week, Daphne sat with Morgan and Royce in the welcoming office of a children's counselor. The walls were adorned with bright paintings and shelves overflowed with stuffed animals and toys designed to put young minds at ease.

Morgan clutched a squishy stress ball while Royce fidgeted with his shoelaces. The counselor—a kind man named Henry—knelt to their level.

"We're going to talk about some tough stuff," he said gently. "But remember, it's okay to have big feelings about them."

Morgan looked up from under a furrowed brow. "Like being mad?"

"Exactly," Henry confirmed with a warm smile. "Or sad or scared or anything else you feel."

Royce peered at his sister before glancing back at Henry. "And we can say it all out loud?"

"You can," Henry assured them. "Your words are safe here."

As they spoke of fears and confusion that had burrowed deep within their young hearts, Daphne watched from across the room—a silent sentinel absorbing every word. She felt both the prick of tears and the burgeoning hope that these small steps would pave the way for healing.

Breaking cycles demanded more than silence; it required courage and conversations laced with honesty and support. And as Daphne guided her children through this labyrinth of recovery, she fortified herself with newfound allies who understood the journey all too well.

♥♥♥

Daphne sat nervously in Dr. Richards' office, her heart pounding in her chest. The memory of Dr. Fischer's betrayal still haunted her, but she was determined to move forward and heal.

Dr. Richards, a kind and empathetic woman, gently guided Daphne through the painful memories. She encouraged Daphne to express her feelings and explore the trauma in a safe and supportive environment.

As they talked, Daphne felt a sense of relief wash over her. She realized that she was not alone in her experience and that there were others who understood what she had been through. This realization gave her strength and hope for the future.

Over time, Daphne began to rebuild her trust in therapy and herself. She learned coping mechanisms to deal with the anxiety and fear that lingered from the assault. With Dr. Richards' guidance, she started to reclaim control over her life and regain a sense of normalcy.

Through it all, Daphne remained committed to protecting her children from harm and providing them with a loving and stable home environment. She knew that breaking the cycle of abuse required not only healing herself but also fostering open communication with her kids about difficult topics like trust, boundaries, and consent.

As Daphne continued on her healing journey with Dr. Richards, she found solace in knowing that she was taking steps towards a brighter future for herself and her family. Though the road ahead would be challenging at times, she was determined to overcome obstacles and create a life filled with love, safety, and happiness for all of them.

♥♥♥

Daphne's eyes fluttered open, her heart pounding in her chest. She was drenched in sweat, the sheets tangled around her body. The dream had felt so real, as if she were back in that dilapidated house in Queens, cowering from her father's rage.

The memory of his cruelty flooded back - the way he would lash out at the slightest provocation, his fists clenched and his face twisted with anger. Daphne had always tried to avoid triggering his temper, but it seemed like there was never a safe moment around him.

She felt a wave of confusion and anger wash over her as she relived those traumatic experiences. How could she have allowed herself to be subjected to such abuse for so long? Why hadn't she fought back or sought help sooner?

Recounting her dream in her therapy session that week, Dr. Richards appeared at her side, placing a comforting hand on her shoulder. "Daphne, it's okay," she said softly. "You're safe now."

She looked up at her, tears streaming down her face. "I had a dream about my father," she whispered hoarsely. "It brought back all these memories... I feel so confused and angry."

Dr. Richards nodded understandingly. "It's completely normal to feel that way," she said gently. "Dreams can often bring up repressed memories and emotions that we haven't fully processed."

She encouraged Daphne to explore the meaning behind the dream, asking her questions about the details and how they made her feel. As they delved deeper into the dream's symbolism, Daphne began to understand that it was not just a random occurrence, but a reflection of unresolved issues from her past that were still affecting her present life.

"I don't want my past to define me," Daphne whispered, her voice barely audible above the hum of the air conditioner. "But some days... it feels like it's all I am."

Dr. Richards squeezed her hand, offering her a lifeline amid the storm of her emotions. "You're so much more than your father's actions, Daphne," she said firmly. "You've come a long way in confronting your past, and you're stronger than you give yourself credit for. Healing takes time, but I truly believe that you can overcome this."

As Daphne listened to her therapist's words, she felt something stir within her—a flicker of hope, buried deep beneath the layers of guilt and shame. She knew that the road ahead would be long and filled with obstacles, but for the first time in her life, she believed that her journey might lead her to a place of peace and redemption.

"Thank you, Dr. Richards," Daphne whispered, wiping the tears from her eyes with a trembling hand. "I want to believe that, too."

"Good," Dr. Matthews said with a smile, her eyes crinkling at the corners. "Now, let's talk about some coping strategies for when these memories become overwhelming."

Dr. Richards helped Daphne see that talking through these buried memories was an essential part of her healing journey - not just for dealing with the trauma of her childhood, but also for breaking free from the patterns of behavior that had been ingrained in her as a result of that abuse. With her guidance and support, Daphne felt empowered to face these truths head-on and work towards healing and growth.

♥♥♥

As Daphne sat across from Dr. Richards, her fingers nervously pleated the fabric of her skirt. The safety of the therapist's office—with its soft lighting and muted colors—usually provided comfort, but today the conversation had veered into territory that made her heart race.

"Daphne, you mentioned having difficulty with certain aspects of personal care," Dr. Richards said gently. "Would you like to talk about where that originated?"

Daphne's throat tightened. She'd never shared this with anyone, not even Reuben. The memory had remained locked away, much like she had been that day.

"I was twelve," she began, her voice barely audible. "We were living in Akron then."

Dr. Richards nodded encouragingly, her pen poised over her notepad but not writing, giving Daphne her full attention.

"I was taking a bath," Daphne continued, her eyes fixed on a point just beyond Dr. Richards' shoulder. "I'd locked the bathroom door—something we weren't supposed to do in our house, but I desperately wanted privacy."

Her hands stilled in her lap as the memory unfurled with startling clarity.

"I heard the doorknob turn, then his voice—my father's voice—on the other side. 'Daphne, open the door. You know we don't have locked doors in this house.'"

She drew a shaky breath.

"I didn't answer. I thought maybe if I stayed quiet, he'd go away. But the knocking became pounding. 'Daphne, let me in. I just want to wash your back for you.'"

Daphne's eyes finally met Dr. Richards', filled with decades-old fear.

"His anger became more intense with each passing second. I could hear it building in his voice, that familiar tone that meant danger. And then—" her voice caught, "—he broke the door. Just burst through it."

Dr. Richards remained silent, creating space for Daphne to continue at her own pace.

"As he moved closer, he started making these horrible accusations about what I was really doing in the bathroom. He began calling out for Miles, convinced my brother was hiding in there with me. The things he said..." Daphne shook her head, unable to repeat the words.

She wrapped her arms around herself, a protective gesture that Dr. Richards had noticed before.

"I didn't bathe for over a month after that," Daphne whispered. "I couldn't bear it. I'd wash quickly at the sink when no one was home, but I couldn't make myself get into a bathtub. My mother eventually noticed, of course, but she just seemed irritated by the inconvenience of it."

Dr. Richards leaned forward slightly. "And now?"

"To this day, I prefer showers. I can't remember the last time I took a bath," Daphne admitted. "And I'm terrified of locking bathroom doors. Even in my own home—especially in my own home—that click of the lock sends me right back to being twelve years old, hearing those fists on the door."

She exhaled slowly, feeling both drained and somehow lighter, as if speaking the memory aloud had diminished its power, if only slightly.

"Thank you for sharing that, Daphne," Dr. Richards said softly. "These intrusions on your privacy and bodily autonomy can have lasting effects. It makes perfect sense that you've developed these protective behaviors."

Daphne nodded, wiping away a tear that had escaped despite her best efforts.

"What we can work on," Dr. Richards continued, "is finding ways to help you reclaim that sense of safety and control. Not to erase what happened—we can't do that—but to create new associations that aren't rooted in fear."

As the session continued, Daphne felt something shift within her—a small release, like a knot finally beginning to loosen after years of constriction. The memory would always be there, but perhaps it didn't have to define her bathing rituals forever.

♥♥♥

Dr. Richards leaned forward slightly, her pen poised above her notepad. "You mentioned control several times, Daphne. Can you tell me more about why having control feels so important to you?"

Daphne's fingers tensed, pleating the fabric of her skirt. "I've told you about my father, about growing up in that environment."

"Yes, but I sense there's more to it," the therapist probed gently. "Was there a specific moment in your adult life when you felt particularly out of control?"

The memory flashed unbidden—Mark sitting on her bed, her teddy bear in his hands, the violation of her private space. She could still feel the chill that had swept through her at the realization that nowhere was truly safe.

"In college," Daphne began, her voice dropping to barely above a whisper. "There was an incident with a stalker. He... he got into my dorm room somehow. I'd already had a run-in with him at a party where he..." She swallowed hard, unable to finish the sentence.

"Take your time," Dr. Richards encouraged.

"He was arrested a few days later. He'd attacked another girl on campus. It could have been me." The last words emerged strangled, as if her throat had constricted around them.

"And after this happened?"

"I started making lists. Organizing everything. Checking locks, windows." Daphne's hand made a unconscious motion, as if turning a key. "If everything was in order, if I could control my environment, maybe I could control who got close to me. Maybe I could be safe."

Dr. Richards nodded slowly. "And when you met Luke?"

"He seemed safe," Daphne admitted. "In control. I didn't realize then that what I thought was protection was actually the beginning of another kind of cage."

♥♥♥

As their sessions progressed over the following weeks, Dr. Richards gently suggested that confronting the past might include speaking directly with those who shared it. "Sometimes healing requires uncomfortable conversations," she explained, her voice steady and reassuring. "Reaching out to Miles might help you both validate each other's experiences and break the silence that has protected your father's behavior for so long." Daphne had nodded, anxiety knotting in her stomach at the thought. But the seed had been planted, and after days of drafting and discarding what she would say, she finally gathered her courage. With trembling fingers, she picked up the phone, the weight of years spent under the same roof with Miles, protecting him, keeping silent about their father's tempestuous rage—it all bore down on her with an intensity that threatened to overwhelm.

Daphne hesitated, the phone heavy in her hand. Sunlight streamed through the kitchen window, casting long shadows across the linoleum floor. The kettle whistled a shrill note, breaking the silence that had settled in the room. She turned off the stove and poured herself a cup of tea, her hands shaking slightly as she wrapped them around the warm ceramic.

She had rehearsed this conversation in her mind a thousand times, but now that the moment had arrived, words eluded her. The weight of years spent under the same roof with Miles, protecting him, keeping silent about their father's tempestuous rage—it all bore down on her with an intensity that threatened to overwhelm.

Daphne took a deep breath and dialed Miles's number. The line clicked and buzzed before his voice came through, casual and unsuspecting.

"Hey Daphne, what's up?" Miles sounded busy; there was always an edge of distraction in his voice.

"Miles," Daphne began, her voice steadier than she felt. "I need to talk to you about something important."

Miles chuckled. "What's up? Did you finally decide to join me for that trip to Vegas?"

"No, it's not that," Daphne replied. She paused, steadying her voice. "It's about Dad."

A silence fell between them—a thick, tangible void as if Miles could sense the gravity of what was coming next.

"Dad?" he echoed. His tone shifted from playful to guarded. "What about him?"

Daphne clenched her jaw. "It's about what he did to us... what he did to me."

There was a shuffling sound on the other end of the line as if Miles had suddenly lost his balance. "What are you talking about?"

"The abuse, Miles," Daphne pressed on, her voice tinged with a pain she couldn't hide. "The violence... I can't keep pretending it didn't happen."

A heavy breath filled the receiver. "Abuse? Daphne, come on." His words tumbled out in a dismissive rush. "Dad always said you were fanciful and you made things up."

Daphne felt her heart sink. She had expected resistance but not outright denial.

"Miles," she said firmly, gripping the phone tighter as if it were an anchor in this storm of denial. "You were there too. You saw how he was."

"Look," Miles interjected, his voice rising slightly in defense or perhaps discomfort. "I remember Dad being strict, sure, but abuse? That's a serious accusation."

The word 'serious' hung between them like an accusation of its own.

"Dad had his moments," Miles continued with an edge of impatience now creeping into his tone. "But we turned out alright, didn't we? I think you're blowing this out of proportion."

Daphne closed her eyes for a moment and leaned against the kitchen counter for support.

"I'm not making this up," she whispered into the phone, each word drenched with decades of suppressed hurt.

There was another pause—a space filled with

unspoken truths and unacknowledged wounds.

"I have to go," Miles said abruptly.

"Miles—"

But he had already hung up.

Daphne slowly lowered the phone and placed it on the counter beside her untouched cup of tea. The light in the kitchen seemed colder now as she wrapped her arms around herself—a solitary figure grappling with ghosts that refused to be laid to rest.

Chapter 9 – Déjà vu
2004

The final divorce papers arrived on a Tuesday, nearly five years after Luke's arrest. Daphne stared at the manila envelope on her kitchen counter, the word "CONFIDENTIAL" stamped across its front in bold red letters. Inside lay the official end to a chapter of her life marked by fear and control—a legal declaration of her freedom.

As she signed the last page, she felt a weight lift from her shoulders. Luke remained at Leavenworth, his military career destroyed alongside his marriage, while she had gradually rebuilt her life piece by piece. The past five years had been a masterclass in resilience—balancing her career in financial crimes risk assessment with the demands of raising three children alone, finding strength she hadn't known she possessed.

Morgan, now fourteen, had grown from a quiet nine-year-old into a teenager with a passion for engineering and space exploration. Twelve-year-old Royce, who had been just seven when his father was arrested, showed increasing promise in the kitchen, experimenting with recipes that sometimes succeeded brilliantly and sometimes set off the smoke alarm. Little Caroline, only three when Luke was taken away, had few memories of her father but at eight years old had blossomed into a spirited child with a natural talent for music, her small hands already confident on the guitar strings. Single motherhood hadn't been easy, but watching her children heal and grow filled Daphne with a fierce pride.

The call from her boss came two weeks after the divorce was finalized. "How would you feel about Sydney?" he asked, his voice crackling with excitement over the phone. "The expansion's going better than projected, and we need someone with your expertise to head up the risk assessment division there. It's a significant promotion, Daphne."

In therapy with Dr. Richards, they had discussed the possibility of a fresh start. "Sometimes physical distance can create the space needed for emotional healing," Dr. Richards had suggested during one of their final sessions. "Not as an escape, but as an opportunity to redefine yourself and your children away from the shadows of the past."

As Daphne packed up their Richmond home, sorting through memories both painful and precious, she felt a mixture of trepidation and hope. Australia was halfway around the world—far from the shadows of her marriage, far from the whispers that had followed her family after Luke's arrest, far from the well-meaning but often suffocating support network that had seen her at her worst.

"Are we really doing this, Mom?" Morgan had asked, looking suddenly younger than fourteen as they taped up another box.

"We are," Daphne had answered, surprising herself with the certainty in her voice. "Sometimes you need to jump into the unknown to find out what you're made of."

Now, as Daphne sat in the window seat of the airplane, her mind a whirlwind of emotions as she gazed out at the tarmac glistening from last night's rain, she allowed herself to feel the full weight of this decision. The anticipation of starting over in Sydney with her children, Morgan, Royce, and Caroline, was a mix of nervousness and excitement.

She had been planning this move for months, ever

since she had been given the opportunity by her boss. The thought of starting a new life in a new country, far from the pain and memories of the past, was both exhilarating and terrifying.

The children were excited too, each with their own Gameboys and snacks, ready to while away the hours on the long flight. Daphne smiled as she watched them, grateful for the chance to give them a fresh start.

♥♥♥

Daphne's fingers tightened around the armrest as she settled into her window seat on the flight to Sydney. The hum of the airplane engines surrounded her, punctuating the mix of excitement and apprehension that coursed through her veins. She gazed out at the tarmac, watching the ground crew scurry about their tasks, their fluorescent vests a vivid contrast against the dull gray concrete. This new chapter in her life loomed before her like an open book, each blank page simultaneously inviting and daunting.

As she fumbled with her seatbelt, trying to find a sense of control in this unfamiliar environment, Daphne felt the presence of someone beside her. She glanced over to see a tall man settling into the aisle seat. His carry-on bag revealed a hint of his personality: a well-worn leather satchel adorned with various travel stickers, hinting at a life filled with adventure and exploration.

"Hi there," he said, extending a hand. "I'm Reuben."

"Nice to meet you, Reuben. I'm Daphne," she replied, shaking his hand firmly. There was something about his easy smile that put her at ease, despite the whirlwind of emotions swirling within her.

"So, what brings you to Sydney?" Reuben asked, stowing his satchel beneath the seat in front of him.

"Work," Daphne answered, her voice reflecting a sense of pride. "I recently got a promotion, and they're transferring me to our office in Sydney. It's a big change, but I'm excited for the opportunity."

"Congratulations! That sounds like an amazing opportunity," Reuben said genuinely. "I'm actually headed to Melbourne for a conference. I'm a machine learning engineer." He paused, tilting his head slightly. "It sounds like we both have some exciting new ventures ahead of us."

♥♥♥

"Indeed," Daphne agreed as the plane leveled off.

"New ventures are always a mix of excitement and apprehension, aren't they?"

"Absolutely," Reuben nodded. He leaned back in his seat and sighed deeply, his eyes momentarily distant. "My wife just called me this morning to tell me she's pregnant with our first child. So, there's that too."

"Wow, congratulations!" Daphne exclaimed, her curiosity piqued. "You must be thrilled. How does your wife feel about it?"

"Thank you," Reuben replied, his face lighting up with joy. "She's over the moon. We've been trying for a while now, so this is such a blessing for us. Do you have kids?"

Reuben's eyes followed Daphne's gaze to the three children sitting across the aisle. He couldn't help but notice the resemblance between them and Daphne. They all had her striking features, with their mother's piercing blue eyes and wavy chestnut hair.

"They look just like you," Reuben commented, his voice soft and genuine. "How old are they?"

Daphne smiled warmly at her children, feeling a surge of pride. "Caroline is 8, Royce is 12 and Morgan is 14," she replied.

♥♥♥

As the plane leveled off, Daphne and Reuben continued their conversation, discovering they shared a love for art, travel, and vintage films. Daphne admired his wit and thoughtful perspectives. Reuben's eyes sparkled as he spoke passionately about his favorite directors and their unique styles.

Daphne found herself drawn to his intelligence and dry humor. They talked about their favorite destinations around the world, sharing stories of breathtaking landscapes and hidden gems. Daphne couldn't help but feel a connection with this man who seemed to understand her in a way that few others did.

As the hours passed, they lost track of time, engrossed in their conversation. The flight attendants served dinner, but neither of them paid much attention to the food as they continued to talk animatedly about their shared interests.

♥♥♥

Daphne took a sip of her airline coffee, the aroma wafting down the aisle as she engaged in conversation with the handsome stranger beside her. Their discussion had deepened, touching on their respective college experiences. Daphne couldn't help but feel an instant connection with Reuben, a sense of familiarity that felt almost like deja vu. It was as if they had met before, in another time and place. The conversation flowed effortlessly between them, each sharing their thoughts and experiences with ease. Daphne felt a warmth spread through her chest as she realized that she had never felt so comfortable with someone so quickly before. It was a strange yet comforting feeling, one that she hoped would continue throughout their journey together.

Hey, this might sound strange," Daphne began hesitantly, "but have we met before? There's something about you that feels so...familiar."

Reuben furrowed his brow, deep in thought for a moment. "I was just thinking the same thing. It's like déjà vu, isn't it?"

They exchanged puzzled glances, trying to pinpoint where and when their paths might have crossed. As memories swirled through Daphne's mind, something suddenly clicked. Her eyes widened with recognition.

"Ben?" she whispered, the nickname emerging from some long-forgotten corner of her memory.

Reuben's face transformed with sudden realization.

"Wait a minute," he said, his eyes lighting up. "We met at UCLA, didn't we? At a lacrosse game?"

Daphne felt her heart race as she nodded, her voice barely above a whisper. "Yes, I remember watching you play. They called you Ben back then. You were incredible out there."

He smiled, a mix of surprise and nostalgia washing over his face. "I can't believe it. You actually remember that? We really did cross paths all those years ago. What are the odds?"

♥♥♥

As the plane began its descent, Daphne's heart raced with anticipation. She couldn't believe the serendipity of their reunion after all these years. Reuben's eyes sparkled as he smiled at her, his expression suggesting he was just as thrilled by their chance meeting.

"I can't believe it's been so long," he said, his voice low and husky. "I never forgot about you, Daphne."

Daphne felt a blush creeping up her neck as she met his gaze. "Me neither," she admitted softly. "It was fate that brought us together again."

As the plane touched down and passengers began to

gather their belongings, Daphne and Reuben hurriedly exchanged contact information, eager to continue their connection in this new chapter. They promised to keep in touch and maybe even meet up again soon. As they disembarked, they shared a warm embrace, both feeling a sense of closure and new beginnings.

As Daphne walked away from the airport, she couldn't help but feel a renewed sense of hope for the future. The past had been painful and filled with darkness, but now she had a glimmer of light shining through the clouds. And who knew? Maybe one day she would find love.... But for now, she was content to focus on her children and building a new life in Australia. After all she had been through, she deserved happiness and peace at last.

♥♥♥

Daphne's children, Caroline, Royce, and Morgan, chattered excitedly as they made their way through the terminal. Caroline's eyes widened at the sight of a giant airplane model, while Royce pointed out a departure board filled with destinations he'd never heard of. Morgan rolled her eyes but couldn't help but smile at her siblings' enthusiasm.

The family followed the signs for customs and

baggage claim. Daphne felt a sense of anticipation building within her as she thought about starting fresh in Australia. She knew it wouldn't be easy, but she was determined to create a safe and nurturing environment for her children.

As they collected their luggage, Daphne couldn't help but feel grateful for the support of her friends and therapists back home. They had helped her heal from the trauma of her past and given her the strength to move forward.

Chapter 10 – Sydney
2004

The first light of dawn filtered through the curtains, casting a warm glow on Daphne's face as she reached for the ringing alarm clock. She silenced the shrill noise and swung her legs over the edge of the bed, her feet finding their way into well-worn slippers. Her eyes were still heavy with sleep, but there was no time to linger in the warmth of her blankets.

The house lay quiet as she padded down the hallway, each step a silent promise to her sleeping children. "Rise and shine, kiddos!" she called out cheerfully. Down the hallway, doors creaked open as her children emerged, rubbing their eyes and stifling yawns. Daphne busied herself in the kitchen, spreading vegemite on toast and arranging orange slices on plates.

Lunch boxes lined up on the counter like soldiers awaiting inspection. With practiced movements, she assembled sandwiches, each precisely cut into halves. Sliced apples nestled next to cheese sticks and juice boxes filled in the gaps—a symphony of routine.

The kettle whistled its readiness and she poured hot water over freshly ground coffee beans, savoring the aroma that began to fill the room.

"Did you finish your math homework, Royce?" she asked her son while pouring coffee into her travel mug.

"Uh-huh," he mumbled around a mouthful of toast.

"Great, remember you have baseball practice after school, and Chris' mum will be picking you up." Daphne glanced at the clock, the ticking seconds urging her forward, never allowing her to pause. "Alright, everyone in the car!"

As they piled into the car, the morning news played softly on the radio. Daphne listened with half an ear, her mind already racing ahead to the day's tasks and meetings. She deposited her children at the school gate with quick hugs and words of encouragement before heading to the office.

At work, Daphne's desk was a fortress of order, every pen and notepad in its designated place. Numbers and graphs filled her computer screen, piecing together a puzzle of financial crimes and risk assessment. But even as she immersed herself in her work, the weight of responsibility never lifted from her shoulders.

"Mrs. Stainthorpe, Caroline's school called," her assistant informed her, peeking around the office door. "She's not feeling well and needs to be picked up."

"Thank you, Jenny," Daphne replied, her heart sinking. She glanced at the meeting reminder on her screen, already calculating the impact of her absence on her workload. "Could you please reschedule my afternoon meetings?"

"Of course," Jenny nodded sympathetically.

Daphne rushed to the school, her thoughts a whirlwind of concern for her daughter and the unfinished tasks waiting at her desk. The rest of the day was consumed by caring for her sick child, tending to her fever and offering comfort. As evening settled, she prepared dinner, folded laundry, and checked homework, her body growing wearier with each passing hour.

"Tomorrow is another day," she whispered to herself, summoning the strength to rise and prepare for the next challenge that awaited her.

In the morning, Daphne returned to her office, her mind focused on the tasks ahead. Her dedication to her work in financial crimes risk assessment was unwavering, and she took pride in helping protect her company's integrity. As she reviewed case files and meticulously analyzed data, a sense of accomplishment bloomed within her. This was something she excelled at, a place where her love for spreadsheets and attention to detail converged.

"Great job on that last report, Daphne," her colleague, Jason Nguyen, said over their regular Zoom meeting. "You really uncovered some crucial information."

"Thank you, Jason," she replied with a smile, feeling a burst of satisfaction. It was moments like these that reminded her why she had chosen this career path, the fulfillment it brought her even amidst the chaos of her life.

Yet, as the day wore on and the sun dipped below the horizon, casting shadows across her workspace, Daphne couldn't ignore the gnawing loneliness that settled deep within her. She missed the companionship of a partner, someone to share her triumphs and tribulations, to offer a warm embrace after a long day.

The silence of her home only amplified her isolation.

The distant hum of appliances and the faint ticking of the hallway clock were constant reminders of the emptiness surrounding her. She tried to fill the void with activities – folding laundry, organizing cupboards, attempting new recipes – but nothing could truly satisfy her longing for connection.

♥♥♥

This Saturday, it was Daphne's turn to host the BBQ. Her backyard buzzed with activity as the Sydney sun bathed everything in a warm glow. Morgan was teaching some of the younger kids a card game on the patio, while Royce helped man the grill alongside Nick, their neighbor from two doors down. Caroline sat cross-legged on a blanket with her friend Emma, both girls giggling over something on Emma's phone.

"Your pineapple upside down cake is divine," Sarah exclaimed, appearing beside Daphne with an empty plate. "I swear, it gets better every time you make it."

Daphne smiled, watching her friends' children intermingle with her own. "Gran's recipe. I think the brown sugar caramelizes better in this climate."

The scene before her was exactly what she'd hoped for when they moved to Sydney—a sense of belonging, of community. Children's laughter mingled with adult conversation as the smell of grilled sausages and the sweet scent of her cake filled the air. The clinking of glasses and cutlery created a familiar melody that echoed through her home.

Yet despite being surrounded by people who cared for her, Daphne felt a subtle emptiness she couldn't quite name. She was mother, hostess, friend—but something was missing.

"You're doing that thing again," Jenny said, joining them with a glass of white wine in hand. "That thousand-yard stare while everyone's having fun."

"Just taking it all in," Daphne replied, accepting the glass Jenny offered.

Later, as she retreated to the kitchen to slice more cake, Daphne found herself alone for a moment. The sounds of conversation and laughter drifted in from outside as she pressed the knife through the sticky sweetness, feeling the warmth of the oven still lingering on her skin. She closed her eyes, letting the familiar taste of home wash over her as she sneaked a small bite.

This was good—this life she'd built for herself and her children. These friends who had become family. But as she stacked slices onto a serving plate, she couldn't help but acknowledge the quiet space in her heart that remained unfilled—a space that belonged to neither her children nor her friends, but was reserved for something else entirely.

With a deep breath, she picked up the plate and rejoined the gathering, her smile firmly back in place. Tomorrow would bring a new week, new challenges at work, and perhaps—though she hardly dared admit it to herself—new possibilities.

♥♥♥

The quarterly financial risk assessment conference room hummed with anticipation as executives from global offices filed in. Daphne straightened her navy blazer and reviewed her presentation notes one last time. As Sydney's newest team lead, she felt determined to make a strong impression.

"Daphne Stainthorpe?" A British accent cut through her concentration.

She looked up to find a tall man with dark hair and intelligent green eyes extending his hand.

"Mason Williams, London office. I've heard

impressive things about your work in identifying that pharmaceutical fraud pattern."

His handshake was firm, his smile genuine. Something about his confidence without arrogance caught her attention immediately.

"Thank you," she replied. "Though I can't take all the credit—it was a team effort."

"Modest too," he said with a slight smile. "I'm here for the Hartwell merger project. We'll be collaborating for the next month."

As the meeting began, Daphne found herself occasionally glancing in Mason's direction. When he spoke, his insights were sharp and thoughtful. She noted how he gave full attention to each speaker, regardless of their rank—a rare quality in their competitive field.

Later, as they walked toward their respective offices, Mason asked, "Any recommendations for a visitor trying to experience the real Sydney, not just tourist traps?"

"Actually," Daphne found herself saying, "a few of us are going to a wine bar in Surry Hills after work on Friday. Very local, great Australian wines. You'd be welcome to join."

The invitation surprised her as much as it seemed to please him. It had been months since she'd extended herself socially beyond necessary work functions. But something about Mason's easy manner made it feel natural.

"I'd like that," he said with a smile that reached his eyes. "It's a date—professionally speaking, of course."

Daphne laughed, the sound unexpected and light. "Of course."

♥♥♥

Three weeks into the Hartwell project, the Sydney office erupted in celebration when the merger cleared its final regulatory hurdle. The conference room transformed into an impromptu party space, with champagne flowing and the usual corporate boundaries softening under the influence of success and alcohol.

Daphne leaned against the window overlooking the harbor lights, watching her colleagues with a small smile. The past weeks working with Mason had been surprisingly enjoyable. Their professional chemistry had made the complex project run smoothly, and she'd found herself looking forward to their meetings.

"Penny for your thoughts?" Mason appeared beside her, offering a fresh glass of champagne.

"Just thinking this view never gets old," she said, accepting the drink. "How are you feeling about the project wrapping up?"

"Satisfied professionally," he admitted, "though I've grown rather fond of Sydney. And its residents." His eyes held hers a moment longer than strictly necessary.

Three glasses of champagne later, they stood close together on the office balcony. The conversation had drifted from work to personal histories, discovering shared loves of jazz and historical biographies.

"It's your children who are the real achievement though," Mason said. "The way you speak about them... they're lucky to have you."

"I'm the lucky one," Daphne replied, feeling the warmth of the champagne and something else spreading through her. "They're my world."

When his fingers brushed hers on the railing, she didn't pull away. The loneliness of the past months seemed to crystallize in that moment—the struggle of building a life in a new country, raising children alone, maintaining a professional facade while aching for connection.

"My hotel is just down the street," he said quietly.

Daphne knew she should decline. Office relationships were messy. Long-distance ones, impossible. Yet she found herself nodding.

"Let me get my purse."

♥♥♥

Sunlight streamed through unfamiliar curtains. Daphne blinked awake, momentarily disoriented until the events of the previous night came rushing back. Mason slept peacefully beside her, one arm flung across the pillow.

Daphne glanced at her watch—6:30 AM. She'd need to be home before Mrs. Henderson, her neighbor who had stayed overnight with the children, needed to leave for her volunteer shift at 7:30.

She slipped from the bed and gathered her clothes, moving quietly to the bathroom. As she dressed, she studied her reflection in the mirror. Her hair was tousled, but her eyes held a mixture of guilt and something else—perhaps relief at having allowed herself a moment of connection.

When she emerged, Mason was sitting up in bed.

"Morning," he said, his voice gentle. "Can I call you a taxi?"

"That would be great," she replied, checking her phone to find three texts from Caroline asking if she'd be home in time to help with her science project. "I need to get back to the kids."

An awkward silence stretched between them as Mason reached for the hotel phone.

"Daphne," he began once he'd arranged the taxi, "about last night—"

"It's okay," she interrupted, not wanting to hear apologies or promises neither of them could keep. "We're both adults. You're leaving for London in three days. Let's not complicate things."

Relief and something like regret crossed his face. "You're remarkable, you know that?"

She smiled, appreciating his honesty. "We had a nice night. But my children are my priority."

"As they should be," he said sincerely. "For what it's worth, I think you're doing an amazing job here—with everything. Not everyone could rebuild their life on the other side of the world while raising three children alone."

His words touched a place in her that had been aching for validation. "Thank you for saying that."

The hotel room phone rang—her taxi had arrived. They parted with a brief hug that held no promises, just appreciation for a moment of connection in a life that sometimes felt overwhelmingly solitary.

Twenty minutes later, Daphne slipped into her apartment, finding Mrs. Henderson dozing in the armchair.

"I'm so sorry," Daphne whispered as the older woman stirred. "The office party ran much later than I expected." The lie tasted bitter, but she managed a grateful smile. "Thank you for staying with the kids."

"No trouble at all, dear," Mrs. Henderson replied, gathering her things. "They were perfect angels. Royce is still asleep, but Caroline and Morgan have been up for a bit."

As the door closed behind her neighbor, Daphne leaned against it, exhaling slowly. The weight of her responsibilities settled back onto her shoulders, along with a new layer of guilt. She promised herself this wouldn't happen again—her children deserved better than a mother who disappeared overnight, regardless of how desperately she might crave adult connection.

"Mum! You're home!" Caroline called, rushing into the living room with a half-assembled science project. "Can you help me finish this? It's due tomorrow!"

Daphne pushed all thoughts of Mason aside and smiled at her daughter. "Of course, sweetheart. Let me just make some coffee first."

This was her real life—not stolen moments in hotel rooms, but science projects and Saturday morning cartoons and being present for her children. Whatever had happened with Mason would remain what it was: a brief escape, nothing more.

Chapter 11 – Justin
2005

Six weeks later, Daphne stared at the pregnancy test in her bathroom, the second pink line unmistakable. Her hands shook as she set it down on the counter.

"This can't be happening," she whispered to the empty room.

But it was. The nausea that had plagued her mornings suddenly made sense. The fatigue she'd attributed to overwork had another explanation entirely.

She sank onto the edge of the bathtub, her mind racing. She was forty-two. She had three children already. She was establishing herself in a new country, a new office. And the father was an ocean away, resumed in his London life.

Mason. Should she tell him? They'd exchanged a few friendly emails since his return, professional and cordial. He'd mentioned a long-term girlfriend once, someone he'd been "taking a break from" during his Sydney assignment. That relationship had apparently rekindled upon his return.

Daphne placed a protective hand over her still-flat stomach. This child hadn't been planned, but in that moment, she knew with absolute certainty that she wanted this baby.

"We'll be okay," she whispered, not just to herself but to the new life growing within her. "We'll make it work."

The decision not to tell Mason wasn't difficult. What would be the point? He lived on the other side of the world, had his own life, his own relationship. This child would be hers—a unexpected gift, a piece of Sydney that would remain with her forever.

She looked around the bathroom of her Sydney home, remembering how alien it had felt when they'd first arrived. Now it was home. They were building a life here, and this baby—this surprise—would be part of that new beginning.

"Justin," she said suddenly, trying the name on her tongue. She'd always liked it. "Justin Mason." A small acknowledgment of his father, even if Mason himself would never know.

Daphne squared her shoulders and stood up. She needed to tell her children they would be getting a new sibling. She needed to make doctor's appointments. She needed to inform her boss eventually.

But first, she needed to absorb this new reality herself: in the midst of rebuilding her life, she had accidentally created another life entirely.

♥♥♥

The evening light faded as Daphne ended another video call with Jason, their usual work discussion having stretched well past office hours again. She leaned back in her chair, rubbing her lower back where a dull ache had settled—a new companion since hitting the ten-week mark of her pregnancy.

"We should probably call it a night," she said, glancing at her watch. "It's getting late here."

"What time is it there now? Nearly nine?" Jason asked from his office in Singapore, looking remarkably fresh despite the hour.

"Half past," Daphne confirmed. "And I still need to help Royce with his science project."

Jason nodded, his expression warm even through the pixelated screen. "How are you feeling? You seem tired."

The question caught her off guard. They'd maintained a strictly professional relationship for months, their conversations revolving around risk assessments and financial algorithms. Yet lately, a subtle shift had occurred—small talk extending beyond pleasantries, genuine concern in his questions.

Daphne hesitated. She was only twelve weeks along, still keeping the pregnancy private outside her immediate family. But something about Jason's genuine concern made her consider confiding in him.

"Actually," she said, her hand unconsciously moving to her still-flat stomach, "I've been better. Morning sickness isn't just for mornings, it turns out."

Jason's eyes widened, his professional composure momentarily slipping. "You're pregnant? Wow, that's... congratulations?"

She laughed at his uncertain tone. "Yes, it's a good thing. Unexpected, but good."

"I didn't realize you were seeing someone," he said carefully.

"I'm not," Daphne replied simply. "It's complicated, but the father isn't in the picture."

To his credit, Jason nodded without judgment. "Well, congratulations all the same. That's wonderful news, Daphne."

As they said their goodbyes, Daphne felt surprisingly lighter for having shared her secret. There was something about Jason—his quiet thoughtfulness, perhaps—that made him feel safe to confide in, even from thousands of miles away.

♥♥♥

"You look better," Jason observed during their weekly team call. The others had dropped off, leaving them alone on the line as usual.

Daphne smiled, running a hand through her newly trimmed hair. At twenty weeks, her energy had returned, and the small but definite bump was now visible beneath her loose blouse.

"I feel better. The second trimester is apparently the golden period."

"I've been reading about that, actually," Jason admitted, then looked embarrassed. "I mean, I was curious after you told me. So I did some research."

Something warm bloomed in Daphne's chest at his words. "You've been reading pregnancy books?"

"Articles mostly," he clarified. "But there's this great pregnancy app I found. It tells you what size fruit the baby resembles each week."

Daphne laughed. "A banana, according to my doctor's app."

"That's exactly what mine said!" Jason's face lit up with enthusiasm. "Did you know the baby can hear your voice now?"

"I did," she said, touched by his interest. "The kids have been reading to my belly every night. Caroline's choice is usually some teen drama, while Royce goes for adventure stories."

"And Morgan?"

"Science journals," Daphne replied with a fond eye roll. "Trying to create a little engineer, I think."

They shared a laugh, and Daphne found herself wishing, not for the first time, that the distance between Sydney and Singapore wasn't so vast. Their friendship had deepened over the past months, with Jason becoming an unexpected source of support through her pregnancy.

"Have you thought about names yet?" he asked.

"Justin," she said without hesitation. "Justin Mason."

"It's perfect," Jason said softly. "Strong but gentle."

Later, after they'd hung up, a notification pinged on Daphne's phone. Jason had sent her a link to a playlist titled "Songs for Justin," filled with classical pieces apparently beneficial for developing minds.

Daphne pressed play, letting the gentle melodies fill her living room as she placed a hand on her growing bump. Distance might separate them, but Jason had found ways to be present nonetheless.

♥♥♥

The Sydney office buzzed with anticipation as the Singapore team arrived for the annual regional summit. At thirty-two weeks pregnant, Daphne moved more slowly through the hallways, one hand supporting her lower back as she directed her team in finalizing presentation materials.

"Daphne?"

The voice was familiar, yet somehow different—richer, more resonant than through video calls. She turned to find Jason standing there, looking both familiar and strangely new in three dimensions.

"Jason," she smiled, extending her hand automatically before he surprised her by leaning in for a gentle hug instead.

"Look at you," he said, stepping back to take in her pregnancy. "You're glowing."

"I'm enormous is what I am," she laughed, but felt a blush warming her cheeks. "It's good to see you in person."

"You too." His eyes held hers a moment longer than necessary. "The photos and videos don't do you justice."

Throughout the day, Jason stayed close by, pulling out chairs for her during meetings, ensuring she had water, even bringing her lunch when she mentioned being hungry. His attentiveness drew knowing looks from colleagues, but Daphne found she didn't mind.

That evening, as the teams gathered for dinner at a waterfront restaurant, Jason claimed the seat beside her.

"So tomorrow's the big presentation," he said, filling her water glass. "Nervous?"

"A little," she admitted. "It's hard to project authority when you waddle rather than walk."

He laughed. "Trust me, no one's thinking about that. They're too busy being impressed by your analysis of the Asian market vulnerabilities."

As the night wore on, their conversation deepened beyond work, touching on childhood dreams, favorite books, and the paths that had led them to their current lives. There was an ease between them that transcended their virtual connection—a comfort that felt both surprising and entirely natural.

"Will you have to rush back to Singapore after the summit?" Daphne asked as they shared a dessert, the Sydney Opera House glittering across the water behind them.

"Actually," Jason said, looking somewhat nervous, "I've put in for a transfer to the Sydney office. It's not final yet, but there's a good chance I'll be relocating within the next six months."

Daphne's heart skipped. "Really? That's... that would be wonderful."

"Would it?" he asked, his expression suddenly vulnerable.

Before she could answer, a sharp pain radiated across her abdomen. She gasped, clutching her stomach.

"Daphne?" Jason's voice sharpened with concern.

"I'm fine," she breathed as the pain subsided. "Braxton Hicks contractions. They're normal."

Jason's worried expression didn't ease. "Maybe we should get you home."

As he helped her to her feet, Daphne felt another rush of warmth for this man who had become such an unexpected presence in her life. Whatever lay ahead for them—friendship or possibly more—she was grateful for the connection they'd forged across time zones and computer screens.

"Thank you," she said as he hailed a taxi. "For everything."

"Don't thank me yet," he replied with a gentle smile. "I'm not going anywhere, Daphne. Not if I can help it."

♥♥♥

"He's perfect," Jason whispered, peering down at the

newborn cradled in Daphne's arms. He'd arrived at the hospital bearing flowers, a teddy bear, and a stack of books for the inevitable waiting periods.

Justin Mason Stainthorpe had entered the world after a mercifully quick labor, his tiny features a blend of Daphne and a man who would likely never know of his existence. At seven pounds three ounces, with a shock of dark hair and alert eyes, he was indeed perfect.

"Thank you for coming," Daphne said, her voice hoarse from the exertion of childbirth. "You didn't have to."

"Wild horses couldn't have kept me away," Jason replied, perching carefully on the edge of the hospital bed. "Besides, I had to meet the little banana in person."

Daphne laughed, then winced as her body protested the movement. "It's been quite a journey from those first video calls, hasn't it?"

Jason's hand found hers atop the hospital blanket. "The best journeys often are the ones we don't plan."

Over the following months, as Daphne adjusted to life with a newborn while balancing three older children and her career, Jason remained a constant presence. Though still based in Singapore, he visited Sydney monthly for work, each time bringing small gifts for Justin and spending evenings helping with dinner, bath time, and bedtime stories.

"You don't have to do all this," Daphne told him one night after they'd finally gotten all four children to sleep—no small feat with a colicky three-month-old.

They sat on her back porch, the Sydney night wrapping around them like a comfortable blanket. Jason's eyes reflected the soft glow of the outdoor lights as he turned to her.

"I know I don't have to," he said simply. "I want to."

"Why?" The question had been on her mind for months. "We're just friends, Jason. And Justin isn't—"

"I know he isn't mine," Jason interrupted gently. "That doesn't matter to me."

He reached for her hand, his touch tentative but warm. "What matters is that I care about you, Daphne. All of you—Morgan, Royce, Caroline, and now Justin too. The how and why of his arrival doesn't change that."

Daphne felt tears prickling behind her eyes. "It's complicated. My life is complicated."

"The best things usually are," he replied, echoing his words from the hospital. "And I'm still not going anywhere—unless you want me to."

As Justin's cries echoed through the baby monitor, Daphne gave Jason's hand a squeeze before rising to tend to her youngest. Whatever lay ahead for them remained to be seen, but having him in her life—in all their lives—felt right in a way she couldn't quite explain.

The relationship with Jason might never progress beyond deep friendship, especially with the distances involved. Yet his steady presence through her pregnancy and Justin's early months had become a touchstone—proof that connection could form in the most unexpected ways, bridging oceans and time zones to create something meaningful.

♥♥♥

Daphne hummed along to a favorite melody as she took the laundry off the line in the backyard, finding comfort in the routine chore. As she shook out one of Morgan's oversized hoodies, she smiled thinking of her child's unique spirit. Daphne heard the creaky back door open and turned to see seventeen year old Morgan hovering in the doorway, uncharacteristically timid.

" Shouldn't you be getting ready for your driving lesson?" Daphne asked, glancing at her watch. "I thought Mr. Patterson was coming at three to take you out for practice before your P-Plates test next week."

Morgan's fingers fidgeted with the edge of their shirt, avoiding eye contact for a moment before responding softly, "I called and rescheduled. I... I need to talk to you about something important. Do you have a minute?"

Daphne set down the half-folded pile of clothes and walked over to Morgan, guiding them to sit together on the faded outdoor chairs. Taking Morgan's nervous hands in hers, she said "Of course, you know you can tell me anything."

Morgan took a shaky breath before speaking again. "So, I've been doing a lot of thinking and learning about myself lately. And I realized that I'm non-binary. I don't fully identify as either male or female. I know this might be confusing, but it's important you know how I feel inside."

Daphne nodded slowly, focusing intently on Morgan's words. She had noticed subtle changes in their style and mannerisms lately but hadn't wanted to pry. Now it made sense. Morgan continued "I also recently discovered that I'm asexual. I'm just not interested in sexual or romantic relationships the way most people are."

Daphne's heart swelled with empathy and appreciation that Morgan trusted her enough to confide these profound truths. She pulled them into a fierce embrace. "Thank you for telling me. I can't imagine how scary and difficult this was to share."

Still holding Morgan tight, she continued "I support you and love you unconditionally, no matter how you identify. All I want is for you to feel comfortable being your authentic self. We can take things slow, but I absolutely want to understand so I can support you better."

Morgan exhaled in relief, eyes glistening with gratitude. "I was so afraid you'd reject me or not understand," they whispered. Daphne stroked their hair lovingly. "The only thing that matters to me is that you're happy and living as your true self. I'm so proud of you for having the courage to tell me. Nothing could ever change my love."

They talked for hours, Morgan explaining the nuances of their identity and answering Daphne's thoughtful questions. Daphne processed it all, mindfully adjusting her language to use Morgan's new pronouns.

She felt closer to her child than ever after this vulnerable sharing of hearts and minds.

Chapter 12 – Growth
2009

As Daphne continued to grow and evolve in her personal life, she also began to explore new interests outside of her work. It had been over a year since Justin's birth when she found herself staring at her reflection one morning, barely recognizing the tired woman looking back at her.

"Time for a change," she murmured to herself, and that afternoon she signed up for membership at a local fitness center near her home. It wasn't just about losing the baby weight—it was about reclaiming a sense of herself beyond motherhood and spreadsheets.

Her first few sessions were humbling. Years of prioritizing everyone and everything else had left her body weaker than she'd realized. But there was something satisfying about the ache in her muscles, the measured progress as she gradually increased her endurance on the treadmill and added weights to her routine.

Three times a week, she carved out time for herself between work and family responsibilities. The gym became her sanctuary—a place where she could focus solely on her own needs without guilt. Her friends noticed the change in her almost immediately—not just the physical transformation as her body grew stronger, but the renewed confidence in her posture and the spark that had returned to her eyes.

It was during a Saturday morning fitness class that she first noticed him. Greg Harper moved with the easy grace of someone completely at home in his body. As the instructor guided them through a particularly challenging sequence, Daphne caught his eye in the mirror and he flashed her an encouraging smile. Something fluttered in her chest that had nothing to do with exertion.

After class, he approached her as she was refilling her water bottle.

"First time?" he asked, his Australian accent thicker than most she'd encountered in corporate Sydney.

"Tenth, actually," she replied with a small smile.

"Though it doesn't get any easier, does it?"

"That's how you know it's working," he said with a wink. "I'm Greg, by the way."

"Daphne."

Their conversation was brief—just enough to establish that they were both regulars, both enjoyed the Saturday morning class, both worked in the city though in different industries. But as Daphne left the gym that morning, she found herself looking forward to the next class in a way that had nothing to do with fitness goals.

Her newfound physical outlet not only became a source of strength and energy but also added another layer to her relationships. Friends who once knew her as the spreadsheet-loving, laundry-folding woman now saw her as someone embracing new challenges and perhaps even new possibilities.

♥♥♥

Despite her successes, Daphne couldn't shake the feeling that something was missing from her life. She longed for someone to share these experiences with - someone who could understand the weight of her responsibilities and appreciate the beauty of their new home. Someone who would challenge her, push her limits, and see past her perfectionism. Someone who would cherish her quirks, like leaving dirty dishes in the sink and wearing sweatpants all day. Someone who would complete her, not just complement her.

Her connection with Greg from the gym had promised something different than her online dating experiences. Their relationship began intensely - hiking coastal trails on weekends, training for the City2Surf race together, and sharing the endorphin high of their workouts. The physical chemistry between them was undeniable, and for a while, Daphne thought she might have found someone who understood the importance of both strength and vulnerability.

But as weeks turned to months, she noticed the pattern. Greg could share his body but not his thoughts, his time but not his fears. Each time she attempted to deepen their connection, he would retreat behind his charming smile and suggest another workout or outdoor adventure. The walls he had built around his heart seemed impenetrable, and eventually, Daphne stopped trying to scale them.

She wanted love that didn't require explanations or translation. Love that wouldn't disappear after a project ended or a holiday weekend was over... but after years of failed relationships and heartbreaks, she had all but given up on finding love again.

♥♥♥

She took a chance and went on a dating app, hoping to find someone who could appreciate her for who she was, flaws and all. Dating in the online world offered a glimmer of hope, but the endless swiping and superficial conversations left her feeling disillusioned. A man named Trevor Mitchell seemed promising, with his kind eyes and gentle demeanor. They shared coffee and conversation, but something felt off. He was too eager to please, always agreeing with everything she said, never offering any real insight into his own life. It was comforting yet suffocating.

Life moved forward despite her romantic disappointments. On a sunny February morning, Daphne stood in Morgan's bedroom doorway, watching as her firstborn carefully arranged textbooks on their desk.

"I can't believe you start university next week," Daphne said, her chest tight with pride and nostalgia. "Macquarie's aerospace engineering program is lucky to have you."

Morgan looked up, a rare smile spreading across their face. "I still can't believe I got in."

"I can," Daphne replied. "You've been designing planes since you were seven."

The commute from their home to Macquarie University would be manageable - just under an hour by train and bus. Though many of Morgan's friends were eager to move out, Morgan had decided to continue living at home through university, a decision that secretly relieved Daphne. She wasn't quite ready to see her firstborn leave the nest entirely.

"I got you something," Daphne said, pulling a small package from behind her back. Inside was a sleek calculator that Morgan had been eyeing for months.

"Mum, this is too expensive!" Morgan protested, even as their fingers ran reverently over the device.

"Nothing's too expensive for my future NASA engineer," Daphne replied, her voice catching slightly.

Downstairs, she could hear Royce chattering excitedly about his latest cooking class. At sixteen, he'd just gotten his Learner's Permit and was alternating between begging for driving practice and attending the culinary program at the community college. His passion for food had blossomed in Sydney, influenced by the city's diverse culinary scene. Just last week, he'd prepared a multi-course dinner that left them all speechless—a fusion of Asian and Australian flavors that demonstrated talents far beyond his years.

As she helped Morgan prepare for this next chapter, Daphne couldn't help reflecting on her own journey. Four years in Sydney had transformed them all. Caroline was discovering her musical talents, and little Justin was growing into a curious toddler with a mischievous streak. Her career had advanced beyond her expectations.

Yet as her children grew more independent, Daphne wondered what the coming years would hold for her. Perhaps it was time to reassess what she truly wanted from this life she'd built so carefully in Australia.

♥♥♥

And that's when she met him—Cameron Reynolds, an intellectual with a passion for problem-solving and a love for ice cream just as strong as hers. They met at the Royal Easter Show, both reaching for the same showbag at a confectionery stand. They clicked instantly, sharing late-night talks about everything from literature to life's mysteries.

As they sat at the table one night, sharing a pint of cookie dough ice cream, she knew she'd found what she'd been searching for all along: a partner, not a project. Life had been waiting for her to make room in her heart for love, and she was finally ready.

But as with any journey, Daphne's path to self-discovery wasn't without its bumps. After a few months of dating Cam, she realized that while they had an undeniable connection, there were aspects of their relationship that needed work. She feared that her need for control and perfectionism might push him away, but instead of retreating, she decided to address it head-on.

"Cam," she said one evening, her voice soft and vulnerable, "I've been thinking about my quirks and the way I can be a bit controlling at times. I want you to know that I'm working on it. I don't want my fears to jeopardize what we have."

He looked at her, his eyes filled with understanding and warmth. "Daphne, nobody's perfect. We all have our flaws, but that's what makes us human. And that's why I love you. We'll grow together, okay?"

His words brought tears to her eyes, and she nodded, grateful for his patience and support.

As the years passed, Cam became woven into the fabric of their lives. He taught Royce how to parallel park for his driving test, helped Caroline master complex chord progressions on her guitar, and became Justin's favorite storyteller at bedtime. He even developed a respectful rapport with Morgan, bonding over physics equations and space exploration theories.

Their relationship evolved with the natural rhythm of seasons. They celebrated Morgan's graduation from Macquarie University, cheered at Royce's first culinary competition win, and supported Caroline as she formed her first band. When Justin started primary school, Cam was there for his first day, camera in hand, capturing moments that would become cherished memories.

By their third anniversary, they had fallen into a comfortable routine. Perhaps too comfortable. The passionate discussions that had once kept them talking until dawn gradually shortened. Date nights became predictable. The spark hadn't disappeared, but it had dimmed to a steady, reliable glow.

"Do you ever wonder if we're settling?" Daphne asked one evening as they sat on the balcony of their apartment, watching the Sydney Harbour lights twinkle across the water.

Cam considered her question thoughtfully. "I think there's a difference between settling and building something lasting," he finally replied. "What we have isn't always fireworks, but it's real. It's honest."

She leaned against his shoulder, knowing he was right. After the chaos of her previous relationships, there was profound value in their stable, supportive partnership. Yet something in his answer left her unsettled.

Their fourth year together brought unexpected challenges. Cam received an offer for his dream job—a research position at a prestigious think tank in Melbourne. The opportunity was too good to pass up, but the distance would be significant.

"We can make it work," Daphne insisted as they discussed their options. "Weekend visits, holidays together."

Cam nodded, but his eyes held a question he was afraid to ask. "And longer term? Would you ever consider moving to Melbourne?"

The question hung between them, heavy with implications. Sydney had become home—not just a place she lived, but the setting for her children's formative years, the foundation of her career, the backdrop to their life together.

"I... I don't know," she admitted honestly. "The kids are established here. My job..."

"It's okay," he said, taking her hand. "We don't have to decide everything now."

But the question had opened a door neither could fully close. As the weeks passed and Cam's departure date approached, they both sensed the crossroads they were facing. Their conversations grew deeper, more intentional, as if trying to store up connection for the coming separation.

On his last night in Sydney, they walked along the harbor, retracing the steps of their first dates.

"I don't regret a single moment," Cam said, stopping to face her under the shadow of the Opera House. "These four years with you, with the kids—they've been the best of my life."

Daphne felt tears threatening. "But sometimes love isn't enough, is it?"

He brushed a strand of hair from her face, his touch achingly familiar. "Sometimes timing is everything. And maybe ours wasn't quite right."

They parted with promises to stay in touch, to visit, to not let go completely. But as Sydney's winter turned to spring and spring to summer, the calls grew less frequent, the visits more complicated to arrange. By the time a year had passed, their relationship had gently faded into a fond friendship, marked by occasional messages and the shared memories of a love that had been real, if not forever.

♥♥♥

"Morgan Stainthorpe, NASA Propulsion Engineer," Daphne read aloud from the official letter, pride making her voice tremble. "I can't believe it."

Morgan looked up from their laptop, a rare, full smile illuminating their face. "I got the call this morning, but I wanted to wait until I had the official offer before telling everyone."

Ten years had passed since their arrival in Sydney. Justin, now nine, bounded around the living room with excitement, although he clearly didn't understand the significance of his oldest sibling's achievement. At twenty-three, Morgan had exceeded even Daphne's high expectations, graduating at the top of their class and completing a prestigious internship at the Australian Space Agency before applying to NASA.

"This calls for a celebration," Daphne declared, already mentally planning a family dinner. She paused, reality setting in. "When do they want you to start?"

"Six weeks," Morgan replied, their excitement tempered by the knowledge of what this meant. "I'll need to move to Houston."

The words hung in the air, both thrilling and devastating. Daphne felt her heart constrict—pride and loss battling for dominance. Her firstborn was truly leaving the nest, not just to another city but another continent.

As the family celebrated over Morgan's favorite vegan meal, Daphne listened eagerly as they described their upcoming role. "I'll be working on developing the next generation of rovers for Mars exploration! Can you believe it?" Morgan gushed. "I'll get to collaborate with such brilliant scientists and engineers every day."

Caroline was about to take her last year 12 exam, Morgan was going off to their dream job, and Royce had just finished culinary school. It was time to go home to Richmond.

♥♥♥

Later, after the dishes were cleared and the younger ones had gone to bed, Morgan found Daphne sitting alone on the back porch.

"Are you okay, Mum?" they asked, settling into the chair beside her.

Daphne smiled through the tears that threatened. "More than okay. I'm incredibly proud of you."

"But sad too?"

"It's a parent's job to raise children who can leave," Daphne said softly. "Doesn't make it any easier when they actually do."

Morgan was quiet for a moment. "I've been thinking... maybe it's time for all of us to think about what's next. Royce is established in his career here, Caroline's band is taking off... but you've always talked about eventually returning to Richmond."

Daphne looked at her child in surprise. "I didn't think you remembered that."

"Of course I do," Morgan said. "And I've seen how you've been since things ended with Cam. Maybe this is the universe telling you it's time for a change too."

As the words settled over her, Daphne felt something shift—a possibility taking shape, a door opening where she'd thought only walls remained. After a decade in Sydney, perhaps it was time to consider what the next chapter might hold.

"Maybe you're right," she said thoughtfully. "Maybe it is."

As the sun began to set on the day of their celebration, Daphne took a moment to reflect on the bittersweet nature of leaving Sydney. She knew that saying goodbye to the life she had built there would be difficult, but she also felt ready to embrace new experiences and opportunities in Richmond.

"Life is full of surprises," she whispered to herself, echoing Cam's words from weeks before. And with her newfound confidence and the unwavering love of her family, Daphne knew that she was prepared to face whatever surprises lay ahead.

The following day, Daphne sat in her home office with the soft morning light streaming through the window. She opened her laptop and began to draft an email to her employer, requesting a transfer to their

Richmond office.

"Dear Mr. Thompson," she typed, her fingers trembling slightly as she composed each sentence, "I hope this message finds you well. I am writing to formally request a transfer to our Richmond office."

She went on to explain her reasons for wanting to relocate, including her desire to be closer to family and the opportunities that awaited her children in Richmond. As she completed the email, Daphne hesitated for a brief moment before clicking 'send.'

"Here goes nothing," she murmured, feeling a mix of anxiety and anticipation.

Days later, Daphne received a response from her employer. Her heart raced as she opened the email, her eyes scanning the words with bated breath:

"Dear Daphne, We understand your request and are happy to accommodate your transfer. You have been an invaluable asset to our Sydney office, and we look forward to having you join our team in Richmond."

A sigh of relief escaped her lips as she closed her laptop. The decision was now final – they were moving back to Richmond. Daphne knew there would be challenges ahead, but she felt ready to face them head-on.

"Goodbye, Sydney," she whispered, wiping away a tear. "Hello, Richmond."

Chapter 13 – Richmond
2015

It was moving day, again, and Daphne stood in the driveway of her Richmond home watching as the movers hauled in boxes. The familiar scent of pine and magnolia filled her nostrils as she took in the sight of their home. It had been a long journey, but they were finally back where it all began.

Caroline, Royce, Morgan, and little Justin joined her on the sidewalk, taking in the sight of their old house with a mix of nostalgia and excitement. For the older children, they had grown up here, and it held countless memories. For Justin, nearly ten years old now, this was an entirely new adventure.

As they watched the movers work, Daphne felt a sense of pride wash over her. They had made it through so much—the abuse, the moves, the struggles—and now they were back together again. It was a testament to their resilience and strength as a family.

"I can't believe we're really back," Caroline whispered, her eyes taking in every detail of the house. The same brick facade, the same oak tree in the front yard, the same creaky step leading up to the porch.

"It's smaller than I remember," Royce commented, his chef's eye already evaluating the kitchen through the window.

Morgan remained quiet, their face a mixture of emotions. In just two weeks, they would be boarding a plane to Houston, embarking on the career they had dreamed of since childhood.

"You okay?" Daphne asked softly, nudging Morgan's shoulder.

"Yeah," they nodded, offering a small smile. "Just taking it all in before I leave. It's strange—coming home only to say goodbye again."

Justin tugged at Daphne's hand. "Is this really where you used to live, Mum?"

"Yes, sweetheart," Daphne replied, ruffling his dark hair. "This is home."

As they made their way to the front door, the house next door opened, and an elderly woman stepped out onto her porch. Her silver hair was neatly styled, and despite her age, she moved with purpose and energy.

"Daphne Stainthorpe, as I live and breathe!" the woman called, her voice warm with delight. "You're finally back!"

"Mrs. Pine!" Daphne exclaimed, her face lighting up with genuine joy. She crossed the lawn to embrace her neighbor tightly. "It's so good to see you."

Helen Pine had been their neighbor since Daphne and Luke had first built the house. She had been there through the birth of each child, had watched them grow, had been a steady presence during the darkest days of Daphne's marriage. When Luke had been arrested, it was Mrs. Pine who had stepped in to help with childcare while Daphne worked.

"Look at you all," Mrs. Pine marveled, glancing over Daphne's shoulder at the children. "My goodness, Caroline, you're the spitting image of your mother at your age. And Royce—so tall! Morgan, I've been following your accomplishments in the local paper. So proud of you, dear."

Her gaze settled on Justin, her expression softening. "And this must be the little one I've only seen in photographs. Hello, Justin."

Justin, normally shy around strangers, felt immediately at ease with Mrs. Pine. There was something about her warm smile and kind eyes that put him at comfort. "Hello," he replied, stepping forward to shake her hand formally, just as Daphne had taught him.

Mrs. Pine laughed delightedly. "Such a gentleman! You'll have to come over for cookies soon. I still make the best chocolate chip cookies in Richmond—just ask your siblings."

"It's true," Royce confirmed with a grin. "No one beats Mrs. Pine's cookies. Not even me, and I'm a professional now."

"So I heard!" Mrs. Pine beamed. "A real chef in the family. Mr Pine would have been so proud, Royce."

As they chatted, Daphne felt a wave of nostalgia wash over her. This was what she had missed during their years in Australia—this sense of community, of belonging, of shared history.

"You all must be exhausted," Mrs. Pine said finally. "I've left a casserole in your refrigerator—just needs fifteen minutes in the oven. And there's fresh bread on the counter. The Pine family welcome wagon is still operational after all these years."

Daphne's eyes filled with tears. "Thank you, Helen. For everything."

Mrs. Pine patted her cheek gently. "That's what neighbors are for, dear. Now, go get settled. We'll have plenty of time to catch up."

Inside, the house was just as Daphne remembered—perhaps a bit smaller after their spacious Sydney home, but filled with familiar nooks and crannies. The children dispersed to claim bedrooms, their voices echoing through halls that had been silent for too long.

"I want the blue room!" Justin called, racing up the stairs.

"That's my old room," Morgan objected, following close behind.

"You're leaving in two weeks," Justin reasoned. "I should get it!"

Daphne couldn't help but smile at the comforting normalcy of their bickering. Some things never changed, no matter how far they traveled or how much time had passed.

♥♥♥

The scent of cardboard and packing tape filled the air as Daphne supervised the movers carrying the last of their belongings into the Richmond house. After years in Sydney, it felt surreal to be standing in the familiar entryway of the home where she and Reuben had built so much of their life together.

"Mum!" Caroline called from upstairs. "Come look what I found in this old trunk!"

Daphne made her way up the staircase, noting how the afternoon sun still cast the same patterns through the stained glass window on the landing. Some things never changed, and there was comfort in that constancy.

She found Caroline in the attic storage space, kneeling beside a battered steamer trunk that Daphne hadn't seen in years. It had been shunted to a corner, somehow overlooked during their previous moves.

"I was clearing space for my music equipment and found this pushed way back in the corner," Caroline explained, gesturing to the open trunk. "Did you know this was up here?"

Daphne shook her head, crouching down beside her daughter. "I'd forgotten all about it, honestly. It must have been packed away before we left for Australia."

Caroline lifted out a bundle of blue and gold fabric, carefully unfolding it to reveal a cheerleading uniform. "UCLA?" she read aloud, her eyebrows raised in surprise. "You were a cheerleader?"

"Yup, all four years," Daphne confirmed with a nostalgic smile, taking the uniform and holding it against herself. "It seems like another lifetime ago."

"I can't believe it still exists," Caroline marveled, digging deeper into the trunk. "Wait, there's something else in here." She pulled out a heavy burgundy jacket, turning it over to reveal TEMPLE UNIVERSITY emblazoned across the back in faded white letters.

"Oh my goodness," Daphne breathed, her fingers tracing the lettering. "I can't believe this survived all these moves."

"Is this Dad's?" Caroline asked, looking more closely at the jacket.

Daphne shook her head slightly, taking the jacket and pressing it to her face. Despite the years, she could almost imagine it still carried a trace of Reuben's scent from that first night. "No, this is Ben's. He gave it to me the night we met after a lacrosse game. I was a freshman cheerleader, and he was playing for the visiting team."

Caroline's eyes widened with interest. "You never told us about someone named Ben!"

Daphne carefully folded the jacket, her fingers lingering on the worn fabric. "It was a long time ago," she said softly, her tone gently closing the door on further questions. "Another life, really."

"But you kept his jacket all these years," Caroline observed, her curiosity clearly piqued. "He must have been special."

"We should finish unpacking the essentials before dinner," Daphne redirected, placing the jacket and uniform back in the trunk with deliberate care. "Justin and Royce will be here soon to help with the furniture arrangement."

Caroline seemed to sense her mother's reluctance and nodded, though her eyes remained on the trunk as Daphne closed the lid. "I'll go check if the kitchen boxes are labeled correctly."

After Caroline left, Daphne reopened the trunk and took out the jacket once more. She ran her fingers over the stitched letters, memories washing over her like waves—the intensity in his eyes when they first met, the warmth of his hand holding hers across a diner table, the electricity of their first kiss under the streetlamp.

"Ben," she whispered, the name feeling both foreign and achingly familiar on her lips after all these years.

She hadn't thought about Reuben "Ben" Feldman in years—had deliberately pushed those memories aside as she built her life with Luke and then focused on raising her children alone. But now, standing in the house where she'd started over so many times, the jacket in her hands felt like a message from her younger self, a reminder of possibilities and paths not taken.

With a deep breath, Daphne carefully refolded the jacket and placed it back in the trunk, closing the lid firmly. The past was the past, and she had a home to organize and children to settle. Yet as she descended the stairs to rejoin Caroline in the kitchen, she couldn't help but wonder what had become of Ben after all these years, and whether he ever thought of the cheerleader who had kept his jacket for decades.

♥♥♥

Later that evening, after Mrs. Pine's casserole had

been devoured and the dishes washed, Daphne sat on the porch swing, a glass of iced tea in hand. The Virginia humidity wrapped around her like an old friend, and the crickets sang their familiar evening chorus.

Morgan joined her, settling onto the swing with a sigh.

"Having second thoughts?" Daphne asked.

"No," Morgan shook their head. "It's my dream job. But..."

"But it's hard to leave again so soon," Daphne finished.

"Yeah." Morgan looked out across the darkening yard. "I feel like I just got you all back, and now I'm the one leaving."

Daphne slipped an arm around her eldest child's shoulders. "That's the thing about family, Morgan. It stretches, but it doesn't break. Houston isn't so far. We'll visit, you'll come home for holidays. And there's always video calls."

"I know," Morgan nodded. "It's just—while we were in Sydney, I kept thinking about coming back here someday. And now that we're here, I'm leaving again."

"Life rarely follows the paths we imagine," Daphne mused. "Sometimes it has better ideas."

They sat in comfortable silence for a while, the swing's gentle creaking a soothing backdrop to their thoughts.

"Did you ever regret it?" Morgan finally asked. "Moving us to Australia?"

Daphne considered the question carefully. "No," she said finally. "It was exactly what we needed at the time. It gave us all a chance to grow, to discover who we were away from the shadows of the past." She squeezed Morgan's shoulder. "And look at the amazing adult you've become. NASA, Morgan. NASA!"

Morgan couldn't help but smile at their mother's enthusiasm. "You've changed too, you know. You seem... lighter somehow."

"Do I?" Daphne raised an eyebrow.

"Yeah. Less..."

"Controlling?" Daphne supplied with a self-deprecating laugh.

"I was going to say 'burdened,'" Morgan corrected.

"But yes, that too."

Daphne laughed, nudging Morgan playfully. "Cheeky."

"Honest," Morgan countered with a grin.

As the evening progressed, the rest of the family joined them on the porch. Caroline strummed her guitar softly, her voice floating through the warm night air. Royce talked excitedly about his upcoming interview at Riverfront, Richmond's most prestigious restaurant. Justin dozed against Daphne's side, exhausted from the day's excitement.

It was perfect—or as close to perfect as life ever got. Yet Daphne couldn't shake the feeling that something—or someone—was still missing from her life. The thought came unbidden, surprising her with its clarity. After years of focusing solely on her children and career, she recognized a longing for companionship that she hadn't allowed herself to acknowledge in a very long time.

♥♥♥

The first week back in Richmond passed in a blur of unpacking, organizing, and settling into new routines. Royce aced his interview at Riverfront and was thrilled to be offered a position as a line cook—a prestigious start for a young chef just out of culinary school. Caroline enrolled in music theory and composition classes at the local community college, her talent having blossomed during their years in Sydney. Morgan spent their days preparing for the move to Houston, organizing paperwork and researching apartments near the NASA facility.

And Justin, after some initial nervousness, started at Richmond Elementary School, where he was placed in Mrs. Pine's granddaughter's fifth-grade class.

"How was your first day?" Daphne asked as Justin burst through the door, his backpack bouncing against his back.

"It was awesome!" Justin exclaimed, his earlier anxiety completely forgotten. "Mrs. Amelia is super nice, and I got to sit by the window, and at recess, I made a friend!"

"You did?" Daphne smiled, helping him take off his backpack. "Tell me about this friend."

"His name is Roman, and he's only six months older than me, but he's the same height," Justin reported, digging into the after-school snack Daphne had prepared. "He likes space too, just like Morgan, and he has all the same video games I do, and he invited me to his house to play sometime!"

"That's wonderful, sweetheart," Daphne replied, her heart warming at her son's excitement. After the move from Sydney, she had worried about Justin making friends in Richmond. "Maybe we can arrange a playdate soon."

"He lives with his dad," Justin continued between bites of apple. "His mom died when he was a baby, but he says he doesn't remember her at all. His dad's really nice, though. He picks Roman up from school every day and helps coach his soccer team."

Daphne felt a pang of sympathy for Roman and his father. She knew all too well the challenges of single parenthood. "Well, it sounds like they're a nice family."

"Can I go to Roman's house this weekend?" Justin asked eagerly. "Please? He said they have a huge backyard with a treehouse!"

"Let me talk to his father first," Daphne laughed. "I'll need his phone number to arrange things properly."

"I already got it!" Justin declared triumphantly, pulling a crumpled piece of paper from his pocket.

"Roman wrote it down for me. His dad said I could come over anytime."

Daphne took the paper, examining the childish scrawl. "Roman Feldman," she read. "And his father's name is..."

But Justin had already moved on, racing upstairs to tell Morgan about his new friend, leaving Daphne with just a phone number and a common surname that triggered no recognition. She tucked the paper into her pocket, making a mental note to call Roman's father later to arrange the playdate.

♥♥♥

The morning of Morgan's departure arrived all too quickly. The family gathered in the driveway, huddled around Morgan's packed car. The early September air carried a hint of autumn, and a few leaves had already begun to turn on the oak tree in the yard.

"You have everything?" Daphne asked for the third time, her eyes scanning the car as if she might spot something critical Morgan had forgotten.

"Yes, Mum," Morgan replied patiently. "And if I forgot something, you can always send it. Or I'll buy a new one.

They do have stores in Houston, you know."

Daphne pulled Morgan into a tight hug, blinking back tears. "I know. I just... I'm going to miss you so much."

"I'll miss you too," Morgan whispered, their voice thick with emotion. "All of you."

Royce stepped forward next, enveloping his sibling in a bear hug. "Call when you get there, okay? No matter what time."

"I will," Morgan promised.

Caroline hugged Morgan fiercely, words failing her for once. When she pulled back, her cheeks were wet with tears, but she managed a watery smile. "You better send pictures of NASA. Lots of them."

"Every day," Morgan assured her.

Finally, Justin approached, his lower lip trembling as he fought to be brave. At ten, he was old enough to understand that this wasn't just any goodbye—Morgan was really leaving, starting a new life thousands of miles away.

"Hey, buddy," Morgan said softly, kneeling down to Justin's level. "You know what? I need a special mission partner in Houston."

"You do?" Justin sniffled.

"Absolutely. I'll be working on rovers for Mars, and I'll need someone to test my ideas with. Think you can help me over video chat?"

Justin's face brightened. "Really? Like a real NASA helper?"

"The most important kind," Morgan confirmed solemnly. "I couldn't do it without you."

Justin threw his arms around Morgan's neck, hugging them tightly. "I'll be the best helper ever!"

As Morgan finally got into the car and pulled away, waving through the open window, Daphne felt a complex mixture of emotions—pride, sadness, excitement, nostalgia. Her firstborn was truly an adult now, embarking on a path they had dreamed of since childhood.

Mrs. Pine appeared at the fence line, a tray of cookies in hand. "Thought you might need these," she said gently, noticing Daphne's tears.

"Thank you, Helen," Daphne managed, accepting the

tray gratefully.

"First one to leave the nest is always the hardest," Mrs. Pine observed, her eyes kind. "But Morgan will be just fine. You've raised a remarkable child there."

"I hope so," Daphne whispered.

"I know so," Mrs. Pine said firmly. "Now, come over for tea later today. I've been saving up all the neighborhood gossip for ten years, and you have a lot of catching up to do."

Daphne laughed despite her tears. "I'd like that."

As they walked back toward the house, Justin suddenly remembered his playdate. "Mum! Can you call Roman's dad today? Roman said I could come over on Saturday!"

Daphne patted her pocket, feeling the crumpled paper with the phone number. "Of course, sweetheart. I'll call this afternoon."

♥♥♥

Later that afternoon, after the children had dispersed to their various activities—Royce to Riverfront for his first shift, Caroline to the college for a campus tour, and

Justin to his room to work on homework—Daphne finally had a moment to herself. She sat at the kitchen counter with a cup of coffee, smoothing out the crumpled paper with Roman's father's phone number.

Taking a deep breath, she dialed the number, listening to it ring several times before a woman answered.

"Feldman residence," the voice said crisply.

"Oh, hello," Daphne replied, slightly taken aback. "This is Daphne Stainthorpe, Justin's mother. Justin and Roman have become friends at school, and Roman invited Justin for a playdate this weekend."

"Yes, of course," the woman replied. "I'm Mrs. Winters, the housekeeper. Mr. Feldman mentioned something about this. He's traveling for business today but will be back tomorrow. Shall I have him call you?"

"That would be lovely," Daphne said. "Or perhaps we could just arrange it now? My daughter Caroline could drop Justin off on Saturday morning if that works."

"Saturday at ten would be perfect. Mr. Feldman usually takes Roman to the park in the afternoon, but they'll be home all morning. I'll let him know it's arranged."

"Wonderful," Daphne said, jotting down the address Mrs. Winters provided. "Thank you so much."

She hung up, feeling a strange disappointment at not speaking directly to Roman's father. Still, the playdate was arranged, and that was what mattered for Justin's sake.

"Mum!" Justin called, racing down the stairs. "Did you call Roman's dad? Can I go?"

"All set for Saturday morning," Daphne confirmed with a smile. "Caroline will drop you off."

Justin pumped his fist in victory before dashing back upstairs, leaving Daphne to wonder about the man whose son had so quickly befriended her youngest.

Chapter 14 – Kismet
2015

Saturday arrived with golden autumn sunshine streaming through the windows. Caroline drove Justin to his playdate, promising to pick him up at one o'clock.

"Have fun, squirt," she said, ruffling his hair as he bounded up the walkway to Roman's front door.

By mid-morning, Daphne's phone chimed with a text from Caroline: "Got a last-minute gig at that cafe near Roman's house! Playing there every weekend. Roman's dad offered to bring Justin home. That work?"

Daphne smiled, happy for her daughter's opportunity. "Perfect. Tell him thanks!" she texted back.

With a rare afternoon to herself, Daphne decided to catch up with Mrs. Pine. She had scarcely knocked on her neighbor's door when Helen pulled her inside.

"Just in time! I've made fresh scones," Mrs. Pine announced, ushering Daphne to a comfortable chair surrounded by photo albums. "These are all the neighborhood children over the years. You'll recognize some of these faces!"

Hours flew by as Helen recounted stories of neighborhood block parties, graduation celebrations, and holiday gatherings. Daphne was so engrossed in the tales of families who had come and gone that she completely lost track of time.

"And here's the Feldman boy when they first moved in," Mrs. Pine said, pointing to a photo of a small child with a gap-toothed smile. "Such a sweet child, though terribly shy after losing his mother. His father has done a remarkable job raising him alone."

"Roman seems like a wonderful boy," Daphne agreed. "Justin hasn't stopped talking about him."

Mrs. Pine's eyes twinkled mischievously. "His father is quite the catch, you know. Brilliant engineer, devoted father, and not hard on the eyes either."

"Helen!" Daphne laughed, feeling a blush creep up her cheeks.

A sudden knock at Mrs. Pine's door interrupted their

conversation. It was Royce, looking for his mother.

"Mum, Justin's been home for hours," he said. "He said you were supposed to be there when he got back."

Daphne glanced at her watch, startled to see it was nearly dinnertime. "Oh my goodness! I completely lost track of time. I'm so sorry, Helen, I should go."

"Don't be silly, dear. Go take care of your boy. And don't forget what I said about Roman's father," Mrs. Pine added with a wink.

Over the next few weeks, a pattern emerged. Caroline, delighted with her new regular gig at the café, happily drove Justin to Roman's house each Saturday. Roman's father always brought Justin home, but through a series of missed connections – Daphne at the grocery store, visiting friends, or absorbed in Mrs. Pine's stories – they never quite crossed paths.

"Mum, Roman's dad said that being an engineer is like solving puzzles all day," Justin reported excitedly after one visit. "He let us take apart an old computer and put it back together!"

"He sounds wonderful," Daphne replied, curious about this man who had captured her son's imagination.

"He asks about you," Justin mentioned casually one evening. "Wants to know if you're settling in okay."

This caught Daphne's attention. "What did you tell him?"

"I said you seem happy to be home but you work too hard," Justin answered honestly. "He said he knows what that's like."

Another Saturday, another missed connection. This time, Daphne had just stepped into the shower when Justin arrived home, full of stories about the treehouse they'd been building.

♥♥♥

On a rainy Sunday afternoon, while Justin was at a classmate's birthday party, Daphne sought refuge from the dreary weather in her favorite coffee shop. She hesitated for a moment before pushing open the door, the bell above chiming softly as she stepped inside. A wave of warmth and familiarity washed over her – this place had always been her refuge from the chaos of her life.

The atmosphere was immediately inviting, with the aroma of freshly brewed coffee wafting through the air and soft jazz music playing in the background. Daphne took a deep breath, letting the comforting scents and sounds envelop her like a warm embrace.

"Hi there, welcome back," greeted the barista behind the counter, offering her a knowing smile. Daphne returned the smile, feeling a sense of belonging that she hadn't experienced in years.

"Thanks, it's been too long," she replied, her voice tinged with nostalgia. She scanned the menu, her fingers twitching slightly – a telltale sign of her ever-present need for control. But here, in this little sanctuary, she allowed herself the luxury of spontaneity. "I'll have the vanilla latte, please."

"Enjoy your latte," the barista said, handing Daphne's her drink. She nodded in gratitude, a bittersweet smile tugging at the corners of her lips.

"Thank you," she murmured, cradling the warm cup in her hands and taking her first sip. The familiar taste brought her both comfort and an inexplicable ache, a yearning for something that had been missing from her life for far too long.

Daphne's heart skipped a beat as she recognized Reuben across the crowded coffee shop. It had been over a decade since they last saw each other, but his face was as familiar to her as her own. She hesitated for a moment, unsure if she should approach him or not. But something inside her urged her to take the chance, to see where this unexpected reunion would lead.

As she made her way through the sea of tables and chairs, Daphne felt a mix of excitement and trepidation. What would Reuben think when he saw her again? Would he remember her? Would there be any lingering feelings between them?

When she finally reached his table, Reuben looked up and his eyes widened in surprise. "Daphne!" he exclaimed, standing up to greet her. "It's been so long! I can't believe it."

They embraced warmly, both feeling a sense of nostalgia wash over them. As they sat down opposite each other, Daphne couldn't help but notice how handsome Reuben still was - his sandy hair slightly grayed at the temples, his eyes crinkling with laughter lines.

Over steaming cups of coffee and flaky croissants, Daphne and Reuben marveled at the coincidence that had brought them together again after all these years.

"I still can't believe it," Daphne said, shaking her head in wonder. "When Justin kept talking about his new friend Roman and his dad, I never imagined..."

Reuben smiled, his eyes crinkling at the corners. "Roman hasn't stopped talking about Justin either. The treehouse they're building has become his obsession."

"The famous treehouse!" Daphne laughed. "Justin's been sketching designs for weeks. I should have connected the dots when he mentioned his friend's dad was an engineer."

They fell into comfortable conversation, the years melting away as if they'd never been apart. Reuben spoke about his engineering work, his voice animated as he described the projects that challenged and fulfilled him. Daphne shared stories of her career journey, the pride she felt in her children's accomplishments, and her recent move back to Richmond.

As they talked, Daphne felt a sense of ease with Reuben that she hadn't experienced with anyone else in such a long time. Their connection was still there, undeniable and magnetic after all these years.

The conversation took a more serious turn when Reuben's expression softened, his eyes reflecting a sadness that tugged at Daphne's heart.

"I lost my wife when Roman was born," he said quietly. "Complications due to childbirth was what they said. It's been... challenging."

Daphne reached across the table, gently covering his hand with hers. "I'm so sorry, Ben."

"We've been finding our way since then," he continued, a quiet strength in his voice. "Roman's an amazing kid."

As he spoke about Roman, Daphne could sense Reuben's deep love for his son. She knew firsthand the challenges of raising children through difficult times and admired how he was navigating this chapter in his life.

"And you?" Reuben asked. "The boys mentioned you're on your own as well?"

Daphne nodded, finding herself opening up about things she rarely shared—the challenges of single motherhood, the joy of watching her children grow into independent adults, the occasional loneliness that crept in despite having people around her.

"It seems impossible that after all these years, our sons would be the ones to bring us back together,"

Reuben said, his gaze meeting hers.

"Some might call it fate," Daphne replied with a small smile.

As they left the coffee shop, walking side by side in the warm afternoon sun, Daphne couldn't help but feel a renewed sense of possibility. Life was unpredictable, filled with unexpected twists and turns. But sometimes, those very twists led exactly where you were meant to be all along.

♥♥♥

As Daphne prepared for her coffee date with Reuben, she found herself lingering longer than usual before the mirror. It had been decades since their paths had crossed on that airplane, yet the flutter in her stomach felt strangely familiar—reminiscent of their first meeting on the UCLA campus.

She applied a touch of lipstick, then paused, studying her reflection. The young woman who had once cheered at lacrosse games was still there somewhere, beneath the layers of experience and heartache. So much had happened since then—the stalker incident during sophomore year that had left her feeling vulnerable and exposed, the relationship with Luke that had promised security but delivered control, the years of rebuilding her life piece by piece.

Would Reuben see those changes in her? Would he sense the walls she'd constructed, brick by brick, around her heart?

Daphne took a steadying breath. This wasn't the frightened college student who had fallen into Luke's arms seeking safety after a traumatic brush with danger. Nor was she the broken woman who had fled to Australia with three children and countless emotional scars. She was stronger now, more assured of who she was and what she wanted.

Whatever happened today with Reuben, she would face it on her own terms—not out of fear, not out of need, but out of genuine choice.

♥♥♥

Daphne and Reuben met for coffee every Sunday morning, their conversations flowing as easily as the steaming lattes they sipped. They shared their hopes, dreams, and fears, finding solace in each other's company. As the weeks passed, a deep connection formed between them. It was more than friendship - there was an undeniable romantic affection that blossomed between them.

One sunny afternoon, after their usual coffee date, Reuben took Daphne's hand as they walked through the park. "Daphne," he said softly, his eyes meeting hers. "I've been thinking...I don't want to lose you."

Daphne looked up at him, her heart racing. "Ben," she replied, her voice barely above a whisper. "I don't want to lose you either."

They stood there for a moment, their hands entwined, gazing into each other's eyes. The world around them seemed to fade away, leaving only this shared breath between them. Reuben's eyes, warm and full of promise, searched her face with quiet wonder. Daphne felt her heart quicken as he gently tugged her closer, eliminating the last bit of space between them.

"Daphne," he whispered, her name like a prayer on his lips.

In response, she lifted her chin slightly, an invitation he didn't hesitate to accept. His mouth found hers with exquisite tenderness at first, then with growing certainty. The kiss deepened as she leaned into him, her free hand coming to rest against his chest where she could feel his heartbeat matching the rapid rhythm of her own.

When they finally parted, breathless and smiling, Daphne knew something fundamental had shifted. What had begun as a chance meeting had blossomed into something profound and undeniable.

"I've never felt this way before," she admitted softly, her fingers tracing the line of his jaw.

"Neither have I," Reuben replied, his voice husky with emotion. "And it terrifies me in the best possible way."

It was a simple moment, yet it held so much promise for the future. They knew that whatever happened between them would be worth the risk—because sometimes in life, you have to take a chance on love. And Daphne and Reuben were ready to do just that.

♥♥♥

Daphne's heart fluttered as Reuben led her and the boys into the planetarium. The dimly lit room was filled with plush seats and a large dome overhead, projecting a breathtaking view of the universe. She felt a sense of wonder and excitement that she hadn't experienced in years.

"This is so cool!" Justin whispered loudly, his eyes wide with amazement as he gazed upward. "Morgan would love this! Do you think they have the Mars rovers here? The ones like she's working on?"

Roman nodded enthusiastically. "Dad said they have a whole exhibit on space exploration after the show. We can see all the NASA stuff then."

"Your sister works for NASA?" an elderly woman seated nearby asked Justin, leaning forward with interest.

"Yes ma'am," Justin replied proudly, puffing out his chest. "She's an engineer working on the next generation of Mars rovers!"

As they settled into their seats, Reuben reached over past the boys and took Daphne's hand. She felt a warmth spread through her as they shared a smile over the children's heads, then turned their attention to the twinkling stars above them. Throughout the presentation, Justin peppered Roman with questions about constellations and planets, his excitement barely contained in whispers.

"Did you know Morgan showed me how the rover cameras work?" Justin told Roman. "They have to be super tough to handle all the dust storms."

"That's nothing," Roman replied. "Dad says the next challenge is creating robots that can repair themselves when they're millions of miles from Earth."

Daphne and Reuben exchanged another glance, both amused and impressed by the boys' knowledge. They spent the evening immersed in the wonders of space, the adults occasionally sharing their own dreams and aspirations when the boys paused for breath, feeling a deep connection that went beyond their shared appreciation of astronomy and their children's friendship.

When the show ended, Daphne couldn't help but feel a sense of longing as they walked out into the night air, the boys racing ahead toward the promised exhibit of space exploration technology.

"Morgan would totally freak out over this model," Justin exclaimed, pointing to a detailed replica of a Mars rover. "Can I take a picture to send her, Mum?"

"Of course," Daphne replied, watching as Reuben helped position the boys for the best angle.

As they finally walked back to the car, the boys chattering excitedly about everything they'd seen,

Reuben's hand found Daphne's again. In that moment, with stars above and their sons ahead, Daphne knew that this was something special, something she had been searching for all her life. She gave his hand a gentle squeeze, silently conveying her desire to explore this newfound connection further.

♥♥♥

Daphne set the table with her finest china, the warm autumn colors of her Thanksgiving decorations creating a festive atmosphere throughout the dining room. Caroline and Royce moved around the kitchen, helping with last-minute preparations while Justin bounced excitedly between rooms.

"Mum, is Roman bringing his new robot to show me?" Justin asked, carefully placing the cloth napkins beside each plate.

"Not today, sweetheart," Daphne replied, sliding the turkey out of the oven. Its golden-brown skin glistened as savory aromas filled the kitchen. "But I'm sure you two will find plenty to talk about."

Caroline looked up from the cranberry sauce she was transferring to a crystal bowl. "I still can't believe you're actually dating someone, Mum," she teased with a gentle smile. "And Roman's dad, of all people."

"It's about time," Royce added, stirring the gravy with expert precision. "You deserve to be happy."

The doorbell rang, and Justin bolted to answer it before anyone could stop him. Moments later, he returned with Reuben and Roman in tow, the November chill clinging to their coats.

"Happy Thanksgiving!" Reuben said warmly, presenting Daphne with a bouquet of autumn flowers. His eyes lingered on hers a moment longer than necessary, conveying a private message of appreciation.

Roman immediately showed Justin something on his phone, the two boys huddling together in conspiratorial excitement. "Dad helped me download that space simulator I told you about," Roman explained. "It shows exactly what the Mars rovers see!"

"That's so cool! Can we show it to Morgan on our video call later?" Justin asked, his eyes shining.

"Absolutely," Reuben replied. "I'd love to hear her professional opinion on it."

As they gathered around the table, the blend of families felt surprisingly natural. Royce carved the turkey with professional skill while Caroline poured sparkling cider into everyone's glasses. When all were seated, Daphne suggested they share what they were thankful for this year.

"I'm thankful for my new school and meeting Roman," Justin said promptly.

"I'm thankful for Dad's pancakes and our treehouse," Roman added, grinning at his father.

"I'm thankful for my first real job at Riverfront," Royce offered.

"I'm thankful for my band getting that regular gig," Caroline said.

When it came to Reuben's turn, he looked directly at Daphne. "I'm thankful for second chances," he said simply, his voice soft with meaning.

Daphne felt a warmth spread through her chest as she completed the circle. "And I'm thankful for all of you, for this moment, for coming home to Richmond, and for unexpected joys."

As they ate, conversation flowed easily between them all. Caroline described her latest musical compositions, while Royce explained the intricate techniques he was learning at Riverfront. Even with the age differences, the connection between them all seemed to deepen with each passing moment.

"Your sweet potato casserole is amazing," Reuben told Daphne. "You'll have to share the recipe."

"Family secret," she replied with a wink. "Though I might be persuaded to share it under the right circumstances."

Later, when they gathered in the living room for the video call with Morgan, Daphne watched as Roman eagerly showed his space simulator to Morgan on the screen, Justin leaning against him to get a better view. Morgan's face lit up as she explained how the actual controls worked, Roman and Justin hanging on her every word.

"They're like they've always known each other," Reuben murmured, sitting beside Daphne on the couch.

"It feels right, doesn't it?" she whispered back. "All of us, together like this."

As the evening wore on, with games and dessert and more laughter than Daphne's house had heard in years, she felt a sense of completion she hadn't experienced in a very long time. This wasn't just a dinner or a holiday—

it was the merging of two families that somehow belonged together, a new constellation forming from stars that had been wandering the sky separately for far too long.

♥♥♥

Daphne stood in the kitchen of Reuben's house, her eyes drawn to a colorful image on the refrigerator door. It was a photo of the four of them—Reuben, Daphne, Justin, and Roman—taken during their visit to the zoo last month. In the picture, both boys were balanced on the adults' shoulders, all four faces beaming with laughter as they posed in front of the elephant enclosure.

She couldn't help but smile as she remembered that day—how the boys had raced from exhibit to exhibit, their enthusiasm infectious; how Justin had insisted on buying ice cream cones for everyone when Roman declared he'd never tried mint chocolate chip; how Reuben had kept his hand in hers as they walked, a small gesture that felt both natural and profound.

Reuben appeared behind her, his arms wrapping around her waist. "I wanted to make sure you saw this," he said softly, pointing to the photo. "My favorite picture of my favorite people."

"Mine too," she whispered, leaning back into his embrace. "I can still hear the boys laughing at that monkey stealing Roman's map."

"And Justin trying to imitate the penguin walk," Reuben added, chuckling against her hair. "They've become inseparable."

"Just like us," Daphne said, turning in his arms to face him. "Thank you for this—for making us feel like we belong here."

Reuben's eyes were warm as he gazed down at her. "You're part of our family now," he said simply. "Both of you."

"I'm so grateful for this," she replied, her voice thick with emotion.

Reuben kissed the top of her head gently. "I'm grateful for you too," he said. "You bring so much light into our lives—both you and Justin."

From the backyard, they could hear the boys laughing as they worked on their latest treehouse improvement. The sound was like music—the soundtrack of their blending family.

As they stood there together, Daphne felt a sense of

peace wash over her. She knew that there would be challenges ahead—raising children and merging their lives was no easy task—but she also knew that she had found someone who would be by her side every step of the way. And for Daphne, that was all she needed to face whatever came their way..

♥♥♥

The morning of their one-year dating anniversary, Daphne woke and walked into the kitchen. She found a note from Reuben telling her to meet him in the park at noon. He had a surprise planned. Daphne smiled, her heart fluttering with excitement about how he would celebrate this special milestone.

At five minutes to noon, Daphne strolled through the park entrance, following the stone path winding through verdant trees and flower beds. In the distance, she spotted Reuben laying out a blanket underneath a canopy of cherry blossoms.

As she approached, Reuben greeted her with a loving kiss and helped her sit down. He had set out all of Daphne's favorite foods - fresh local fruits, imported cheeses, chocolate-dipped strawberries, and a bottle of champagne chilling on ice.

Daphne was touched that he went to such lengths to create her ideal romantic picnic. Soft guitar music played from a speaker as pink and white petals drifted gently down around them. "This is so beautiful, thank you my love," Daphne said, leaning over to cradle Reuben's face in her hands and kiss him tenderly.

Over lunch, they reminisced joyfully about the life they'd built together so far - the cozy dates, family celebrations, late night talks laying in each other's arms. "This past year with you has been the happiest of my life," Reuben declared, eyes brimming with emotion. Daphne wiped away a stray tear, overwhelmed by how cherished he made her feel.

As the afternoon sun filtered through the trees, they snuck in kisses between sips of champagne. Daphne wished she could press pause, make this blissful day last forever. But she found comfort knowing a lifetime of anniversaries awaited them. Each milestone would only deepen their love.

Later, enveloped in Reuben's arms as gentle guitar strums played on, Daphne thanked the universe for this man who saw and accepted her wholly. "I fall more in love with you each passing day," she whispered. He answered by holding her tighter, profoundly grateful for the gift of each other.

When the light began to fade, they packed up slowly, stealing a few more kisses beneath the cherry blossom canopy. Hand-in-hand, they strolled back along the path changed forever by this profound day, ready to start year two wrapped in newly deepened love.

♥♥♥

Daphne and Reuben's relationship deepened over time. They shared their hopes, dreams, and fears with each other, finding solace in the other's understanding presence. They explored Richmond together, discovering hidden gems and revisiting old haunts. Daphne felt a sense of belonging she hadn't experienced in years.

One evening, as they sat on Daphne's porch swing watching the sun set over the treetops, Reuben took her hand. "Daphne," he said softly, "I love you." His words hung in the air between them like a promise.

Daphne looked into his eyes, seeing the depth of his feelings reflected there. "I love you too, Ben," she replied, her voice barely above a whisper. They leaned in and shared a tender kiss under the fading light of day.

As their relationship progressed, they faced challenges together. Daphne struggled with feelings of guilt and shame from her past experiences with abuse and betrayal. Reuben was patient and supportive, helping her navigate these emotions and find healing through therapy and self-care practices.

Meanwhile, Reuben juggled his responsibilities as a single father to Roman while also pursuing his career. Daphne admired his dedication to both his work and his son, seeing in him the kind of father she had always wanted for her own children.

Their blended family grew closer over time as well. Caroline, Royce, Morgan, Justin and Roman bonded over shared interests while also supporting each other through life's ups and downs. Daphne felt grateful for this newfound sense of family that had come into her life after so many years of struggle and loss.

As they celebrated their second anniversary together, Daphne realized that she had finally found the love she had been searching for all these years - a love that was strong enough to heal old wounds and build a new future filled with hope and happiness for all of them. And as they danced under the stars on that warm summer night, she knew that she was exactly where she was meant to be - in Reuben's arms, surrounded by the love of her family, finally at home in her own skin once again.

♥♥♥

Daphne woke up feeling achy and feverish, her body wracked with chills. She groaned softly, pulling the covers tighter around herself. She knew she should get up and take some medicine, but the thought of moving was too daunting.

As the day wore on, her symptoms worsened. Her head throbbed, her body felt heavy, and she was drenched in sweat. She tried to call in sick to work, but her voice was too weak to form coherent sentences.

When Daphne didn't answer his calls, Reuben knew something was wrong. Dropping everything, he arrived at her house. He could tell she was sick and immediately sprang into action. He made her a cup of hot tea with honey and lemon, brought her a bowl of chicken soup, and fetched her some over-the-counter cold medicine from the pharmacy.

As Daphne lay in bed, Reuben tenderly cared for her. He made sure she took her medicine on time, brought her warm blankets to keep her comfortable, and even massaged her sore muscles to ease the pain. His gentle touch brought solace to Daphne's aching body.

Throughout the day, Reuben stayed by Daphne's side, reading books aloud to distract her from the discomfort of being ill. He told stories about their travels together and shared his dreams for their future as a family. His soothing voice and kind words helped lift Daphne's spirits amidst the misery of being sick.

As night fell, Daphne's fever finally broke, and she began to feel a little better. Reuben helped her into bed and tucked her in tightly under the covers. As he kissed her forehead gently, Daphne felt an overwhelming sense of gratitude for having him in her life. In his loving arms, she knew she had finally found the person she had been waiting for all along - someone who would care for her not just as a partner but as a soulmate who would stand by her through thick and thin.

♥♥♥

Daphne and Reuben sat in a quiet corner of Riverfront, the upscale restaurant where Royce had recently been promoted to sous chef. The elegant space was filled with soft lighting, sophisticated decor, and the gentle murmur of conversation. Daphne couldn't hide her pride as diners at nearby tables raved about their meals, knowing her son had helped create the culinary masterpieces.

"It was so thoughtful of you to arrange this dinner," Daphne said, looking around the restaurant appreciatively. "Royce must be thrilled we're here."

"I thought it would be nice for all of us," Reuben replied with a smile that seemed to hold a secret. "A family celebration."

Royce had briefly emerged from the kitchen earlier, his chef's whites pristine as he greeted them with professional courtesy undercut by a conspiratorial wink at Reuben. Since then, they'd been treated to course after course of Riverfront's finest offerings, each dish more impressive than the last.

As they finished their main course, Daphne noticed Reuben growing increasingly distracted, checking his watch and glancing toward the kitchen.

"Is everything alright?" she asked.

"Perfect," he assured her, reaching across the table to squeeze her hand. "Just perfect."

When dessert time arrived, Daphne eagerly anticipated the restaurant's renowned chocolate cake.

"I've been saving room all evening," she confessed. "Royce says their flourless chocolate cake is heaven on a plate."

The waiter approached with a knowing smile, setting down not only the expected chocolate cake but also an ornate box beside her plate.

"What's this?" Daphne asked, looking between the waiter and Reuben.

"A little something extra for you," the waiter explained before stepping away.

Daphne's attention was immediately drawn to the decadent chocolate cake, garnished with fresh raspberries and a dusting of powdered sugar.

"Aren't you going to open the box?" Reuben asked, a hint of nervousness in his voice.

"Oh, I'll check it out in a minute," Daphne replied, her fork poised over the cake. "But this dessert looks too good to wait."

Reuben shifted uncomfortably. "Daphne, don't you want to see what's inside?"

"I'm sure it's lovely," she said, taking her first bite of

cake and closing her eyes in bliss. "Oh my goodness, this is amazing."

"But don't you want to know what it is?" Reuben persisted, his eyes darting between her and the box.

After several more exchanges and Daphne's continued focus on the chocolate cake, Reuben finally said, "There might be something important in there."

With a sigh, Daphne set down her fork and picked up the box. Inside was an oversized fortune cookie decorated with pink sprinkles. Her eyebrows rose in surprise.

"It's a fortune cookie," she said, setting it aside and reaching for her cake again.

"Aren't you going to open it?" Reuben asked, his voice strained.

"I'll save it for later," Daphne replied, savoring another bite of cake.

"But don't you want to know what your fortune says?" he pressed, his knuckles white as he gripped the edge of the table.

After more gentle prodding, Daphne finally relented

and broke open the cookie. Inside was a small slip of paper. As she read the words written there, her breath caught in her throat:

"The whispers of my heart have led me to you. Will you marry me?"

When she looked up in shock, Reuben was no longer across the table but kneeling beside her, a velvet box open in his palm. Inside nestled a beautiful diamond ring that caught the restaurant's soft lighting.

"Daphne," he said, his voice thick with emotion, "you've brought joy and love back into my life when I thought those days were behind me. Will you do me the extraordinary honor of becoming my wife?"

Tears filled Daphne's eyes as she finally understood his persistence about the fortune cookie. With her heart overflowing with love, she nodded and whispered, "Yes."

The restaurant erupted in applause as Reuben slipped the ring onto her finger and kissed her tenderly. Moments later, Royce emerged from the kitchen with two flutes of champagne, his face beaming with happiness for his mother.

As Daphne gazed into Reuben's eyes, the chocolate cake momentarily forgotten, she realized that sometimes life's sweetest moments come in unexpected packages—and it's worth setting aside even the most tempting dessert to discover them.

Chapter 15 - Wedded Bliss
2017

Daphne took a deep breath as she stood just outside the vineyard ceremony space, clutching her bouquet with trembling hands. In just moments, she would walk down the flower-adorned aisle to join the man she was poised to spend the rest of her life with.

"You look beautiful, mum. Don't be nervous," said Royce as he took her arm.

"Thank you sweetheart," she replied.

As the music swelled, signaling her cue, Daphne focused on putting one foot in front of the other, not wanting to trip. As soon as her eyes met Reuben's at the end of the aisle, her nerves melted away. His eyes radiated pure love and wonder.

Daphne floated towards him, taking in the beaming faces of loved ones surrounding them. She and Reuben chose this intimate venue because of the way the vines twisted together, symbolizing two souls joining in love.

The officiant guided them through reading the vows they had crafted straight from their hearts. Before they began, he paused and looked out at the gathered guests.

Traditionally, I would ask who gives this woman to be married," the officiant said with a warm smile. "But today, I ask: who gives this bride and groom to be joined in marriage?"

Without hesitation, Morgan, Caroline, Royce, Roman, and Justin all rose to their feet as one, their faces beaming with pride and joy.

"We do," they declared in unison, their voices blending in perfect harmony across the generations they represented.

Daphne's eyes filled with tears at this beautiful affirmation from their children. Reuben squeezed her hand, equally moved by the moment. This wasn't just a union of two people, but truly a binding together of their entire family.

As the children sat down, Daphne turned back to Reuben, her heart overflowing with love for this man and the beautiful, blended family they had created together.

"From our first meeting at UCLA," Reuben murmured, his voice steady and sincere, "to finding each other again on an airplane and finally reconnecting in Richmond, it feels like fate has always been guiding us together."

Daphne squeezed his hand tighter, her heart swelling with emotion as she responded, "Reuben, you are the love I've searched for all my life. I promise to cherish and support you, just as you have always cherished and supported me."

Their words hung in the air, echoing the commitment and devotion that bound them together. As they sealed their vows with a tender kiss, the venue erupted in applause, and the newlyweds stepped hand-in-hand into their future.

♥♥♥

The weeks following the wedding were a blur of laughter, joy, and organized chaos. Daphne's love for organization came in handy as they merged Reuben and Roman's belongings with the existing household, determining what would stay, what would go, and what needed to be purchased anew.

"I think we need a bigger dresser," Reuben observed one evening as he stared at the pile of clothes that wouldn't quite fit in the master bedroom furniture.

"Already ordered," Daphne replied with a smile, showing him the confirmation email on her phone. "Should be here Wednesday."

The merger of their households wasn't without its challenges. Roman and Justin, despite their close friendship, still had to adjust to sharing a bathroom. Occasional squabbles over hot water usage and toothpaste cap etiquette erupted, but they were always resolved with a mixture of compromise and good humor.

"Boys," Reuben had said one evening after mediating a particularly heated debate about proper shower scheduling, "remember that this is new for all of us. We're building something special here, but it takes patience."

As weeks turned into months, their routines evolved. Sunday breakfasts became a family affair, with Royce teaching Roman the art of perfect pancakes while Caroline entertained Justin with stories about her latest gigs. Morgan joined via video call when possible, their NASA schedule permitting.

One rainy Saturday afternoon, as Roman and Justin huddled over a complex LEGO creation in the living room, Reuben found Daphne in the kitchen, staring out the window at the downpour.

"Penny for your thoughts?" he asked, slipping his arms around her waist.

Daphne leaned back against him, finding comfort in his solid presence. "I was just thinking about your house," she admitted. "It's been empty for three months now. We should probably decide what to do with it."

The question of Reuben's house had been hovering at the periphery of their conversations since the wedding. It was a beautiful property—a modernist design with sleek lines and floor-to-ceiling windows—that reflected Reuben's engineering aesthetic. While not as spacious as Daphne's family home, it held its own charm and memories.

"I've been thinking about that too," Reuben said, his chin resting on her shoulder. "Part of me wants to keep it. It was the first real home I made for Roman after his mother died."

Daphne nodded, understanding the emotional attachment. "And the other part?"

"The other part knows that holding onto it doesn't make practical sense. We're here now, together. This is our home."

They moved to the kitchen table, where Daphne, true to form, had prepared a spreadsheet outlining the financial implications of selling versus renting.

"If we rent it out, the income could go toward Roman's college fund," she pointed out, scrolling through the calculations. "Property values in that neighborhood have been climbing steadily."

Reuben studied the numbers, his engineer's mind appreciating the detailed analysis. "That's a good thought. But managing a rental property comes with its own challenges."

"Mrs. Pine's son William is a property manager," Daphne reminded him. "He could handle the day-to-day issues for a reasonable fee."

They discussed the options back and forth, weighing emotional attachment against practical considerations. Roman wandered into the kitchen for a snack, catching part of the conversation.

"Are you talking about our old house?" he asked, reaching for the cookie jar.

Reuben and Daphne exchanged a glance, realizing they should have included him in the conversation earlier. "Yes, buddy. We're trying to decide whether to sell it or rent it out," Reuben explained.

Roman thought for a moment, his young face serious. "Could we go there one more time? Before you decide? There are some things I'd like to get."

The following weekend, the three of them visited Reuben's house, with Justin tagging along out of curiosity. Roman walked through the rooms with a quiet reverence, collecting small mementos—a seashell from their trip to the Outer Banks, a smooth stone he'd found on their first hike after moving to Richmond, the height markings on the door frame of his bedroom.

As Reuben watched his son gathering these pieces of their past, he made his decision. "I think we should sell," he told Daphne softly. "These memories," he gestured to Roman carefully wrapping the seashell in tissue paper, "they come with us. The house itself is just walls and a roof."

Daphne squeezed his hand in understanding. "Are you sure?"

"I'm sure. Our home is with you now—with all of

you." His eyes swept the space, taking in the empty rooms that had once been filled with his and Roman's life. "Besides, another family could make new memories here. That seems right somehow."

When they presented their decision to Roman, he nodded thoughtfully. "I thought that's what you'd choose," he said with the wisdom of a child who had already learned about life's transitions. "It's okay. I like our new home better anyway. Justin and I have bigger plans for the treehouse, and Mrs. Pine makes the best cookies."

Daphne felt a rush of love for this thoughtful boy who had become such an integral part of their family. "You're pretty special, you know that?" she told him, pulling him into a hug.

"I know," Roman replied with a grin, the serious moment passing as quickly as it had come. "Can we stop for ice cream on the way home?"

The house sold within weeks, to a young couple expecting their first child. When Reuben handed over the keys, there was a momentary pang of nostalgia, but it was overshadowed by the certainty that they had made the right choice. The proceeds were invested, half in Roman's college fund and half in renovations to expand the treehouse and update the boys' bathroom—investments in their present joy and future security.

As their first anniversary approached, Daphne sometimes marveled at how seamlessly their lives had blended together. The transition hadn't always been smooth—Reuben's organizational system was decidedly more chaotic than her own, and she still couldn't fathom why Roman and Justin needed quite so many exotic LEGO pieces—but the challenges were far outweighed by the happiness they'd found together.

"I was thinking," Reuben said one evening as they sat on the porch swing, watching the sunset paint the sky in shades of orange and pink, "we should take a family vacation this summer. All of us, including Morgan if they can get the time off. Maybe the Outer Banks?"

Daphne smiled, leaning into his embrace. "I'd like that. New memories for our new chapter."

He kissed the top of her head gently. "Exactly what I was thinking."

♥♥♥

Another year passed in what seemed like the blink of an eye. The boys, once barely reaching Reuben's shoulders, now stood nearly as tall as he did, their voices deepening and their interests evolving. At fourteen, Justin had developed a passion for skateboarding, while Roman, six months older, divided his time between robotics club and playing guitar—a hobby he'd picked up from Caroline during her performances around Richmond.

The summer before they were to enter high school brought noticeable changes, particularly in Justin. The sweet, space-obsessed boy who had once spent hours video chatting with Morgan about NASA missions had begun to withdraw, spending more time with a new group of friends that neither Daphne nor Reuben had met.

"It's just a phase," Reuben assured Daphne one evening after Justin had come home well past his curfew, his eyes suspiciously red and unfocused. "All kids test boundaries at this age."

Daphne wasn't so certain. She'd been noticing subtle shifts in Justin's behavior for months—declining grades, secretive text messages, and a newfound defensiveness that emerged whenever she asked about his day. "Maybe," she conceded, "but I can't help worrying."

As they celebrated their second wedding

anniversary with a special family dinner at home, Daphne couldn't help but notice how Justin barely touched his food and kept checking his phone under the table. Caroline had prepared a beautiful cake, and Royce had come home early from his shift at Riverfront to join them, yet Justin seemed elsewhere, mentally and emotionally.

One Saturday morning, Roman knocked softly on the door of Daphne and Reuben's bedroom, his expression unusually serious. "Can I talk to you guys about something?"

They sat at the kitchen table, morning sunlight streaming through the windows as Roman fidgeted with his cereal spoon.

"It's about Justin," he finally said, eyes fixed on the table. "I didn't want to say anything because I didn't want him to be mad at me, but..." He hesitated, clearly torn between loyalty to his stepbrother and concern for his welfare.

"It's okay, Roman," Daphne encouraged gently. "You can tell us."

Roman took a deep breath. "He's been hanging out with these guys from Westfield High School. The ones who are always getting suspended." He glanced toward the stairs to ensure Justin was still asleep. "Last week, when he said he was staying at Trevor's house, he was actually at some party in the old warehouse district. There was drinking and..." he lowered his voice, "I think he's been smoking weed. I found a baggie of something that smelled weird in his backpack when I was looking for my USB drive."

Daphne felt her stomach tighten with anxiety. "Are you sure about this?"

"I saw pictures on someone's social media," Roman admitted. "And... Justin's been asking me to cover for him. He says I owe him because he didn't tell on me when I broke the window playing baseball."

Reuben placed a reassuring hand on his son's shoulder. "You did the right thing telling us, Roman. This isn't about getting Justin in trouble; it's about keeping him safe."

After Roman left to meet friends at the library, Daphne and Reuben remained at the kitchen table, the gravity of the situation settling between them.

"I've seen this before," Daphne said quietly, her fingers nervously tracing patterns on the tabletop. "Miles was around the same age when he started using drugs. My mother always made excuses for him, said it was my fault for abandoning them to go to UCLA." Her voice caught. "As if my decision to go to college somehow caused Miles to make those choices."

"Justin isn't Miles," Reuben said gently, "and we're not your parents."

"I know that," she replied, though the tremor in her voice betrayed her uncertainty. "But there are patterns, Reuben. My father's drinking, my mother's enabling, Miles following in those footsteps... I can't bear to see Justin go down that same path." She looked up at him, her eyes shimmering with unshed tears. "You didn't see what happened to my father. How the drinking and the anger consumed him until there was nothing left of the man he could have been."

Reuben took her hands in his, his grip firm and reassuring. "We won't let that happen to Justin. We'll get ahead of this."

♥♥♥

Their conversation with Justin that afternoon was tense, to say the least. He denied everything at first, then lashed out when confronted with the evidence Roman had shared.

"So now you're spying on me?" he demanded, glaring at them from across the living room. "And Roman's a snitch. Great to know where I stand in this family."

"That's not fair, Justin," Daphne said, fighting to keep her voice calm despite the surge of anxiety his words triggered. "Roman cares about you. We all do."

"Right," Justin scoffed, slouching deeper into the couch. "You care so much you're interrogating me like I'm some criminal."

Reuben leaned forward, his expression serious but compassionate. "Nobody's calling you a criminal, Justin. But we're concerned about the choices you're making. These kids you're hanging out with—"

"Are my friends," Justin interrupted. "And they get me a lot better than anyone in this house does."

The conversation continued in circles, with Justin alternately defensive and dismissive. By the end, they'd established new ground rules—earlier curfews, no more unexplained absences, and a temporary hiatus from unsupervised time with the Westfield group—but Daphne couldn't shake the feeling that they were only addressing symptoms, not causes.

That night, after Justin had retreated to his room with a slammed door that rattled the family photos in the hallway, Daphne sat on the edge of their bed, her posture betraying the weight of her concerns.

"He reminds me so much of Miles sometimes," she whispered as Reuben joined her. "The same defensiveness, the same ability to twist a situation until somehow he's the victim. Miles would always blame me whenever he got caught doing something wrong. 'If you hadn't gone away to college, I wouldn't be like this.' Even my mother believed him."

Reuben wrapped an arm around her shoulders. "Justin's a good kid going through a rough patch. We'll get through this."

But the "rough patch" showed no signs of smoothing over. As the school year continued, Justin's behavior only worsened. His former enthusiasm for family activities was replaced by reluctant participation and frequent attempts to escape to his room or to meet with friends Daphne and Reuben had expressly forbidden him to see.

The situation came to a head on a cool March evening when Officer Daniels from the Richmond Police Department rang their doorbell at 11 PM. Justin had been caught attempting to buy what he thought was marijuana from an undercover officer.

"It turned out to be oregano," Officer Daniels explained, his expression a mixture of concern and mild amusement as Justin slouched behind him, refusing to meet anyone's eyes. "But he was already intoxicated when he tried to make the purchase. No charges this time—he's a minor, and technically he was trying to buy a legal kitchen herb—but I'm required to file a report. Next time won't be just a warning."

After the officer left and a stone-faced Justin had been sent to his room, Daphne paced the kitchen, anxiety coiling tightly in her chest.

"I can't ignore the signs anymore, Ben," she said, her voice strained. "This isn't normal teenage rebellion. He's spiraling, and I'm terrified of where it leads."

Reuben watched her with concern. "What are you thinking?"

"I've tried everything I know—grounding him, taking away privileges, heart-to-hearts, even that adolescent psychologist Dr. Richards recommended. Nothing's getting through." She stopped pacing, a sudden thought crystallizing. "Maybe what he needs is a fresh start.

Somewhere away from these influences."

♥♥♥

Daphne's heart raced as she read the email from her boss. Her expertise in financial crimes risk assessment had been recognized, and she was offered a significant promotion – one that required relocation to Dallas, Texas.

The promotion had come at the perfect time, like an answer to her unspoken prayers. With Justin's behavior becoming increasingly concerning, the opportunity to start fresh in a new city felt like divine intervention.

That evening, Daphne shared the news with Reuben over dinner after the children had gone to bed.

"Dallas," Reuben said thoughtfully, swirling the last of his wine in the glass. "It's a big change, but it could be exactly what Justin needs right now."

"You'd be willing to move?" Daphne asked, surprised by his immediate support. "Your engineering firm—"

"Has offices in Dallas," Reuben finished with a small smile. "I already checked. I could transfer within the company, though I'd have to start over in some ways." He reached across the table, taking her hand. "This family comes first, Daphne. If Dallas is what Justin needs, then Dallas is where we'll go."

The family meeting the next day proved more challenging. Caroline, deep into her final year at the community college, was hesitant about the disruption.

"What about my band? My degree?" she asked, her brow furrowed with concern.

"You and Royce would stay here," Daphne explained gently. "The house stays in the family—you'd take care of it while we're in Dallas. Finish your degree, focus on your music."

Royce, already building his career at Riverfront, nodded in agreement. "I've been meaning to move back home to save money anyway. We can hold down the fort here."

Roman approached the news with characteristic optimism. "I looked up the robotics programs at Dallas high schools," he announced, his eyes bright with excitement. "They're nationally ranked! And there's this really cool engineering summer camp I could apply for."

Justin, however, was furious. "This is so messed up," he spat, pushing away from the table. "You're ruining my life! I'm not going to some stupid school in Texas where

I don't know anyone!"

"Justin—" Daphne began, but he was already storming out of the room, the slam of his bedroom door reverberating through the house.

♥♥♥

The weeks that followed were tense. While Daphne and Reuben made arrangements for the move, Justin grew increasingly withdrawn and hostile. His behavior at school deteriorated further, resulting in two suspensions before the semester was half over.

"He's self-sabotaging," Dr. Richards said during their final family therapy session. "It's a common response to perceived loss of control. By making the situation worse, he's trying to either force you to change your minds or justify his anger."

Despite the challenges, plans for the move proceeded. Daphne's company arranged for a corporate apartment in Dallas while they looked for permanent housing. Reuben secured a transfer to his firm's Texas office. Roman researched extracurricular activities and neighborhood amenities with infectious enthusiasm.

One week before their scheduled flight to Dallas,

disaster struck. Justin didn't come home from school. Hours turned into a full day with no word. Frantic calls to his friends yielded nothing—or at least nothing they were willing to share. The police took a report but explained that with Justin's history of behavioral issues, he was likely classified as a runaway rather than a missing person.

"He'll come back when he's hungry or cold," the officer assured them, but his words brought little comfort.

Three agonizing days passed. Caroline and Royce joined the search, checking skateparks, abandoned buildings, and anywhere else teenagers might congregate. Daphne barely slept, jumping at every sound that might be the door opening or a text notification.

♥♥♥

It was Roman who finally received a message—a strand of incomprehensible gibberish from Justin, sent at 2 AM. Using the location tracking app that the boys had installed for gaming purposes, Roman was able to pinpoint Justin's location to an abandoned warehouse where teens were known to gather. As they pulled up, Daphne's heart hammered in her chest. Roman spotted a group of teenagers lingering outside.

"I recognize some of them from school," he said quietly.

Before they could even exit the car, a boy with a pallid face and bloodshot eyes approached Roman, his expression frantic.

"Roman? Man, I'm so sorry. I didn't know he'd take that much. I swear," he stammered, backing away as Reuben emerged from the driver's side.

"Where is he?" Reuben demanded, his voice tight with concern.

The boy pointed toward the warehouse entrance. "Inside. He's been acting weird for like fifteen minutes."

They hurried through the rusted doors into the dimly lit space. The scene that greeted them froze Daphne's blood. Justin was pacing in a large, erratic circle, muttering incoherently to himself. His movements were jerky and unpredictable, like a marionette with tangled strings. Occasionally, he would stop to engage with another teen who stood nervously to the side, clearly out of his depth.

Roman recognized the second boy. "That's Chris from my biology class."

Chris looked up, relief washing over his face when he spotted them. "Thank god you're here. He won't sit down or drink water. He's been like this for fifteen minutes."

"What did he take?" Reuben asked, his voice deliberately calm despite the panic evident in his eyes.

"LSD," Chris admitted, unable to meet their gaze. "But he was supposed to take one tab. He took seven."

Daphne's knees weakened at the information. Seven times the normal dose. Before she could process this, Justin suddenly veered off his circular path, lurching toward a side room.

"Justin!" she called, but he didn't respond, disappearing through the doorway.

A heartbeat later, they heard a scream followed by the unmistakable sound of shattering glass. Daphne's body moved before her mind could catch up, rushing toward the sound with Reuben close behind.

Justin emerged from the room, even more agitated than before, blood streaming down his arm in alarming rivulets. It dripped onto the concrete floor, creating a macabre trail behind him.

"Oh my god," Daphne gasped, the sight of her son covered in his own blood causing her legs to give way. She slumped to the ground, fumbling for her phone as sobs wracked her body. "We need an ambulance," she managed to tell the 911 operator, her voice barely functioning.

Roman took charge, gathering the other teenagers together, his voice low and urgent. "What exactly happened? I need to know everything."

While Roman pieced together the events, Reuben attempted to get close enough to Justin to examine his wounds. The boy continued his erratic movements, now leaving smears of blood on whatever he touched.

"Justin, son, I need you to stay still for a moment," Reuben pleaded, trying to grab a clean shirt someone had offered to wrap around the bleeding arm.

Justin's only response was a string of disconnected words, his eyes wide but unfocused, clearly not registering his surroundings. Reuben followed him into the room where the injury had occurred.

The sight that greeted him was chilling—a shattered window with blood-stained shards, pieces of glass scattered across the floor like cruel confetti. Justin had apparently put his entire arm through the window in his drug-induced state.

Minutes later, the wail of sirens announced the arrival of help. Paramedics rushed in, followed by police officers who immediately began clearing teenagers from the premises. Some fled, others were corralled for questioning.

From the side room came renewed shouts and the sounds of a struggle. Reuben emerged, tears streaming down his face as he made his way to Daphne, who was still on the floor, her body shaking with silent sobs.

"Don't go in there," he whispered, kneeling beside her and pulling her into his arms. "You don't need to see him like that."

The paramedics wheeled Justin out strapped tightly to a gurney, a mesh spit mask covering his face to prevent him from spitting at or biting the medical staff. His body thrashed against the restraints, unintelligible sounds emanating from behind the mask. The sight was nothing short of heartbreaking—their son, reduced to this feral state by chemicals and poor choices.

As they passed Daphne, something remarkable happened. Justin's eyes, which had been darting wildly around the room, suddenly locked onto hers. For the briefest moment, clarity seemed to return to his gaze.

"I'm sorry, mum," he said, his voice cracking before he slipped back into agitation, continuing to struggle against his restraints as they wheeled him toward the ambulance.

♥♥♥

The following days were a blur of hospital corridors and psychiatric evaluations. Justin was placed on a two-day psychiatric hold for observation and to allow the drugs to fully leave his system. Their carefully laid moving plans were thrown into disarray.

"We'll need to change our flights," Reuben said as they sat in the hospital waiting room, exhaustion etched into every line of his face. "I think we should look at a direct flight, maybe next week after Justin's released."

Daphne nodded numbly, unable to form words. The image of her son, blood-covered and restrained, had burned itself into her memory.

Roman, desperate to be helpful in a situation where he felt powerless, had spent hours on his laptop researching treatment options.

"There's a place called Bridgewater Center outside Dallas," he told them, showing them the website on his phone. "They specialize in teen addiction and have really good success rates. Maybe when we get there, Justin could..."

He trailed off, uncertain if his suggestion was welcome or intrusive. But Daphne reached for his hand, squeezing it gratefully.

"Thank you," she whispered. "We'll look into it."

The warehouse incident had changed everything. What had started as a family move had now become a desperate race to save Justin from himself, and none of them were certain of the outcome.

Chapter 16 – Dallas
2019

Daphne awoke to the sound of rain pattering against her bedroom window. She lay there in the comforting warmth of her bed, feeling the heavy weight of sadness and exhaustion settle over her like a thick blanket. Her chest tightened as she stared at the ceiling, the morning light filtering through the curtains casting a dim glow across the room.

She sighed, knowing that she should be getting up and starting her day. But it felt impossible to summon the motivation to do anything beyond lying there, her thoughts flickering between memories of happier times and the oppressive reality of her worsening depression.

"Come on, Daphne," she whispered to herself, attempting to muster some energy. "You can do this."

The first task was always getting out of bed, which

seemed to grow more daunting with each passing day. She swung her legs over the edge, allowing her feet to brush against the plush carpet. For a moment, she allowed herself to remember how she used to dance around her bedroom, music blaring and laughter bubbling from her lips. But now, even standing up felt like an insurmountable challenge.

With a deep breath, she forced herself upright, the familiar twinge in her back reminding her that time had taken its toll on more than just her mental state. Her once-organized bedroom now looked like a monument to all the tasks she could no longer bring herself to complete – piles of laundry waiting for her careful folding, unopened mail littering her desk, and stacks of books she'd lost interest in halfway through.

"Small steps," Daphne reminded herself as she shuffled towards the bathroom. Each movement felt heavy, as if she were wading through waist-deep water. The simple act of brushing her teeth took longer than usual, her mind wandering to past conversations with Reuben and the love they shared. Yet even his support couldn't seem to lift her spirits.

As she stared at her phone, Daphne's finger hovered over Dougie's name in her contacts. Her cousin had always understood the darkness that sometimes engulfed her—they'd spent countless late-night calls talking each other back from the edge over the years. But Dougie was gone now, another casualty of this terrible year. Uncle Doug's cancer had taken him just weeks ago, and Dougie, unable to imagine a world without his father, had followed him two days later by his own hand. The grief was still too raw, the loss of these anchors in her life compounding the helplessness she felt watching Justin spiral.

In the kitchen, Daphne stood before the coffee maker, remembering how she'd once taken pride in her ability to craft the perfect cup. Now, even measuring out the grounds felt like an overwhelming task. She hesitated, her fingers trembling slightly as she held the scoop. The smell of coffee beans, which used to bring her joy, now only served as a reminder of how much had changed.

"Damn it," she muttered, finally managing to pour the grounds into the machine. As the aroma of brewing coffee filled the room, she leaned against the counter, feeling the cool granite beneath her fingertips. It grounded her for a moment, before she was swept away again by memories and regrets.

"Morning, Daphne," Reuben's voice called from the doorway, pulling her back to reality. He sauntered into the kitchen, his eyes heavy with concern.

"Morning," she replied, forcing a small smile onto her face. But even this simple act felt strained, another reminder that happiness was becoming an increasingly elusive concept.

As they shared their morning routine, the ghost of who Daphne once was seemed to linger over each mundane task. Her love for spreadsheets and organization now overshadowed by the unending struggle to find motivation and fight off the oppressive weight of her depression. And with every passing day, the distance between her past self and present reality seemed to grow ever wider.

She sat down at the table across from him, taking a sip of her coffee, careful not to scald herself as it was too hot. "It's becoming harder and harder to get out of bed in the mornings," she confessed, her voice barely above a whisper.

Reuben reached across the table and took her hand. "It's been six weeks, Daphne. You can't keep blaming yourself for Justin."

At the mention of her son's name, Daphne's composure cracked. "They won't even let me talk to him, Ben. My own son, and I don't know if he's okay, if he's angry, if he's..." Her voice broke, unable to complete the thought.

"The Bridgewater Center knows what they're doing,"

Reuben assured her, though his own eyes betrayed his worry. "The first phase of treatment is isolation from triggers. We knew that going in."

"I know what we agreed to," Daphne replied, pulling her hand away. "That doesn't make it any easier."

Reuben sighed, running a hand through his hair. "Roman's struggling too, you know. He misses Justin, but he's also angry at him for what happened."

The mention of Roman pierced through Daphne's fog of depression. The boy had become increasingly quiet over the past weeks, spending more time in his room with his robotics projects and less time engaging with the family. He'd been the one to find Justin that night—unconscious on the bathroom floor, an empty pill bottle by his hand. The image had traumatized the fifteen-year-old in ways they were still discovering.

"Is he still having nightmares?" she asked.

"Last night was bad," Reuben admitted. "He came into our room around three. I set up the trundle bed for him."

Guilt washed over Daphne, fresh and sharp. She'd been so consumed by her own emotional pain that she'd failed to notice Roman's midnight visit. "I should have woken up."

"You needed the sleep," Reuben said kindly. "You haven't been sleeping well either."

Later that evening, as they cleared the dinner plates, Roman finally spoke about what was weighing on him. "When do we get to see Justin?" he asked, his voice small but determined.

Daphne exchanged a glance with Reuben. "The center called yesterday," she said carefully, not wanting to build false hope. "They said Justin has completed the first phase of his treatment program. If everything continues to go well, we can visit next weekend."

Roman's face brightened momentarily before clouding over again. "What if he doesn't want to see us? What if he's still mad?"

"He asked about you," Reuben said, placing a reassuring hand on his son's shoulder. "The counselor said he specifically wanted to know how you were doing."

Roman nodded, processing this information. "I'm still kind of mad at him," he admitted, his voice thick with emotion. "Is that okay?"

"Of course it's okay," Daphne said, drawing him into a hug. "We're all dealing with this in our own way."

"Dr. Thompson said it's normal to feel angry," Reuben added, referencing their family counselor. "Remember what we talked about in our session on Tuesday?"

Roman nodded against Daphne's shoulder. "That feelings aren't right or wrong, they just are."

"Exactly," Daphne murmured, stroking his hair. "And Justin's going to need time to heal, just like all of us."

♥♥♥

The following week brought their first scheduled visit to the Bridgewater Center, a sprawling facility nestled among the pine trees outside Dallas. The two-hour drive passed in tense silence, each of them lost in their own thoughts and anxieties about the reunion.

Daphne clutched a small photo album she'd

assembled—pictures of home, of Caroline's latest band performance, of Royce in his chef's uniform, of Morgan standing proudly in front of the NASA logo. She wanted Justin to know that despite the distance, he remained connected to the family.

The center itself was surprisingly beautiful, more like a retreat than a rehabilitation facility. Gardens and walking paths wound through the property, and the buildings were designed to feel homey rather than institutional.

Justin's counselor, Ms. Lara Jenkins, met them in a comfortable visiting area decorated with potted plants and artwork created by the residents. "Justin's made significant progress," she informed them, her tone both professional and warm. "He's been working hard in his individual therapy sessions and has become quite engaged in our group activities."

"How is he? Really?" Daphne asked, unable to hide the tremor in her voice.

Ms. Jenkins smiled reassuringly. "He's doing better than most teens at this stage. The detox was difficult, as we expected, but he's shown remarkable resilience. There's still a long road ahead, but he's taking those first steps willingly now."

When Justin finally entered the room, Daphne barely recognized her son. Gone was the sullen, angry teenager with bloodshot eyes and unkempt appearance. In his place stood a thinner but clearer-eyed young man, his hair neatly trimmed and his posture straighter than it had been in months.

"Hey," he said softly, his gaze darting between them before settling on Roman.

The boys stared at each other for a long moment before Roman lunged forward, throwing his arms around Justin in a fierce hug. "You idiot," Roman whispered, his voice breaking. "You could have died."

"I know," Justin replied, his own arms coming up to return the embrace. "I'm sorry."

Watching her son hold his step-brother, seeing the genuine remorse and relief in that embrace, Daphne felt something inside her begin to thaw. The numbness that had encased her heart since that terrible night started to recede, replaced by the first tendrils of hope.

The visit wasn't without its difficult moments. Justin was still Justin—quick to deflect with humor when conversations turned too serious, defensive when discussing certain aspects of his choices. But there were also moments of surprising candor, like when he admitted how scared he'd been when he woke up in the hospital.

"I thought I was going to die," he told them, his voice small. "And then I was mad that I didn't."

Daphne reached for his hand then, half-expecting him to pull away. Instead, he gripped her fingers tightly. "I'm glad you're still here," she said simply, her voice thick with emotion.

"Me too," he replied after a moment. "Most days, anyway."

As they prepared to leave, Ms. Jenkins pulled Daphne and Reuben aside. "Justin's made enough progress that we're considering transitioning him to our day program. He would live at home but come here for treatment five days a week."

The prospect of having Justin home again filled Daphne with both joy and trepidation. "Is he ready?" she asked.

"We believe so," Ms. Jenkins replied. "But the home environment needs to be structured and supportive. We'd need your full commitment to family therapy and maintaining firm boundaries."

Reuben squeezed Daphne's hand. "We're committed to whatever Justin needs."

The following weeks were a flurry of preparation. Under Dr. Thompson's guidance, they established clear house rules and expectations. Daphne threw herself into creating a healing environment, researching nutrition to support recovery and arranging her work schedule to accommodate Justin's treatment program.

Slowly, the fog of depression that had enveloped her began to lift as she focused on concrete tasks. The laundry piles diminished, one load at a time. The unopened mail was sorted and filed away. Small steps, as she had reminded herself that morning that now felt so long ago.

On a crisp autumn morning, exactly ten weeks after he had entered the Bridgewater Center, Justin Stainthorpe came home. His belongings fit into a single duffel bag—personal items strictly limited by the center's policies to discourage materialism and encourage introspection.

As he stood in the entryway of their Dallas home, looking both older and younger than his fifteen years, Daphne felt a surge of fierce protectiveness. This boy, her son, had walked through fire and emerged singed but alive. Now it was up to all of them to help him build a new life from the ashes of his old one.

"Welcome home," she said simply, opening her arms.

Justin hesitated for just a moment before stepping into her embrace. "It's good to be back," he murmured against her shoulder.

Behind them, Reuben and Roman waited their turn, the four of them forming a constellation of broken pieces slowly being mended together—not perfect, but whole in all the ways that truly mattered.

♥♥♥

Despite these efforts, Daphne found herself struggling with the weight of uncertainty. Each time Justin left the house for his treatment program, anxiety gnawed at her. Would today be the day he relapsed? Had she missed some subtle sign that morning? The constant vigilance was exhausting.

"You need support too," Dr. Thompson told her during one of their family sessions. "Parents of recovering addicts often neglect their own mental health while focusing on their child."

The therapist recommended a support group that

met weekly at a community center not far from their home. Daphne was skeptical at first—the thought of sharing their private struggles with strangers made her uncomfortable—but Reuben encouraged her to give it a try.

"Just one meeting," he urged. "If you hate it, you never have to go back."

The following Thursday evening, Daphne found herself sitting in an uncomfortable folding chair, surrounded by parents whose faces reflected the same mix of worry, exhaustion, and cautious hope that she saw in her own mirror each morning.

"Welcome, everyone," the group facilitator began. "For those joining us for the first time, I'm Gail Henderson. I'm a social worker by profession, but I'm here tonight as the mother of a son who's been in recovery for seven years."

As the meeting progressed, Daphne listened to stories that echoed her own fears—parents who had discovered drugs hidden in teddy bears, who had received middle-of-the-night phone calls from emergency rooms, who had watched their bright, loving children transform into strangers before their eyes.

When it was her turn to speak, words failed her at first. "I'm Daphne," she finally managed. "My son Justin is fifteen. He's been home from residential treatment for two weeks."

A woman sitting across the circle caught her eye, offering an encouraging nod. "The early days are the hardest," she said gently. "I'm Ellen, by the way. My daughter Lily has been clean for thirteen months now."

Something about Ellen's calm presence drew Daphne in. Unlike some of the other parents who spoke with an almost evangelical fervor about their children's recovery journeys, Ellen's quiet confidence suggested a hard-won wisdom that Daphne desperately needed.

After the meeting, Ellen approached her. "First time's always tough," she said, handing Daphne a tissue she hadn't realized she needed. "But it gets easier."

"Does it?" Daphne asked, unable to imagine a time when this wouldn't be the central focus of her existence.

"Not in the way you're hoping," Ellen admitted with a rueful smile. "The worry never completely goes away. But you learn to live alongside it rather than letting it consume you."

They exchanged phone numbers, and over the

following weeks, Ellen became Daphne's lifeline. Her late-night texts when Justin seemed distant, her practical advice for handling difficult conversations, her unflinching honesty about her own daughter's setbacks—all of it helped Daphne navigate this unfamiliar terrain.

Ellen introduced her to Gail outside the context of the support group, and the three women formed an unlikely friendship bound by shared experiences. Gail, whose work at the homeless shelter had given her perspective on the broader social issues surrounding addiction, invited Daphne to volunteer.

"Many of our clients are struggling with substance abuse alongside homelessness," she explained. "Seeing that side of recovery might be helpful for you—and eventually, for Justin too."

Daphne was hesitant to involve Justin, worried that exposure to people still in active addiction might trigger him. But when she mentioned the idea to his counselor, Ms. Jenkins surprised her.

"Volunteer work can be incredibly therapeutic," she said. "Especially when it allows Justin to see himself as someone who can offer help rather than just receive it."

Justin's initial reaction was predictably resistant. "So I'm supposed to go hang out with a bunch of homeless addicts to make myself feel better? That's messed up, Mum."

"That's not what this is about," Daphne countered, keeping her voice level despite the flash of anger his dismissive tone provoked. "It's about being of service to others."

"Whatever," Justin muttered, but Daphne noticed he didn't outright refuse.

♥♥♥

His first visit to the shelter was awkward. He stood stiffly in the kitchen area, robotically spooning mashed potatoes onto plates as people filed through the dinner line. But somewhere between the second and third hour, something shifted. Daphne watched from across the room as an elderly man stopped to chat with Justin, their conversation eventually drawing a reluctant smile from her son.

On the drive home, Justin was unusually quiet. "What are you thinking about?" Daphne asked, trying to sound casual.

"That old guy, Mr. Garcia," Justin replied after a moment. "He used to be an engineer. Built bridges and stuff. Now he lives in his car."

"Life can change quickly," Daphne said carefully.

Justin nodded, staring out the window. "He told me I reminded him of his grandson." Another pause, longer this time. "He said I had good hands for building things."

The shelter became a regular part of their routine—twice monthly at first, then weekly as Justin's interest grew. There he met Frank Donovan, a master electrician who volunteered his Saturdays teaching basic trade skills to shelter residents.

"Your boy's got an aptitude for this," Frank told Daphne after Justin had successfully rewired a broken lamp under his supervision. "He's patient, detail-oriented. Those are rare qualities in someone his age."

As months passed and Justin's recovery solidified, school remained a fraught subject. Despite the Bridgewater Center's recommendation that he return to a normal educational environment, Justin resisted.

"I can't go back there," he insisted during a particularly tense family meeting. "I don't know anyone and I'm afraid I'll fall into old patterns with friends and start using again."

Dr. Thompson, who had continued as their family therapist, suggested a compromise. "What about completing your GED? It would give you a goal to work toward without the social pressures of traditional high school."

The idea appealed to Justin, who had always been bright despite his academic struggles. With Reuben's help, he began studying for the exam, his natural intelligence finally channeled into something constructive.

♥♥♥

Justin threw himself into studying for the GED with unexpected determination. While his peers navigated the social complexities of junior year, he worked with tutors and spent long hours at the kitchen table with practice tests spread before him.

"I've never seen him this focused," Reuben remarked to Daphne one evening as they watched Justin hunched over his books.

"He wants to prove something to himself," Daphne replied. "And to us."

When Justin passed his exams with surprisingly high scores, the family celebrated with a dinner that felt like a turning point. For the first time in years, Justin's smile reached his eyes as he accepted their congratulations.

"So what now?" Roman asked his step-brother as they cleared dishes afterward. "Early graduation means early freedom."

"Frank says I can start working with him part-time," Justin replied, referring to the electrician who had taken him under his wing at the shelter. "Learn the trade properly."

Months passed, seasons changed. Justin's apprenticeship with Frank grew into a genuine career path as he discovered an aptitude for the precise, methodical work. Meanwhile, Roman entered his senior year, his evenings now consumed with college applications and the anxious waiting that followed.

"I applied to five schools," Roman announced over dinner one night. "But Drexel's my first choice."

Reuben tried to hide his pleasure at this statement, but his proud smile betrayed him. "The engineering program there is excellent," he said with forced casualness. "Though I'm sure all your options are good."

When the thick envelope from Drexel University arrived in early spring, the family gathered around as Roman tore it open with trembling fingers. The acceptance letter inside triggered a celebration that filled their home with more genuine laughter than they'd heard in years.

"Dad's alma mater," Roman said, his eyes bright with excitement. "Philadelphia, here I come!"

"You'll love Philadelphia," Reuben told his son, pride evident in his voice. "The engineering program is challenging, but the co-op opportunities are unmatched."

Roman's excitement was tempered only by his concern for Justin. The boys had grown closer through the ordeal of Justin's addiction and recovery, their stepbrother bond strengthened by shared trauma and healing.

"What if you need me and I'm not here?" Roman asked Justin late one night, their voices carrying through the thin walls of their adjoining bedrooms.

"I'll be fine," Justin assured him. "Besides, you can't put your life on hold because of my screwups."

"They weren't just your screwups," Roman replied. "We're family. That means we share the good stuff and the hard stuff."

The day before Roman was set to leave for Drexel, Frank offered Justin an official apprenticeship in his electrical contracting business.

"I don't normally take on kids without a diploma," Frank explained, his weathered face serious. "But you passed your GED with flying colors, and I've seen your work. I need someone with your attention to detail."

Justin, at eighteen now taller than Reuben and beginning to fill out his lanky frame, stood a little straighter at the offer. "I won't let you down," he promised, the phrase carrying weight beyond its simple words.

♥♥♥

That evening, as the family gathered for a farewell dinner for Roman, Daphne looked around the table at these people who had weathered the worst storm of their lives together. Roman animatedly describing the robotics lab he'd be working in at Drexel; Justin listening intently, occasionally asking questions that showed genuine interest; Reuben watching his boys with quiet pride.

The road had been unimaginably difficult, paved with fear and guilt and countless sleepless nights. There would be challenges ahead—addiction recovery was a lifelong journey, not a destination—but for the first time since they'd moved to Dallas, Daphne felt genuine hope blooming in her chest.

She caught Ellen's words echoing in her mind: "You learn to live alongside it rather than letting it consume you." Somehow, without realizing it, that's exactly what they had begun to do.

Later, after the dishes were cleared and Roman had gone upstairs to finish packing, Justin approached her in the kitchen. "Hey, Mum?"

"Yes, sweetheart?" Daphne replied, turning from the sink where she'd been rinsing glasses.

"I just wanted to say..." he hesitated, searching for words. "Thanks. For not giving up on me. I know I didn't make it easy."

Daphne dried her hands on a dishtowel and pulled him into a hug. For once, he didn't resist or make a joke to break the moment.

"I would never give up on you," she whispered fiercely. "Never."

"I know that now," he said, and Daphne heard in those simple words the promise of a future she had once feared they'd never have.

Chapter 17 – A Writer is Born
2024

The seasons changed and years passed since the difficult days in Dallas. The house they had once viewed as temporary had become a true home, holding memories of both struggles and triumphs. Roman was away at Drexel University pursuing his engineering degree, and though Justin remained in Dallas, his electrical apprenticeship kept him busy with long hours and new responsibilities. Caroline's music career had taken her to Nashville, where her band was gaining traction in the local scene, while Royce had risen to head chef at a prestigious Richmond restaurant. Even Morgan, though constantly busy with NASA projects in Houston, managed to visit occasionally, bringing tales of Mars rovers and space exploration that left them all in awe.

Daphne found herself standing in the doorway of Roman's empty bedroom one Sunday afternoon, dust motes dancing in the sunlight that streamed through the window. She ran her fingers along the bookshelf where his robotics trophies once stood, now replaced by a few engineering textbooks he hadn't taken to Philadelphia.

The house felt too big, too quiet. Even with Reuben's comforting presence, the spaces once filled with laughter and teenage arguments now echoed with a hollowness that Daphne couldn't quite fill with her work spreadsheets or household organization projects.

"Missing the boys?" Reuben asked, appearing behind her and wrapping his arms around her waist.

She leaned back against him, drawing comfort from his warmth. "Is it that obvious?"

"Only to someone who knows you as well as I do," he replied, resting his chin on her shoulder. His breathing seemed slightly labored, even from this small exertion, but Daphne was too lost in her thoughts to notice.

"I just didn't expect the empty nest to feel so... empty," she admitted.

"They'll be home for Thanksgiving," Reuben reminded her, giving her a gentle squeeze before wincing almost imperceptibly.

"That's still weeks away," Daphne sighed. "I need to find something to occupy my mind besides work and laundry."

Reuben turned her in his arms to face him, his eyes warm despite the new lines of fatigue etched around them. "You'll find something, love. You always do."

♥♥♥

Thanksgiving brought a whirlwind of activity to the house. Roman arrived first, taller than when he'd left and sporting a new, more mature haircut that made him look startlingly like Reuben at that age. Justin joined them as well, no longer commuting to the dinner table from his room but from his own apartment across town, his confidence evident in the easy way he now carried himself.

Watching her family gathered around the dining table, Daphne felt a fullness in her heart that almost—but not quite—eclipsed the knowledge that in a few short days, the house would fall silent again.

The morning after Thanksgiving, she found Roman and Justin huddled together in the kitchen, their conversation stopping abruptly when she entered.

"Morning, Mum," Justin said, a little too brightly. "We were just heading out for a bit."

"Both of you?" Daphne asked, raising an eyebrow. "Where to?"

The brothers exchanged a look that Daphne recognized from their teenage years—the universal signal of conspiracy.

"Just some errands," Roman replied vaguely. "Dad's in on it."

"In on what?" Daphne pressed, but the boys simply grinned and slipped past her, grabbing their jackets from the hook by the door.

"Back in a few hours!" Justin called over his shoulder as they disappeared outside.

When they returned later that afternoon, it was with a large pet carrier and bags from the local pet store. Daphne looked up from her book as they entered the living room, Reuben trailing behind them with an amused expression.

"What's this?" she asked, setting her reading aside.

Roman placed the carrier carefully on the floor and

unlatched the door. "We thought you might like some company when we're not here."

From the depths of the carrier emerged two tiny kittens—one with sleek black fur and emerald eyes, and one with a patchwork calico coat featuring tabby stripes, creamy white patches, and splashes of ginger. They blinked in the light, tentatively stepping onto the carpet.

"We've already named them," Justin announced proudly. "The black one is Stan, and the calico is Loretta."

Daphne's heart melted as the kittens explored their new surroundings, Loretta immediately pouncing on a piece of lint while Stan surveyed the room with dignity.

"They're perfect," she whispered, tears pricking at her eyes as she gathered both tiny felines into her lap. The kittens settled against her, their small bodies vibrating with contented purrs.

Reuben sat beside her on the couch, his breathing slightly labored from the excitement. "The boys thought you needed someone to take care of when they're not around to keep you busy."

"And someone to keep you company," Roman added, his expression softening. "So you don't get lonely."

As she stroked the kittens' soft fur, Daphne felt a surge of gratitude for her family's thoughtfulness. These tiny creatures couldn't replace her children, but they would certainly bring new life and energy to the quiet house.

♥♥♥

The kittens quickly established themselves as permanent fixtures in Daphne's daily routine. Stan, true to his dignified demeanor, preferred to observe the household activities from elevated perches, while Loretta became a whirlwind of energy, chasing invisible prey and tumbling through the house with abandon.

Their antics brought laughter back to the quiet rooms, but as winter deepened into a particularly cold January, Daphne still found herself seeking something more. The spreadsheets at work, once a source of satisfaction, now felt repetitive. Even her carefully maintained household systems seemed to run on autopilot, requiring less of her attention than she was accustomed to giving.

After a quiet Sunday dinner, as Reuben's leg bounced rhythmically under the table—a habit that had become more frequent lately—he mentioned a book club flyer he'd seen at the local library.

"You've always been a reader," he said, placing his hand on the offending leg to slow the bouncing. "Might be nice to discuss books with other people instead of just those two furballs."

Daphne glanced at Stan and Loretta, who were engaged in a complex game of chase around the living room. "They're not the most literary conversationalists," she admitted with a smile.

The suggestion took root, and the following Thursday found Daphne walking through the doors of the Dallas Public Library, a space she hadn't visited since the boys were young. The book club met in a cozy corner of the building, with comfortable chairs arranged in a circle and soft lighting creating an intimate atmosphere.

"Welcome!" A woman with warm hazel eyes greeted her. "I'm Patty Donovan. First time?"

"Yes," Daphne replied, suddenly feeling nervous. "I'm Daphne Feldman."

"Well, you're just in time—we're starting a new book today," Patty said, guiding her to an empty chair. "We're a friendly bunch, I promise."

The group consisted of eight people, ranging from a college student to a retired schoolteacher. As they discussed the selected novel—a contemporary fiction piece about family secrets—Daphne found herself drawn into the conversation, her perspective valued and her comments met with thoughtful responses.

By the end of the evening, she had not only enjoyed a stimulating discussion but had also made connections with several members, particularly Patty and a married couple, Brent and Alex Mitchell.

"You should join us for coffee sometime," Patty suggested as they gathered their belongings. "We usually meet at Riverside Café after work on Tuesdays."

"I'd like that," Daphne replied, surprised at how easily the words came. Making new friends had never been her strong suit, but something about this group felt right.

As the book club became a regular part of her schedule, Daphne found herself reading more widely than she had in years. The discussions often lingered in her mind long after the meetings ended, sparking ideas and reflections that she began jotting down in a notebook.

One evening, as Reuben massaged his stiffening fingers—a gesture that had become more frequent lately—Daphne shared one of these reflections, a personal response to the memoir they'd been discussing in the book club.

"You should write that down more formally," Reuben suggested, flexing his hand with a barely perceptible wince. "You've always had a way with words."

"I don't know about that," Daphne demurred, though the idea appealed to her more than she wanted to admit.

"I'm serious," Reuben insisted. "Your letters to the kids when they were away at camp were practically literature. Morgan still has them, you know."

The thought of writing something more substantial than notes or emails both excited and terrified Daphne. "I wouldn't know where to begin."

"Begin with what you know," Reuben advised, his breathing slightly labored as he stood. "Write about your experiences, your feelings. The rest will follow."

That night, after Reuben had fallen asleep (earlier than usual, she noted absently), Daphne sat at the kitchen table with her notebook open before her. The blank page was intimidating, but as she began to write about her childhood in Brooklyn, then Queens, the words flowed more easily than she expected.

Hours passed unnoticed as she filled page after page, memories and reflections pouring out in a cathartic stream. When she finally looked up, the first light of dawn was filtering through the kitchen window, and Stan was watching her from atop the refrigerator, his green eyes seemingly approving of her new endeavor.

♥♥♥

The next book club meeting took an unexpected turn when the discussion veered from the assigned novel to the craft of writing itself.

"I've always thought about trying to write something," Patty admitted to the group. "But I wouldn't know where to start."

"There's a writing workshop at the community center," offered Alex, his husband Brent nodding in agreement. "It's led by Beth Reynolds and Stephanie Carter—they're both published authors. Beth writes romance, and Stephanie specializes in thrillers."

Daphne's interest was piqued. "When does it meet?"

"Saturday mornings," Alex replied. "Brent and I went to a few sessions last year. It's very supportive, especially for beginners."

The following Saturday, Daphne found herself entering the community center with her notebook clutched to her chest, apprehension and excitement warring within her. The workshop space was bright and welcoming, with a circle of chairs arranged around a large table.

Beth Reynolds, a woman with an infectious enthusiasm for storytelling, greeted each participant warmly. "Welcome, everyone! Whether you're writing your first sentence or your fifth novel, you're in the right place."

Stephanie Carter, more reserved but no less passionate, outlined the structure of the workshop. "We'll start with some exercises to get the creative juices flowing, then move into sharing and constructive feedback."

By the end of the session, Daphne had not only shared a snippet of her writing but had received encouraging feedback from both the instructors and other participants. Beth's warm praise of her descriptive abilities and Stephanie's thoughtful suggestions for deepening her character development left her feeling both validated and inspired.

"You should definitely come back next week," Beth

told her as they were packing up. "You have a natural voice—authentic and compelling."

"I'd like that," Daphne replied, a sense of purpose taking root within her.

As she drove home, her mind buzzed with new ideas and perspectives. For the first time since the children had left home, she felt genuinely excited about something that was just for her—not work, not family, but a creative pursuit that challenged and fulfilled her in unexpected ways.

When she arrived home, she found Reuben and Justin (who had stopped by for the afternoon) huddled over something in the spare bedroom, the door hastily closing as she approached.

"What are you two up to?" she asked, suspicion coloring her voice.

"Nothing!" Justin called through the door. "Just guy stuff!"

"Guy stuff that requires power tools?" Daphne questioned, hearing the distinctive whir of a drill.

"It's a surprise," Reuben's voice replied, followed by a muffled cough. "Give us another hour."

True to their word, an hour later Reuben and Justin emerged, both looking pleased with themselves despite Reuben's slightly pale complexion and the fatigue evident in his eyes. Daphne had been too preoccupied with her thoughts about the writing workshop to notice these signs.

"We have something to show you," Justin announced, taking her hand and leading her to the spare bedroom.

When they opened the door, Daphne gasped. The formerly utilitarian space had been transformed into a cozy office. A beautiful desk—clearly new—sat beneath the window, a comfortable chair pulled up to it. Bookshelves lined one wall, while the opposite corner featured a reading nook with a small armchair and lamp. Two cat trees stood near the window, positioned to catch the best sunlight.

"Roman helped design it over video call," Justin explained proudly. "Dad and I just put it together."

"We thought you might need a proper space for your writing," Reuben added, slightly out of breath from the exertion but smiling broadly. "A room of your own."

Daphne turned slowly, taking in every thoughtful

detail—the desk positioned to capture the natural light, the ergonomic chair, the small touches that showed how well they understood her needs. On the desk sat a beautiful leather-bound journal and an elegant pen, a card propped against them.

With trembling fingers, she opened the card to find messages from all three sons—Roman, Justin, and Royce—along with Reuben's familiar handwriting:

"For all the stories you've helped us write with your love and guidance, it's time for you to write your own. We believe in you. —Your boys"

Tears welled in Daphne's eyes as she turned to embrace Reuben and Justin. "It's perfect," she whispered, overcome with emotion. "Absolutely perfect."

Daphne sat at her new desk, surrounded by the soft glow of a lamp and the comforting scent of fresh paint. The room was cozy, with bookshelves lining the walls and a small window overlooking the backyard. Roman and Reuben had transformed this space into a sanctuary for her, and she felt grateful for their thoughtfulness.

Picking up her pen, Daphne began to write. The words flowed easily, as if she had been waiting for this outlet all along. She wrote about her struggles with depression and anxiety, about her fears and insecurities. She wrote about her love for Reuben and the boys, about the joy they brought into her life despite the challenges they faced.

As she wrote, Daphne felt a sense of catharsis wash over her. The act of putting her thoughts onto paper allowed her to process her emotions in a way that talking or medication couldn't quite achieve. She felt lighter, as if a weight had been lifted from her shoulders.

Justin entered the room quietly, carrying a steaming cup of tea. "Here you go," he said softly, placing the cup on Daphne's desk. "I heard writing can be thirsty work."

Daphne smiled gratefully at him, taking a sip of the tea. It was just what she needed to help clear her mind further. As she continued to write, she felt a renewed sense of hope and determination. She knew that this new form of therapy would be instrumental in helping her navigate through the difficult times ahead. And with Reuben and her sons by her side, she felt confident that they could face anything together as a family.

♥♥♥

Daphne's fingers hovered over the keyboard, the

cursor blinking steadily on the blank document before her. Stan observed from his perch on the windowsill, his green eyes reflecting the morning light as it filtered through the curtains.

The writing workshop had encouraged them to explore formative experiences—moments that had shaped who they were. Daphne had initially planned to write about her childhood, about Preston's looming presence and Rosie's distant affection. But another memory kept pulling at her consciousness, demanding to be acknowledged.

She began to type, hesitantly at first, then with increasing confidence:

"The first time I truly understood danger didn't wear a monster's face was when I was nineteen. He had brown eyes and a smile that crinkled at the corners. He knew my name before I offered it, appeared outside my classrooms as if by coincidence, made me question my own instincts until the day I found him waiting in my most private space. Some violations leave no visible marks, yet alter the architecture of your soul..."

The words flowed now, releasing a story that had remained largely untold for decades. She wrote about fear and paralysis, about the violation of safety and the desperate scramble for control that followed. She wrote about how that experience had colored her perceptions, making her susceptible to Luke's particular brand of protection-turned-possession.

When she finally stopped typing, the sun had shifted across the room, and three pages stared back at her. Reading them over, she felt a weight lifting—not entirely gone, but lighter, more manageable. The account wasn't just about victimhood; it was about survival, about the strength she had found in the aftermath.

"This is good," she whispered to Stan, who had moved to the desk to lie across her research notes. "Really good."

For the first time, Daphne understood what Beth had meant about authentic writing connecting with readers. These weren't just her words; they were her truth. And in sharing that truth, perhaps she could help others recognize their own strength.

♥♥♥

As spring bloomed across Dallas, Daphne's writing routine became as essential to her day as her morning coffee. She rose before dawn, padding quietly to her office while Reuben still slept (he seemed to need more rest these days, though he dismissed her concerns with a casual wave). In the stillness of those early hours, with Stan often curled on the windowsill and Loretta batting at her pen, Daphne found her voice.

Her friendship with Beth and Stephanie blossomed beyond the Saturday workshops. The three women often met for coffee afterward, sharing insights about their writing processes and challenges. Beth's warmth and encouragement balanced perfectly with Stephanie's analytical approach, providing Daphne with the support and constructive criticism she needed to grow as a writer.

"You should submit some of your shorter pieces to literary magazines," Stephanie suggested one bright April morning as they huddled over steaming mugs in a corner café. "Your vignettes about childhood are particularly strong."

"I don't know," Daphne hesitated, the old insecurities resurfacing. "They're very personal."

"The best writing usually is," Beth assured her, her eyes kind. "And you have a way of making the specific feel universal. Readers will connect with that authenticity."

With their encouragement, Daphne selected three short pieces and submitted them to a respected online literary journal. When the acceptance email arrived two weeks later, she stared at her screen in disbelief, reading the editor's praise of her "evocative prose and emotional honesty" several times before the reality sank in.

"I knew it!" Reuben exclaimed when she showed him the email, his pride evident despite the fatigue that seemed to settle more heavily on his shoulders these days. He pulled her into a hug, his embrace slightly weaker than it once had been. "This calls for a celebration."

That evening, they video-called the children to share the news. Morgan's face filled the screen first, their NASA lab visible in the background.

"That's amazing, Mum!" they exclaimed. "Send us the link as soon as it's published."

Roman and Justin joined the call next, their faces splitting into identical grins of pride.

"Does this mean we get to say our mum is a published author now?" Roman asked, his voice teasing but his eyes serious.

"It's just a few short pieces," Daphne demurred,

though the warmth of their collective pride filled her with joy.

"It's the beginning," Reuben said firmly, his hand resting on her shoulder. As he shifted his weight to stand, he swayed slightly, catching himself on the edge of the table. "Just stood up too quickly," he murmured with a dismissive smile when he noticed Daphne's concerned glance. "Mark my words."

As spring gave way to the intense heat of a Texas summer, Daphne's writing flourished. The journal publication led to requests for more pieces, and her confidence grew with each acceptance. The character sketches and vignettes gradually coalesced into something larger—a narrative that wove together the fragments of her life experiences into a coherent whole.

"You're writing a novel," Beth observed one Saturday after workshop, reading over the latest pages Daphne had shared. "Whether you meant to or not."

The realization both terrified and exhilarated Daphne. A novel seemed so much more substantial, more intentional, than the pieces she'd been crafting. Yet as she reviewed her work that evening, she could see the truth in Beth's words. The characters had taken on lives of their own, their stories intertwining in ways that demanded a larger canvas.

"I think you're right," she admitted to Reuben later that night as they prepared for bed. "It's becoming something bigger than I expected."

Reuben, sitting on the edge of the bed as he caught his breath after climbing the stairs (had the climb always winded him so? Daphne wondered fleetingly), smiled. "That's how the best things often happen—they sneak up on you when you're busy making other plans."

As Daphne's manuscript took shape, Reuben's health began to show more obvious signs of decline. His once-energetic stride slowed; stairs became more challenging; his workday shortened as fatigue claimed him earlier and earlier. Yet caught up in the momentum of her writing and the excitement of discovering this new part of herself, Daphne noticed these changes only peripherally, attributing them to the normal aging process or perhaps the lingering effects of a summer cold.

It was Roman who first voiced concern during his August visit before returning to Drexel. "Dad seems really tired, and his hands seem a little bit shaky," he observed, keeping his voice low as they worked together in the kitchen. "Has he seen a doctor recently?"

"He had his annual checkup in January," Daphne replied, frowning slightly as she recalled how Reuben had downplayed the visit. "He said everything was fine."

Roman didn't look convinced, but he didn't press further, changing the subject to her novel's progress instead.

The manuscript consumed more and more of Daphne's time and energy as fall approached. Beth and Stephanie became her trusted first readers, offering feedback and encouragement as the story evolved. The writing workshop participants celebrated each milestone with her, creating a community of support that nurtured her growing confidence.

"You should start thinking about submitting this to agents," Stephanie advised as they reviewed the latest chapters over lunch. "It's really coming together beautifully."

"I still have so much to do," Daphne protested, though the thought of professional validation sent a thrill through her. "The ending isn't quite right yet."

"No manuscript is ever truly finished," Beth said wisely. "At some point, you have to let it go and see what happens."

That evening, as Daphne related this conversation to Reuben, she noticed how he leaned heavily against the kitchen counter, his breathing slightly labored even at rest.

"Are you feeling alright?" she asked, concern finally breaking through her creative absorption.

"Just tired," he assured her, though his smile didn't quite reach his eyes. "Nothing to worry about. Tell me more about the submission process—how does it work?"

The deflection worked, and Daphne was soon explaining what she'd learned about query letters and literary agents, her excitement momentarily overshadowing her concern.

Later that night, as Reuben slept restlessly beside her, Daphne lay awake, her mind replaying the subtle signs she'd been overlooking. The fatigue. The breathlessness. The way he sometimes massaged his left arm as if working out a cramp. She watched as he thrashed in his sleep, his limbs jerking unpredictably against the sheets—something that had been happening with increasing frequency over the past few months. Tomorrow, she resolved, she would insist he see a doctor.

But morning brought news that drove all other concerns temporarily from her mind. An email from a prestigious New York publisher expressed interest in her manuscript based on the excerpts published in the literary journal.

"They want to see the full manuscript," she told Reuben, her voice trembling with excitement as she read the email again to ensure she hadn't misunderstood.

Despite his obvious exhaustion, Reuben's joy for her was genuine and expansive. "I knew it," he said, pulling her close. "Your writing is too good to go unnoticed."

In the whirlwind of preparing her manuscript for submission, Daphne's worries about Reuben's health receded once more. She worked furiously to polish the final chapters, incorporating feedback from her writing group and making last-minute revisions.

When the completed manuscript finally went out, a curious calm settled over her. She had done all she could; now it was in the hands of fate—or more accurately, in the hands of publishers who received hundreds of submissions each week.

To her surprise, she didn't have long to wait. Just two weeks later, an email arrived requesting a meeting with the editor who had initially contacted her.

"Ben, they want me to come to New York," her voice faint with disbelief.

"Of course they do," he replied, his pride evident despite the pallor that had become his constant companion. "They'd be fools not to sign you."

Daphne's heart raced as she read the email from the prestigious New York publisher. After months of tireless work, her novel had finally caught their attention. She could hardly believe it. With trembling hands, she carefully printed and packaged the manuscript, making sure every detail was perfect.

The next morning, Daphne woke up before dawn, her mind racing with anticipation. She checked her email once more, and there it was - a message from the publisher. They loved her voice and wanted to meet to discuss a possible book deal! Daphne gasped aloud, her heart pounding in her chest. This was it - the opportunity she had been waiting for all these years.

She spent the rest of the day preparing for the meeting, going over every detail of her novel once more. She practiced her pitch until she could recite it in her sleep. Finally, the day arrived, and Daphne made her way to the publisher's office in Manhattan.

As she sat across from the editor, Daphne felt a mix of excitement and nerves. But as she began to speak about her novel, something clicked. The editor listened intently, nodding along as Daphne shared her vision for the story. By the end of their meeting, they had agreed on a book deal - Daphne's first!

Overwhelmed with joy and disbelief, Daphne left the publisher's office that day feeling like all her hard work had finally paid off. She knew that this was just the beginning of a new chapter in her life - one filled with possibilities and endless opportunities for growth as a writer. And with Reuben and her family by her side for support, she felt ready to take on whatever challenges lay ahead.

♥♥♥

The book contract arrived two days later, a thick document filled with legal terminology that Daphne and Reuben pored over together at the kitchen table. The advance was modest but respectable for a first-time author, and the proposed publication timeline would see her novel on shelves within a year.

"This calls for champagne," Reuben declared, though

he looked more fatigued than celebratory as he rose to fetch glasses. He swayed slightly, catching himself on the counter.

"Reuben?" Daphne was at his side instantly, alarm finally breaking through the haze of excitement that had enveloped her for weeks. "What's wrong?"

He tried to smile reassuringly, but the effort fell flat. "Just stood up too quickly," he said, but his voice lacked conviction.

"No more excuses," Daphne said firmly, guiding him to a chair. "Something's wrong, and we're going to find out what it is."

The diagnosis came three days later: Parkinson's disease. Early stages, the neurologist assured them, but progressive and requiring immediate treatment to manage symptoms.

"Many patients lead full, active lives for years after diagnosis," the doctor explained, her voice compassionate but matter-of-fact. "The medications we have now can control symptoms very effectively in most cases."

The drive home was silent, both of them processing the implications of this new reality. It wasn't a death sentence, but it was a fundamental change to their expectations for the future—one that demanded adjustments and accommodations.

"I'm sorry I didn't tell you sooner," Reuben finally said as they pulled into their driveway. "I didn't want to overshadow your success with my health issues."

"Don't you dare apologize," Daphne replied, her voice thick with emotion. "We're a team, remember? In sickness and in health."

The following weeks brought a crash course in managing Parkinson's—medications, lifestyle adjustments, physical therapy. Reuben's neurologist recommended he reduce his work hours to conserve energy, a suggestion he initially resisted but eventually accepted as the fatigue became more pronounced.

Working from home became Reuben's new normal, his engineering firm accommodating his needs with flexible hours and remote access. This arrangement allowed him to rest when needed while still contributing his expertise to ongoing projects.

As winter approached, bringing with it the final preparations for Daphne's book publication, they faced another decision. The publisher was planning a modest book tour, with stops in major cities along the East Coast. Ordinarily, Reuben would have accompanied her, but his health made such travel challenging.

"I should cancel," Daphne said one evening as they sat on the porch, watching the sunset paint the sky in vibrant hues of orange and pink. "The book will still be published whether I do the tour or not."

"Absolutely not," Reuben replied, his voice stronger than it had been in days. "This is your moment, Daphne. I won't let my condition hold you back."

"But who will help you with—"

"I'm not an invalid," he interrupted gently. "I can manage for a couple of weeks. Besides, the boys have already volunteered to take turns staying here while you're gone."

The conversation prompted deeper reflections about their future. Dallas had been their home for years, but with Reuben's condition and the children scattered across the country, they began to consider alternatives.

"I've been thinking," Reuben said one night as they prepared for bed, his movements slower but still purposeful as he laid out his medication for the following day. "Maybe it's time for a change."

"What kind of change?" Daphne asked, though she had been having similar thoughts.

"I'm not getting any younger," he said with a wry smile that reminded her of the charming young man she'd met so many years ago. "And neither are you, though you wear it better. Maybe we should think about downsizing, moving somewhere that would be easier for both of us as we age."

"Like where?"

"Like back to Richmond," he suggested. "The house is still in the family with Royce living there. We could reclaim the master bedroom, be closer to familiar medical facilities, have family nearby."

The idea took root, growing stronger as they discussed the practical aspects. With Daphne's writing career blossoming and Reuben's ability to work remotely, they weren't tied to Dallas professionally. The memories of their time there—both challenging and rewarding—would remain with them wherever they went.

"It feels right," Daphne said finally, the decision settling in her heart with a sense of rightness. "Going home."

As winter deepened, they started making plans. Daphne's book tour would come first, then they would begin the process of listing their Dallas home and preparing for the move back to Richmond. Royce was thrilled at the prospect of having them back, already offering to help prepare the master suite for their return.

One crisp January morning, as Daphne sat in her office putting the finishing touches on her acknowledgments page, she felt a profound sense of gratitude wash over her. The journey that had brought her here—from the frightened young mother fleeing an abusive husband to a published author with a loving family and supportive community—seemed almost miraculous in retrospect.

Stan sauntered into the office, jumping onto the desk with his usual dignity and settling beside her keyboard. Loretta followed, batting playfully at a pencil before curling up in a patch of sunlight on the windowsill.

"We're going on an adventure, you two," Daphne told them, scratching Stan behind the ears. "Back to where it all began."

The cats seemed unperturbed by this announcement, their peaceful presence a reminder that home wasn't just a place but a feeling—one that Daphne had finally found within herself through her writing, and one that she would carry with her back to Richmond, where new chapters waited to be written.

Chapter 18 – Together
2030

Daphne and Reuben sat across from each other at their small kitchen table, the steam from their mugs of coffee rising into the air. The sun streamed in through the window, casting a warm glow on the room. They both knew that today would be another challenging day, filled with doctor visits and emotional hurdles as they navigated Reuben's Parkinson's diagnosis. But for now, they cherished this quiet moment together, savoring the simple pleasure of each other's company.

Daphne reached out to take Reuben's hand, her fingers interlacing with his. His hand was steady but frail, a stark contrast to the strong engineer she had married years ago. She squeezed his hand gently, offering him comfort and support.

Reuben looked into Daphne's eyes, his own filled

with gratitude and love. "Thank you for being here with me," he said softly. "I don't know what I would do without you."

Daphne smiled at him, her heart swelling with affection. "I'm not going anywhere," she replied. "We're in this together."

They sat in silence for a few moments more, their hands still entwined. The sound of birds singing outside the window provided a soothing backdrop to their quiet conversation. As they prepared to face another day of challenges ahead, they found solace in each other's presence and the knowledge that they were facing these trials as a team.

♥♥♥

Daphne gently took Reuben's hand, guiding it to the buttonhole. She could feel the tremors in his fingers as they fumbled with the small fastener. With a soft sigh, she took over, carefully buttoning his shirt for him. Reuben watched her with a mix of gratitude and sadness in his eyes. Though it pained her to see him struggle with such simple tasks, she found solace in being able to care for him in this way. It was a small act of love that reminded them both that they were in this together, facing the challenges of Parkinson's as a team. As

Daphne stepped back, Reuben looked at her with a smile that spoke volumes. "Thank you," he said softly, his voice barely above a whisper. Daphne smiled back at him, her heart swelling with affection for the man she loved so deeply. She knew that their journey ahead would be difficult, but she also knew that they would face it together, hand in hand. And as they stood there, side by side, facing the day ahead, Daphne felt an overwhelming sense of gratitude for their love and their strength. They may be facing an uncertain future, but they were doing it together - and that was all that mattered.

♥♥♥

Daphne's eyes fluttered open, though she hadn't truly been sleeping. She stared at the ceiling, counting the familiar cracks that had become her companions during these sleepless nights. Beside her, Reuben's breathing was labored, even in rest.

She turned to look at him, her heart constricting at how the disease had already begun to claim pieces of him. His once-steady hands now trembled even in sleep, and the lines on his face had deepened with each new medication, each new limitation.

Reuben stirred, somehow sensing her gaze. Despite his own suffering, his first concern was for her. "You haven't slept," he observed, his voice rougher than it used to be.

"I'm fine," she lied, the words automatic now. The weight in her chest had been building for weeks, a familiar darkness she'd hoped never to face again. It wasn't just sadness—it was a physical heaviness that made even breathing feel like an insurmountable task.

Reuben reached for her hand, his movements slower and more deliberate than before. The tremor was worse this morning. "Daphne," he said softly, "you don't have to be strong all the time."

A bitter laugh escaped her lips before she could stop it. "Says the man fighting Parkinson's with more grace than I've ever managed at anything."

"This isn't a competition," he reminded her, his eyes still holding that warmth she'd fallen in love with decades ago. "And you've faced more in your life than most could imagine."

Daphne closed her eyes, unable to bear the kindness in his gaze. The darkness had been growing within her for months as she watched him struggle—first the slight stiffness in his movements, then the tremors, then the diagnosis that had confirmed her worst fears. With each new symptom, each new medication adjustment, the familiar tendrils of depression had tightened their grip on her mind.

"I should be taking care of you," she whispered, her voice breaking. "Not falling apart when you need me most."

Reuben shifted closer, wrapping his arms around her. His embrace wasn't as strong as it once had been, but it still enveloped her in comfort. "We take care of each other," he insisted. "That's what we've always done."

As they lay there in the dim morning light, Daphne felt tears sliding silently down her cheeks. The medications had helped Reuben's physical symptoms, but nothing could ease the ache of watching the man she loved face a degenerative disease. The helplessness was overwhelming, crushing her beneath its weight.

"I'm scared," she admitted finally, the words barely audible. "I can't lose you, Ben. I can't."

"You're not losing me," he promised, though they both knew the disease would progress no matter how much they fought it. "I'm right here, and we'll face this together, just like we've faced everything else."

Daphne nodded against his chest, trying to believe him, trying to find that spark of hope that had always guided her through dark times. But the depression that had crept back into her life was a heavy shadow, dimming even the brightest moments of love between them. It whispered insidious doubts, reminding her of every loss she'd ever suffered, every time she'd been abandoned.

And yet, in the circle of Reuben's arms, there was still a flicker of warmth—not enough to dispel the darkness, but enough to help her face another day by his side, whatever challenges it might bring.

♥♥♥

Daphne and Reuben stood in their kitchen, both trying to navigate the meal prep with their respective physical challenges. Daphne's anxiety was mounting as she struggled to chop vegetables with her trembling hands, while Reuben's Parkinson's made simple tasks like buttoning his shirt a daunting feat.

Despite the difficulties, they laughed through their frustration, finding solace in each other's company. Their eyes met, filled with love and gratitude for having each other during these trying times. It was a small moment of joy amidst the chaos of their lives, but it meant everything to them both. They shared a tender kiss, knowing that they would face whatever came their way together.

♥♥♥

Daphne and Reuben sat side by side on the porch swing, their bodies relaxed as they watched the sun dip below the horizon. The sky was painted in hues of orange and pink, a breathtaking display of nature's artistry. The gentle creaking of the swing was the only sound that broke the peaceful silence between them.

As they gazed at the sunset, Daphne felt a sense of contentment wash over her. She had found her soulmate in Reuben, and together they faced whatever challenges life threw their way. Their hands were intertwined, a symbol of their unbreakable bond. No words were needed to express the love and gratitude they felt for each other in that moment.

As the last rays of sunlight disappeared beyond the horizon, Daphne leaned her head against Reuben's shoulder. They sat there in silence, basking in each other's presence and enjoying the tranquility of the fading day. It was a simple moment, but it was one that Daphne would cherish forever - a testament to the love and connection she shared with her husband.

♥♥♥

Autumn had always been Daphne's favorite season, and as she stood in the kitchen of the home she had shared with Reuben for nearly two decades now, she couldn't help but feel a bittersweet warmth enveloping her. The sun cast a golden glow through the windows, illuminating the cozy space adorned with family photos chronicling their journey together—Caroline's wedding, Royce with his partner and their daughter Emily, Morgan at NASA, and Roman's graduation from Drexel so many years ago.

The scent of cinnamon and nutmeg wafted through the air, mingling with the comforting aroma of freshly brewed coffee. She'd been baking more often lately, finding solace in the preciseness of recipes while so much else in life felt uncertain.

"Morning, love," Reuben said, his movements deliberate as he shuffled into the kitchen, the stiffness in his joints more pronounced in the cooler weather. His hair, now more silver than sandy brown, was tousled from sleep. Despite the changes Parkinson's had brought, his eyes still held that same warmth as he wrapped his arms around her from behind, planting a tender kiss on her cheek.

"Good morning," she replied, leaning into his embrace, savoring his solidity despite how much thinner he'd become over the past year. She turned back to the stove, carefully flipping a pancake in the pan, its edges perfectly crisp and golden-brown.

As they settled down at the small kitchen table, Reuben cleared his throat and hesitated for a moment, choosing his words carefully. "So, I got a call from Roman last night," he began, his voice slightly hoarser than it once had been.

"Really? How is he?" Daphne asked, concern lacing her voice. They hadn't heard much from him in the weeks since the divorce was finalized.

Reuben sighed, running a hand through his silver hair. "He's... struggling, Daphne. The divorce hit him harder than he let on, and now he's lost his job at the engineering firm. Katherine's taken most of their savings, and he's feeling pretty lost. He asked if he could come stay with us for a while, just until he gets back on his feet."

"Of course he can stay with us," Daphne said resolutely, meeting Reuben's gaze. The guest room had been empty since Caroline's twins had visited last month. "We have the space, and heaven knows we both understand how hard it is to rebuild after life falls apart."

Reuben smiled gratefully, reaching across the table to squeeze her hand, his fingers trembling slightly with the familiar tremor. "Thank you, Daphne. I wasn't sure, with everything else going on..." He didn't need to finish the sentence. They both knew he meant his health.

"Family comes first," she said firmly. "Besides, it might be nice having someone else around the house again. It's been too quiet since Justin moved into his own place."

As they finished their breakfast, thoughts of the future swirled through Daphne's mind. She knew that welcoming Roman home would bring challenges, but after all these years of marriage and blending their families, they'd weathered far worse. With Reuben by her side—for however long they had left together—she felt confident they could navigate this new chapter with the same grace that had carried them through all the others.

Chapter 19 - Moving Day
2030

The warm hues of the setting sun painted the familiar Richmond house in a golden glow as Daphne stood in the doorway, triumphantly crossing off the last item on her meticulous checklist. The home, once filled with echoes of the past, now stood ready to embrace a new chapter. It was a labor of love, a symphony of memories and renewed hopes that danced in the air.

As if on cue, the door swung open, Reuben and Roman stepped through. The warmth of their embrace transcended words, a silent acknowledgment of the shared journey that had led them to this moment.

"Thanks for taking me in, Mum," Roman's words, laden with sincerity, hung in the air, marking a poignant shift in their relationship. The weight of the acknowledgment settled on Daphne's heart, and a tender smile played on her lips.

"Anytime, Roman," she replied, her voice carrying the echoes of years spent navigating the complexities of blended families and healing wounds. The journey had been tumultuous, but in that simple phrase, 'Thanks for taking me in, Mum,' a bridge had been built, connecting the dots of their shared experiences.

A truck engine rumbled outside, followed by the slamming of a car door. Daphne glanced out the window to see Justin climbing out of his pickup, toolbox in hand. Despite his earlier reluctance about Roman moving back home—old sibling rivalries dying hard—he'd promised to help set up the electrical work in Roman's room.

"Just in time," Daphne called as Justin entered, his tall frame filling the doorway. The years of apprenticeship had broadened his shoulders, and the confidence of mastering a trade had erased the last vestiges of the troubled teenager he once was. "Roman's trying to figure out where to put his desk for optimal outlet access."

Justin nodded, his expression softening slightly at the sight of his mother. "Figured he'd need help with that. Where is he?"

"Upstairs," Reuben answered, descending the stairs with careful, measured steps—his Parkinson's medication working well today. "Good to see you, son."

The word 'son' still brought a flicker of something warm to Justin's eyes, even after all these years. He clasped Reuben's hand briefly before heading upstairs, toolbox swinging at his side.

Daphne and Reuben exchanged glances, their silent communication a testament to the years they had spent learning each other's rhythms. The healing of their family had been slow, sometimes painful, but moments like these—Justin showing up unasked, Roman accepting help—were the reward for their patience and love.

♥♥♥

The evening unfolded with a symphony of activity as Daphne and Reuben orchestrated the seamless transition of Roman's belongings into the Richmond house. The rhythmic hum of the movers carrying boxes resonated in harmony with the sunlight streaming through the open windows. It was a dance of transitions, a choreography of new beginnings that unfolded in the rooms they had painstakingly prepared.

Daphne and Reuben moved in unison, their silent communication a testament to the years they had spent learning each other's rhythms. As Roman's boxes found their places, Daphne marveled at the way her home transformed into a haven, not just for her and Reuben but for a young man seeking solace in the familiar.

Their coordinated movements spoke volumes about the bond they shared, a love that transcended the spoken word. With every exchanged glance and shared smile, Daphne and Reuben communicated a silent understanding of the significance of this moment.

Reuben, with his easy charm, wrapped his arm around Daphne's waist, pulling her into a moment of shared reflection. The quiet sanctuary of their love radiated through the touch, a tangible connection that needed no verbal affirmation. They stood together, observing the ebb and flow of life within the walls that held their collective history.

As Roman's room took shape, Daphne stole a glance at Reuben, his eyes reflecting a pride that mirrored her own. The air was thick with the weight of shared accomplishments and the promise of a future crafted from resilience and devotion.

A contented sigh escaped both of them simultaneously, a synchronized exhale that released any lingering tension. The house, now brimming with the energy of change, seemed to sigh along with them, as if acknowledging the seamless fusion of past and present within its walls.

"I gotta bolt, mum. I promise I'll be back in time for dinner, though!" Justin shouted over his shoulder as he ran out the door.

♥♥♥

As the doorbell chimed, Daphne's heart skipped a beat. She opened the door to find her daughter Caroline, followed by her husband Dan and their two-year-old twins. The sight of them filled her with joy and nostalgia.

"Mum!" Caroline exclaimed, throwing her arms around Daphne in a tight hug. "We've come to help Roman move back home."

Dan stepped forward, his eyes scanning the familiar surroundings. "It's good to be back," he said with a smile.

The twins, their chubby cheeks rosy from the cold, clung to Dan's legs, giggling as he picked them up one by one. Daphne couldn't help but feel a pang of longing for the days when her own children were this small.

As they all filed into the house, laughter and lively conversation filled the air. Roman emerged from his room, looking both nervous and excited at the prospect of living with his family again.

Together they set about unpacking boxes and arranging furniture, working in harmony like a well-oiled machine. The warmth of their shared history was palpable as they chatted and joked, catching up on each other's lives over the past few years. It was clear that this reunion was more than just a practical solution - it was an emotional homecoming for all involved.

♥♥♥

The doorbell chimed, and Daphne's heart skipped a beat as she heard Royce's voice. She hurried to open the door, her eyes widening in delight as she saw Royce, Stacie, and little Emily standing on the porch. They had brought a delicious home-cooked meal, and Daphne couldn't help but smile at the thought of sharing it with her family.

As they settled around the table, the sound of a motorcycle engine cut through the evening air, followed by silence, then the familiar tread of boots on the porch steps. Justin appeared in the doorway, his work clothes exchanged for a clean button-down shirt, though he hadn't been able to completely remove the traces of electrical work from beneath his fingernails.

"Sorry I'm late," he said, nodding to everyone before his eyes settled on Emily. A genuine smile spread across his face as his niece squealed "Uncle Justin!" and ran to him, arms outstretched. He scooped her up, fatigue vanishing as he spun her around.

"I saved you a seat next to me," Emily declared importantly, pointing to the empty chair.

As they all gathered around the table, Daphne felt a sense of warmth and contentment wash over her. Caroline, Dan, the twins, Royce, Stacie, Emily, Justin, Reuben, and Roman sat down together, chattering happily as they dug into the food. The aroma of roasted chicken and fresh vegetables filled the air, making everyone's mouth water.

Daphne watched as her family enjoyed the meal, feeling a deep sense of gratitude for having them all together under one roof. It was a moment she had dreamed of for years - her blended family coming together to share a meal and each other's company. She felt an overwhelming sense of love and happiness as she looked around at their faces.

Midway through the meal, there was a knock on the door. Daphne's heart skipped a beat again as Morgan walked in with an apologetic grin on their face. "Sorry

I'm late!" they exclaimed as they joined everyone at the table. The room erupted in laughter as everyone welcomed them back into their midst.

As they continued to eat and chat, Daphne felt a deep sense of contentment wash over her once more. This was what she had always wanted - a loving family that supported each other through thick and thin. And now that it was finally here, she knew that nothing could ever break this bond between them.

♥♥♥

As the evening wound down, Stacie and Royce stood up holding hands. They announced their engagement, prompting cheers of congratulations. Emily exclaimed, "Finally!"

Daphne's eyes glistened with tears of joy as she watched her son and his fiancée embrace. She felt a sense of peace and contentment, knowing that her family is complete. The room was filled with love and laughter, a testament to the resilience and strength of this tight-knit group. As they gathered for group photos, Daphne couldn't help but feel grateful for the journey that brought them all together in this moment. Life may have thrown them curveballs, but they emerged stronger and more united than ever before. And as they posed for the camera, Daphne knew that no matter what challenges lie ahead, they would face them together, as a family.

♥♥♥

The sun cast a warm, golden glow upon Daphne and Reuben as they sat in their beloved garden, the scent of blooming flowers enveloping them like an embrace. With each passing year, this shared sanctuary had flourished under their careful nurturing, much like their own love for one another.

"Ben," she whispered, her voice thick with emotion, "I can't imagine my life without you. You've been my rock, my guiding star, my one true love."

"Likewise, Daphne," Reuben replied, his voice warm with sincerity. "You've brought so much joy and light into my life. Together, we've built something truly beautiful here."

As they sat together in their garden oasis, hand in hand, Daphne felt the bittersweet tug of memories past – the laughter of their children, the whispers of secret dreams shared beneath the stars, the quiet moments of comfort when words were not enough.

Chapter 20 - Royce and Stacie
2031

As Caroline lovingly arranged floral centerpieces, her hands moved with the grace of a seasoned florist. The vibrant colors of the flowers stood out against the soft green leaves, creating a stunning display that would undoubtedly be the centerpiece of the wedding reception.

Reuben, Roman, Justin, and Morgan worked diligently to string twinkling lights through the trees that surrounded the venue. The soft glow of the lights cast a warm and inviting ambiance over the area, adding to the festive atmosphere.

Emily and the twins ran around the venue, their laughter filling the air as they played amongst the chairs that were set up for guests. Their joy was infectious, mirroring the happiness that filled everyone's hearts as they prepared for the couple they had all come to celebrate.

Stacie and Royce arrived at the outdoor wedding venue hand-in-hand, their eyes locked in a loving gaze. Daphne stepped forward to embrace them both, her heart swelling with pride for the man her son had become. She could see the nervous excitement in Royce's eyes as he looked around at the beautiful setting they had chosen for their special day.

Daphne and Reuben helped the couple practice their first dance, moving in graceful turns under the twinkling stars above. Royce playfully dipped Stacie, kissing her tenderly as they twirled around the dance floor. The laughter echoed through the air, filling everyone present with a sense of joy and celebration.

As they continued to practice, Daphne couldn't help but feel a deep sense of contentment. Through all life's joys and trials, they had built a family grounded in devotion and love. And now, as she watched her son prepare to marry the love of his life, she knew that their bond would only grow stronger with each passing day.

♥♥♥

The wedding guests began to arrive, their laughter and chatter filling the air. Daphne and Caroline greeted them with warm smiles, recognizing faces from years past. Some were old friends, their faces now etched with lines of age like fine wine. They hugged each other tightly, catching up on lost time as they reminisced about the good old days. The warmth of their reunion was palpable, a testament to the enduring bonds of friendship and family.

Daphne couldn't help but feel a sense of contentment wash over her. All around her were people she loved and cherished, gathered together to celebrate the union of Royce and Stacie. It was a moment she had dreamed of for years - her family reunited in one place, filled with love and happiness.

As the afternoon progressed, Daphne watched as her children danced with their spouses and partners, their joy infectious. She felt a swell of pride in her chest as she saw how far they had all come - from a broken family torn apart by circumstances beyond their control to a loving, supportive unit that stood together through thick and thin.

Looking around at the sea of smiling faces, Daphne knew that this was what life was all about - creating memories with those you love and cherishing every moment together. And as she stood there under the twinkling lights, surrounded by her loved ones, she felt an overwhelming sense of gratitude for everything that had brought them to this place - both the joys and the hardships that had shaped them into who they were today.

♥♥♥

As the final preparations for the ceremony were underway, Daphne spotted Justin meticulously checking the string lights and audio equipment. His brow furrowed in concentration as he tested connections and adjusted settings.

"Everything working properly?" she asked, approaching him with two glasses of lemonade.

Justin accepted the drink with a grateful smile. "Just making sure nothing shorts out during the vows. Wouldn't want the speakers cutting off right when Royce says 'I do.'"

Daphne studied her son's face, noting how the years had transformed him. The troubled teenager from Dallas had become this confident, skilled craftsman who took pride in his work. The electrical apprenticeship that had once been just a lifeline had become his passion.

"You've come a long way," she said softly.

Justin's eyes met hers, understanding passing between them. "We all have, Mum."

Before she could respond, Emily came bounding over, her flower girl dress swishing around her ankles. "Uncle Justin! Can I help with the lights?"

"Sure thing, squirt," he laughed, lifting her up to see the control panel. "See this button? This makes the lights twinkle like stars."

Daphne stepped back, watching as Justin patiently explained the simple electrical concepts to his niece, Emily's eyes wide with wonder. In moments like these, she could see all the pieces of their family story coming together - the struggles, the healing, the love that had brought them through.

"Looks like we're almost ready," Daphne said, her eyes sparkling as they scanned the carefully arranged tables, each draped with crisp white linens and dotted with elegant centerpieces. Reuben gave her hand a reassuring squeeze, his own eyes filled with warmth and love.

"Everything's coming together beautifully," he agreed. "I'm so glad we could all be here to help."

"Beautiful," Daphne whispered, her eyes misting over with emotion. Reuben wrapped his arm around her shoulders and pulled her close, planting a tender kiss on her temple.

"Almost as beautiful as you," he murmured, earning a playful swat from Daphne as she laughed through her tears.

♥♥♥

Turning to Stacie, Royce took her hand in his, his eyes never leaving hers as he spoke the words that would bind them together forever. "Stacie, you are the love of my life, the reason I wake up every morning with a smile on my face, and the person I want by my side for all eternity. I promise to cherish you, support you, and laugh with you through thick and thin. I vow to be your rock, your partner, and your best friend until the end of our days."

Tears welled in Stacie's eyes, her lip trembling as she responded, "Royce, from the moment we met, I knew there was something special about you. Your sense of humor brought light into my darkest moments, and your unwavering love has given me strength I never knew I had. I pledge to stand by your side, to celebrate our victories and weather our storms, and to always choose us, no matter what life throws our way. I love you more than words can say, and I am honored to become your wife."

As Royce slipped the ring onto Stacie's finger, his voice trembled with emotion as he recited. "My partner, my soulmate, my very best friend." The words hung in the air, heavy with the weight of their meaning.

The guests erupted in applause, their joy and love for the couple filling the air like a palpable force. Daphne looked around, her senses tingling with the heady scent of flowers, the sound of laughter, and the sight of twinkling fairy lights that enveloped them all in a world of magic and happiness. She marveled at the tapestry of memories woven throughout the day - each smile, embrace, and tear a testament to the love that bound them all together.

Daphne watched from the sidelines, her heart swelling with pride as she saw her son take this significant step in his life. She had been there through every stage of Royce's journey, from his early years to his adulthood. Seeing him stand before her now, a man in love and ready to commit to a lifelong partnership, filled her with a sense of accomplishment and joy that was hard to put into words.

Reuben stood beside Daphne, his hand gently squeezing hers as they both watched the ceremony unfold. He too felt a deep sense of satisfaction and happiness for Royce and Stacie. Their love story had been a long time in the making, and seeing it culminate in this beautiful moment was truly special.

♥♥♥

"Hey, careful with that!" Reuben called out, breaking into her reverie. He rushed over to help steady a wobbly table, joking with the cousins as they worked together to fix it.

"Teamwork makes the dream work!" Daphne chimed in, joining them in their laughter. And as they continued to set up for the wedding reception, she couldn't help but feel that everything was falling into place – just as it should be.

Amidst the flurry of activity, Royce and Stacie made their grand entrance, arm in arm, their faces radiating with excitement and love.

"Welcome to the party!" Daphne called out, beaming at her son and daughter-in-law.

"Mum, this looks incredible!" Royce exclaimed, his

eyes sweeping over the vibrant floral arrangements and twinkling fairy lights. He wore a tailored navy-blue suit with a crisp white shirt and a playful polka-dotted tie, while Stacie looked radiant in a flowing champagne-colored dress, her dark hair cascading down her shoulders in loose waves. Their fingers were entwined, the warmth of their connection palpable even from a distance.

"Thank you, sweetheart," Daphne replied, her heart swelling with pride. "We wanted everything to be perfect for your special day."

♥♥♥

The speeches at Royce and Stacie's wedding were a heartwarming blend of humor and emotion. Each speaker highlighted the couple's unique qualities, with tales of their quirks and adventures that left the guests chuckling and wiping away tears.

Royce's kind heart was a recurring theme, with stories of his selflessness and generosity. One friend recounted how Royce had once given his last $20 to a homeless man, insisting that it was the right thing to do. Another shared how Royce had always been there to lend a listening ear or offer a helping hand whenever anyone needed it.

Stacie's adventurous spirit was also celebrated, with tales of her daring feats and fearless attitude. One story involved Stacie skydiving on a whim, much to the horror of her friends who were watching from the ground below. Another recounted how she had once hitchhiked across Europe, relying solely on the kindness of strangers for shelter and sustenance.

As the speeches drew to a close, the room was filled with a palpable sense of love and admiration for the newlyweds. The guests clapped enthusiastically as each speaker took their seat, ready to enjoy the rest of the reception in honor of Royce and Stacie's special day.

Daphne sat at her table, her head resting on Reuben's shoulder as she listened to the speeches with a mix of pride and nostalgia. She thought back on all the challenges she had faced over the years - from her own health struggles to navigating life in Dallas - but now she felt an overwhelming sense of peace and contentment. As she looked around at her family gathered together in celebration, she knew that all those hardships had been worth it for this moment right here. She closed her eyes, taking in Reuben's comforting presence beside her, grateful for everything they had been through together and everything they still had ahead of them.

Slipping away from the crowd, they found sanctuary beneath a canopy of oak trees, the dappled light playing across their faces. Reuben gently brushed a stray curl from Daphne's forehead, his fingertips lingering on her skin like a whispered promise.

"Are you alright?" he asked softly, his eyes searching hers for any hint of unease.

Daphne smiled, the warmth of his concern flooding her heart. "More than alright," she replied, her voice a tender murmur. "I just needed a moment with you."

"Me too," he admitted, leaning in to press a gentle kiss to her temple.

As they stood there, wrapped in each other's arms, Daphne reflected on the love she had found in Reuben. The way he knew when to give her space and when to hold her close, how he could make her laugh even on the darkest days, and the quiet strength that anchored their relationship. He was her rock, her confidante, and the partner she had always dreamed of finding.

"Thank you," she whispered into his chest, her words muffled by the soft fabric of his dress shirt. "For being here, for loving me, and for helping to create this beautiful day for Royce and Stacie."

Reuben's arms tightened around her, his breath warm against her hair. "It's an honor," he said, his voice husky with emotion. "And I'm grateful every day that we found each other."

They lingered in that intimate embrace, drawing sustenance from one another as the sun continued its slow descent toward the horizon. And though the festivities carried on around them, for that brief moment, Daphne and Reuben existed in a world entirely their own—a world built on love, trust, and the promise of a shared future.

Epilogue – Tahiti
2032

The late afternoon sun cast long shadows across the garden as Daphne sat at the patio table, her notebook open before her. The pages were filled with lists—meticulously organized columns of items to pack, arrangements to make, people to notify. Stan lounged nearby on a sun-warmed flagstone, while Loretta batted playfully at a dangling vine.

Daphne looked up at the sound of the back door opening. Reuben emerged, moving with the careful deliberation that had become part of his daily rhythm. His medication was working well today; the tremor in his hands was barely noticeable as he carried two glasses of iced tea.

"Any space at that table for me?" he asked, his eyes crinkling with the smile that still made her heart flutter after all these years.

"Always," she replied, shifting her notebook to make room. "I think I've got everything covered. Roman's going to check on the house while we're away, and Royce promised to come by every few days to feed the cats."

Reuben took a sip of his tea, studying her over the rim of his glass. "We don't have to do this, you know. If you're worried about me—"

"I'm not," she interrupted, though they both knew it wasn't entirely true. She reached across the table to cover his hand with hers. "Or rather, I am, but not enough to cancel. The neurologist said you're stable, and we've been planning this trip for months."

"The islands of Tahiti wait for no man," Reuben agreed with a wry smile. "Especially not one whose left side is increasingly uncooperative."

Daphne squeezed his hand, grateful for his ability to address his condition with humor rather than bitterness. When they'd first received his diagnosis, they'd made a pact to focus on living fully in whatever time they had, rather than dwelling on what might come. This trip—this last great adventure before his Parkinson's potentially progressed to a stage where long-distance travel would be too difficult—was part of that promise.

"Justin called earlier," she said, changing the subject. "He wanted to know if we needed a ride to the airport."

"Always the responsible one these days," Reuben chuckled. "Who would have thought?"

"People change," Daphne said softly, thinking of her own transformation over the years. "They heal. They grow."

"Some things don't change, though," Reuben replied, his eyes holding hers with an intensity that still took her breath away. "Like how much I love you."

Later that evening, as they finished packing the last of their suitcases, a wave of familiar anxiety washed over Daphne. She had always been a meticulous planner, finding comfort in organization and preparation, but no amount of list-making could prepare them for the uncertainties that lay ahead. How would Reuben's body respond to the long flight? Would the resort be as accessible as they'd been promised? What if his medication schedule was disrupted by the time difference?

As if sensing her thoughts, Reuben appeared in the doorway of their bedroom, his movement slower after a long day of preparations. "Come here," he said, opening his arms to her.

Daphne stepped into his embrace, breathing in the familiar scent of him—a blend of sandalwood cologne and the indefinable essence that was uniquely Reuben. His arms encircled her, not as strong as they once were but just as comforting.

"We'll figure it out together," he murmured into her hair. "Just like we always do."

♥♥♥

The morning of their departure dawned clear and bright. Their children had insisted on seeing them off, creating an impromptu family gathering at the airport. Roman had driven in from his apartment across town, while Royce and Stacie arrived with little Emily in tow. Justin was there too, having taken the day off work to ensure everything went smoothly.

As they waited at the gate, Daphne watched her family with a full heart. Their journey had not been easy—there had been pain, struggle, and moments of darkness so profound she'd feared they might never find their way back to the light. Yet here they were, surrounded by love, about to embark on a new adventure.

The announcement for priority boarding crackled over the speakers, and Reuben rose to his feet, balancing carefully before finding his stride. "That's us," he said, his excitement palpable despite the fatigue that often shadowed him these days.

Their goodbyes were quick but heartfelt—hugs, kisses, and promises to check in when they landed. As Daphne and Reuben made their way down the jetway, she felt a peculiar blend of emotions—anticipation, gratitude, and a bittersweet awareness of time's passage.

The flight was long but comfortable in their first-class seats. Reuben dozed intermittently, the gentle hum of the engines lulling him into rest despite the occasional tremor that disturbed his sleep. Daphne read for a while, then simply watched the clouds below, thinking about the journey that had brought them to this moment.

When they finally landed in Tahiti, the humid air enveloped them like a warm embrace. Palm trees swayed against a backdrop of mountains so lush and green they seemed almost surreal. Their waterfront bungalow was everything the travel brochure had promised—perched on stilts over crystalline lagoon waters, with a private deck and steps leading directly into the sea.

♥♥♥

The first few days passed in a blissful haze of relaxation. They woke to breakfasts of fresh tropical fruits, spent lazy mornings reading on their deck, and cooled off with gentle swims in the protected lagoon. Reuben's mobility was better in the water, the buoyancy easing the stiffness in his limbs, and they developed a routine of afternoon floating sessions that left him refreshed and more flexible.

On their fifth evening, they arranged for a private dinner on their deck. The resort staff set up a table adorned with local flowers, lit candles that flickered in the gentle breeze, and served a meal of freshly caught fish and island vegetables before discreetly withdrawing.

As they dined under a canopy of stars, the moon casting a silver path across the water, Daphne marveled at the beauty surrounding them. "I wish we could stay here forever," she said, the words escaping before she could censure the wistful thought.

Reuben reached across the table, his movements more fluid in the warm evening air. "We can, in a way," he said softly. "This moment, this feeling—we can carry it with us."

Daphne understood what he meant. Throughout their relationship, they had created spaces of love and sanctuary that transcended physical locations. Whether in the Richmond house that had seen so much of their history or this paradise halfway around the world, home was wherever they were together.

After dinner, they settled on the cushioned lounger on their deck, Daphne nestled in the protective circle of Reuben's arms as they listened to the gentle lapping of waves against the stilts of their bungalow. The Southern Cross glittered above them, a celestial landmark in an unfamiliar sky.

"Thank you," Reuben said after a comfortable silence.

"For what?" Daphne asked, tilting her face up to his.

"For this trip. For convincing me we should come, even when I was worried about the difficulties." His voice was reflective, tinged with a depth of emotion that spoke to all they'd faced together. "For seeing possibilities instead of limitations."

"That's what you taught me," she replied, thinking of how Reuben had always encouraged her to reach beyond the boundaries she'd set for herself. "To look for the light, even in the darkest times."

They lay together in comfortable silence, the rhythm of the waves a soothing backdrop to their thoughts. Tomorrow they would take a boat excursion to see the island's hidden waterfalls. The day after, they had arranged for a local guide to show them the island's interior. Each day was a gift, each experience a memory to treasure.

"Never stop whispering to my heart," Daphne whispered softly, her voice barely above a whisper.

Reuben smiled and pressed his lips gently against her forehead, promising that his love would always surround her like a protective shield.

ABOUT THE AUTHOR

Amy N. Kaplan is an award-winning author who brings imagination to life through her diverse portfolio of children's books, RPG supplements, memoirs, poetry, and fiction. Her writing journey began in childhood when she drafted poems, scripts, and even a neighborhood newspaper, laying the foundation for a lifelong love of storytelling.

Drawing inspiration from her global adventures, family experiences, and favorite fandoms, Amy crafts narratives that explore themes of resilience, self-discovery, and the enduring human spirit. Her writing captures the complexities of relationships, the challenges of building a meaningful life, and the hope that comes from finding one's own path.

When she isn't writing, Amy can be found playing tabletop games, antiquing at local shops, or enthusiastically discussing Star Wars and Monty Python. She lives with her supportive husband, beloved cats, and divides her time between writing and cherishing moments with her children and grandchildren. A passionate literacy advocate, Amy actively supports reading programs in her community.

With ink-stained fingers and a heart full of stories, Amy invites readers to discover worlds that spark creativity and inspire—tales that remain with you long after the final page.

http://www.amynkaplan.com

OTHER BOOKS BY AMY N KAPLAN

Free Range Pigs: An Interactive Adventure Story about Three Little Pigs

Free Range Bears: An Interactive Adventure Story about Three Bears

Chronicles of Adventure: The Ultimate RPG Player's Companion

Chronicles of Adventure: The Ultimate RPG Game Master's Companion

Chronicles of Adventure: The Ultimate RPG Campaign Builder

Chronicles of Adventure: The Ultimate RPG Campaign Creator Guidebook

Reflection's Reckoning (The Mirror Kingdom, Book 1)

Becoming Jewish

WATCH FOR THESE EXCITING NEW TITLES

Free Range Goats: An Interactive Adventure Story about Ten Little Goats

Free Range Wolves: An Interactive Adventure Story about Three Wolves

Carnival of Shadows (The Blackthorn Series, Book 1)

Harbinger of Terror

Binding Flames

Whispers of the Heart